CW01113228

INTO THE DARK

CHARLES BUTLER

BOXTREE

Dedication:
For Maggie and Sophie

First published in the UK 1991
by BOXTREE LIMITED, 36 Tavistock Street,
London WC2E 7PB

1 3 5 7 9 10 8 6 4 2

TM & © 1991 Twentieth Century Fox Film Corporation

All rights reserved

ISBN: 1 85283 607 5

Typeset by Litho Link Limited,
Welshpool, Powys

Printed and bound in Great Britain by
Cox & Wyman, Reading, Berkshire

Except in the United States of America, this book is sold subject to the condition that it shall not, by way of trade or otherwise, be lent, resold, hired out or otherwise circulated without the publisher's prior consent in any form of binding or cover other than that in which it is published and without a similar condition including this condition being imposed on a subsequent purchaser.

A catalogue record for this book is available from the
British Library

Prologue

Grace Van Owen drove her dark blue Ford sedan into the short stay car park at Los Angeles Airport, opposite the terminal for Internal Flights.

Beside her sat Victor Sifuentes. He was wearing his dust-coloured suit – the one he never appeared in at the office – and a loose shirt of brown Indian silk. He looked relaxed and happy. He was flying to Las Vegas to handle the case of a Mexican blackjack dealer who was claiming wrongful dismissal from a small outfit called 'The White Magic Club'.

Victor Sifuentes was looking forward to the trip. The summer smog was at its worst and his relationship with Grace was getting just a little too heavy for comfort.

They were ten minutes early. She parked the car and switched off the ignition; then turned and looked at him. Full-face he was even better-looking than in profile. At such times she no longer thought of him as the smooth trouble-shooting new Partner of McKenzie Brackman, Attorneys-at-Law. Even sober-suited at the office his appearance suggested something wild and alien; there was a look of the pirate about him, with his earring and widely spaced black eyes. Spanish nobility with a touch of Indian blood, perhaps.

She knew, of course, that he was too handsome for his own good. He knew it too – finding it difficult to make others believe there was really anything serious behind those fine eyelashes set in the gaunt Aztec face. Grace looked at him lovingly, but her expression was not happy. She hated him going off like this – even for a few days. In such moods her expression took on a certain heaviness, the shadows under her eyes looking like faint bruising. Victor thought – although he didn't make too much fuss telling her – that she was one of the loveliest women he'd ever seen.

He leant over and kissed her gently on the mouth. 'Time to go!' He got his leather grip out of the trunk and they began to walk through the muggy heat towards the terminal. He had his ticket in his hand as he reached the Las Vegas desk. The first call was just going out. He turned and kissed her again.

'Grace, I just hate these airport farewells!'

'Me too.' She looked miserable. 'So I'll say good-bye now, Victor?'

'Please. But don't worry – we'll see each other very soon!'

They kissed a third time, and Grace hung on just a second too long, her hand reaching up and feeling his glossy black hair over the nape of his neck. For a moment she thought she was going to cry.

'Bye, Victor darling! And good luck with the case!'

Grace turned and ran through the doors, out into the gritty yellow glare of Los Angeles.

Grace drove back downtown on the raised San Diego Freeway, trying to keep her mind a blank. She kept to the fast lane, at slightly above the speed limit, almost hoping that some traffic cop would stop her – anything to take her mind off her new lover, Victor. If she were stopped she could probably talk herself out of trouble – after all, until joining McKenzie Brackman as a Partner, she'd been a judge on the L.A. County Court – something most cops in this violent city took seriously.

But there were no cops. And after a few minutes she began to glance instead at the landscape around her. She'd driven this road many times but never noticed its immediate surroundings. It was as though the speed and the comfortable, air-conditioned interior of the car had hitherto insulated her, like a time traveller in a spacecraft.

It was a truly dreadful area of the city – though not necessarily the worst. A place most of the city treated as though it were a bad smell that civilised people chose not to notice. Unlike the sprawling shanty-towns to the south of L.A., this place was almost entirely deserted except for a crowd of kids fooling about amongst the trash and rubble where everything was ash-grey and nothing grew except stunted weeds – all else stifled by fumes from the Freeway and trails of kerosene from planes landing and taking off every few minutes at the airport.

Grace shuddered. This was the underbelly of Los Angeles – the effluent of the great city which the rest of the population was too busy making money to be bothered to clean up. She looked out again and saw, in front of where the children were playing – looming high above the drifting ash and smog – the giant reclining image of a naked girl on a beach. She was a good forty feet long, supported on a trestle of rusted girders, with her head and feet lopped off at each end of the hoarding. Her nakedness was concealed only by a pair of huge designer sunglasses with great round, pink frames, which were held loosely in one enormous hand across her crotch. Below, was the message: SEE THE WORLD THRU DIFFERENT EYES!

Grace took a last look at the scampering children beyond. They looked so tiny. *Poor little kids!* she thought. To be brought up in a place like this! And with what hope for their future? How could their mothers bring them into the world and allow them to run wild like that? She found herself thinking again of Victor. What chance did they have? Would they marry and have children? Would Victor be the right man? Would he enjoy sacrificing his freedom and settling down to bring up kids? But at least they wouldn't be like those ones back there! Their kids would be loved and cared for, brought up in comfortable affluence by two successful, rising young Partners in the law firm of McKenzie Brackman.

Grace began to relax, to feel more safe and protected, as the Freeway snaked away from the desolation of the ash pit, and plunged towards downtown L.A. Somewhere out there, amid the dull-brown blur of the smog, lay the sanctity of her office. Freedom – money – the good life. She'd soon forgotten the kids on the wasteland.

Chapter One

It happened early in the evening, after another baking hot July day, at the end of the second week of the school vacation.

Candy Turner was just nine years old, an agile little girl with scraggy blonde hair, gap-toothed, and a pert nose freckled like a gull's egg. That evening, along with the rest of the neighbourhood kids, she wore the standard uniform of T-shirt, tracksuit bottoms and trainers; she was riding her mountain bike. The bike and her *Reeboks*, costing more than $100 a pair, represented a small fortune for Candy Turner's mother, Rita, a divorcee in her mid-thirties, living on the margins of Welfare, in a run-down tract-house in Inglewood, near the San Diego Freeway on the way to the airport.

Because Rita was too poor to afford a child-minder, let alone the luxury of play school – even if there had been such things in this neighbourhood – Candy, like hundreds of other kids in this great, sprawling, heartless city, spent hours each day, often late into the evenings, playing wild. Totally unsupervised, totally careless of the risks and dangers, seen or unseen. Out of sight, out of mind . . .

*

Their favourite place to play was called *La Caldera*, which in Spanish means a burnt-out crater of a volcano. In English it was known as the 'ash pit', which was a pretty fair description. Situated a mile from the ocean, and about five hundred yards from the airport road, from which it was sheltered by a high crumbling rampart of ruined factory walls and derelict warehouses, it was a great stretch of wasteland that resembled a city ravaged and abandoned after a long war.

Criss-crossed with deep ditches, some overgrown, others full of foul water, it was a hideous, man-made nightmare of desolation. The stacked carcasses of automobiles, oil drums and great graveyards of rusting household appliances, were all overlaid with a rich growth of vegetation like a lush mould.

Several real-estate companies had thought at one time or another of developing the area, but had all shied off. It was too close to the really bad parts of town – not only were these parts No-Go Areas for the respectable citizens of L.A., but also for most of the local police. But because it was shielded from the road, most of the serious city gangs, the pimps, whores, pushers and muggers, didn't bother with it. It was too desolate, even for crime. The rich pickings were elsewhere; and besides, it stank. There were rumours of hidden, illegal dumpings of toxic waste – even some said, of atomic sludge from an old nuclear reactor, long closed down. In short, it was dangerous. An adventure playground with no boundaries, no supervisors, no rules. The kids loved it.

*

On that July evening the kids ventured further than usual. They'd crossed the raised cinder track which until now had been recognised as the unofficial boundary of *La Caldera*. Then they'd started nosing about on a stretch of smoother, tidier wasteland which stopped abruptly at a high forbidding fence. Chicken wire was stretched taut between concrete stanchions, cantilevered at the top and strung with wicked-looking razor wire. High up, well beyond their reach, was a sign stencilled in black on dirty yellow:

PRIVATE PROPERTY. KEEP OUT!

Then below, in smaller lettering:

THE TRITON CORPORATION.

But the kids didn't bother with this, since few of them could read. Beyond the wire was a jumble of low concrete buildings with rusty corrugated iron roofs, dark metal doors and mean little windows backed with creosoted wooden panels. The children had noticed the place before, and once some of them had tried breaking in; but it appeared impenetrable, with steel doors locked from the inside. Since then they had kept away.

Candy Turner stood in awe. Then she shrugged, 'C'mon you guys, this place is *boring!'* And for the next half-hour or so, until the light began to fade, they resumed one of their favourite games. The older kids, with their mountain bikes – those lucky enough to have them – positioned themselves into pairs, or sometimes threes, up on the cinder track. Each team faced the other about a hundred yards apart; then, at a shout from the referee, both would begin pedalling at break-neck speed on a direct collision course, while the rest of the kids lined the way, cheering or holding their breath.

At the last minute both teams would jack their front wheels round and rear up in a spectacular 'wheelie', as perfectly synchronised as a ballet-on-bikes; then, with the snarl of cinders and in a cloud of choking dust, the riders would crash diagonally down the steep slopes on either side of the embankment, often landing in a tangle of wheels and bodies.

The first priority was not to damage one's machine. Personal injuries were rated very low indeed, and were always borne stoically, so as not to lose face. More serious accidents, such as those causing concussion, torn ligaments, and at least two bad fractures, were treated with 'medi-evac' efficiency: the injured child supported or carried away by a group of his peers, usually to the home of a friend with relatives who could be trusted to have the injury treated with discretion, if possible without the child's family knowing.

They had been playing this particular game for nearly a

year now, unimpeded and more or less unscathed; not once had it occurred to any of them – even the brightest, like Candy Turner, that they had all been remarkably fortunate to have survived so long, without serious injury.

But things like luck and survival were taken for granted. Winning was what mattered. The main object of the game was either to be the last to leave the cinder track, if only by a split-second, or, mightiest victory of all, to remain upright; and when the dust had cleared, to be seen riding on, in solitary triumph, pursued down the track by the high-pitched shrieks of applause from the whole gang.

This evening Candy had been denied her usual victory by a tough, mean-eyed little boy, who looked like a miniature Mexican bandit, and who at the last second had deliberately crashed his front wheel straight into Candy's, at the same time delivering a smart kick at her leg, sending her into a spinning crash which brought two other riders tumbling down on top of her.

Candy responded with gallant cool, picking herself up, dusting herself down, and challenging the little thug to a re-run – just the two of them, *mano a mano*. The light was already bad, as the two of them lined up, at least a hundred yards apart. There was a breathless pause. They could hear the distant roar of traffic from the Freeway. A jet airliner roared down towards the airport, its light winking through the warm dusk. Somebody shouted, 'Go!' and an excited scream went up: 'Go take him, Candy!'

The tyres hummed over the cinders. Both kids had their heads down, legs working like pistons on full throttle. Candy's eyes were fixed on her front wheel, keeping it firmly in the centre of the track, never once looking up, as the shrieking began to fall away behind her: 'C'mon, Candy! *Take him,* Candy! Candy! Candy, Candy . . .!'

She felt the *whoosh* of air passing her leg, heard a tyre sizzle and crash a few inches away – then the sound of fifty little voices howling with excitement, loud enough to be heard half-way to the airport . . .

Only then did she lift her eyes. She was alone, feeling the warm air on her face, a trickle of sweat crawling under her T-shirt. But even now she did not slacken her pace. A dozen or so kids were running after her, still cheering, but one by one dropping back, panting and waving.

Candy kept on down the track, round the side of the jumble of buildings which lay dark and grim now in the thickening twilight. She was dimly aware of an enormous billboard, which rose on stilts high above the ground facing the Freeway, showing the brown body of a naked blonde girl holding a pair of sunglasses across her groin.

At the same time Candy noticed something else. Beyond the last of the buildings a couple of concrete stanchions had been broken, while between them the chicken-wire sagged almost to the ground. It was too good a chance to miss. To cap her triumph she suddenly veered off the track and crashed straight down towards where the wire lay nearest the ground, doing a 'wheelie' at the last moment so that her front tyre cleared the wire and carried her hurtling through the gap.

In the gathering darkness she saw looming ahead a jumbled pile of yellow oil drums. They appeared huge and were painted a dirty yellow. She was too frightened to scream. Then at the last moment something happened to check her headlong rush to disaster. Or so it seemed.

Her rear wheel had snagged in the collapsed razor-wire and she felt herself pulled up with a sudden, terrible jerk. It was as though a huge man had grabbed her from behind, sending her skimpy little body flying over the handle bars and splaying it out in a slimy pool of mud, within inches of the wall of yellow drums.

Both hands and one side of Candy's face were scraped raw. She lay dazed for several seconds, as the mud and slime oozed between her fingers and down her face. She was aware of a horrible choking smell that made her feel sick. Her face and hands were burning like fire. Candy began to moan and tried to open her eyes. This time she did scream. It was the most terrible pain she had ever experienced – worse even than the time she'd spilt boiling water over her bare arm and had been in bandages for three weeks.

But this pain was something different. Candy felt as though her eyes were being poked out with burning sticks. She couldn't scream any more because she couldn't even breathe. She tried to wipe her eyes, but this only made the pain worse. Somewhere, dimly, through a red film of fire, she could see the foul mud glinting with little sparks of oily light, like the shifting images at the bottom of a kaleidoscope. She started to vomit; then lost consciousness.

Chapter Two

The first children reached Candy a few minutes later. They picked their way carefully down the cinder bank, several of them holding back as they reached the slumped wire and saw the little body crumpled in the stinking pool of mud. They noticed the smell almost at once, sharp and tangy – a 'sick smell', as they were later to call it – making their throats sting and their eyes start streaming tears.

One of them – a bright-eyed little boy called Manuel who was particularly close to Candy – found himself distracted for a moment by the sight of a sign fixed to a post near the yellow drums: a black skull-and-crossbones grinning down at him out of a yellow triangle.

The other children were hanging back, wiping their eyes and coughing while they stared at Candy's still body.

'Is she dead?' someone whispered.

'She looks real bad,' another said.

Manuel was the first to touch her. He bent over her, retching with the smell, his grubby trainers now black with stinking slime. He put his hands under Candy's shoulders and lifted her gently, his fingers burning at the touch of the mud.

He thought he heard Candy groan; her shoulders gave a quick shudder that passed through her whole tiny body. 'She's alive,' he called, lifting her bodily and dragging her backwards, feeling sick and dizzy as he went; but not stopping until he'd pulled her back over the wire. Then he collapsed forward, vomiting between his feet.

It was another twenty minutes before they got Candy out of *La Caldera* on to a minor road that led back into the city. Several cars drove deliberately past, some at speed, their drivers not liking what they say in their headlamps; a huge crowd of ragged kids spread out along the sides of the road, waving and screaming, and four of them carrying one of their number who looked badly hurt.

But it was already dark, in a bad area where you didn't stop unless you absolutely had to – and besides, kids were always trouble, even small ones. They could still mug you for the price of drugs, like the best of 'em – and this was an awful lotta kids . . .

Finally, an unmarked pick-up pulled over and stopped. The driver got out slowly. She was a large black woman who looked as though she could pitch Arnold Schwarzenegger through a plate-glass window. 'What you kids think you're doin'?' she growled, advancing heavily.

Special Patrolwoman Donna Johnson of the L.A.P.D. Urban Protection Unit took one look at Candy Turner, caught a poisonous whiff from her clothes, lifted the child like a feather and carried her back to the truck. She laid Cindy carefully along the front seat with her small torso partially gripped under the seat-belt. She was not sure if the child was still alive.

Inside the cab Donna called headquarters. 'S.P. Johnson of the U.P.U.,' she grunted. 'On Melton Road, edge of Inglewood – gang of kids, about two dozen, and one's badly burned. Maybe a DOA. Am proceeding Washington Casualty. Send two ambulances, – she gave her position from a numbered grid-map – 'for the rest o' the kids. It may be a gas case – so make it fast!'

She wiped her hands on her dungarees and went back to the kids, selecting Manuel and one of the others who'd helped carry Candy, and ordered them into the back of the truck; then she told the rest of the gang to stay put and wait till someone came for them.

They all stared as their friends climbed aboard, sitting crouched down with their hands pressed to their ears, as the siren suddenly came alive and the truck roared off with a squeal of tyres.

They waited only until the headlights began to fade, then turned and fled in the opposite direction, silently and very fast. They weren't gonna hang around waiting for no cops. Not even if Candy was hurt bad. *Especially* if Candy was hurt bad!

In their excitement none of them had even thought of the child's precious mountain bike still lying a few feet from the ghastly pool of mud.

*

It was 8.05 pm when Candy Turner was rushed from the unmarked police truck into L.A.'s Washington Hospital. Even as the stretcher was being trundled at speed through the stark corridors towards the Burns Unit, a couple of interns were already cutting away her clothes and trainers, while another had fixed an oxygen mask over her tiny, filthy face. She was only just breathing.

In the Burns Unit she was immediately laid in a shallow tub and her whole body was washed swiftly and carefully in saline solution, a drip was attached to her arm, and her eyes were bathed and bandaged with paraffin gauze. The doctors and nurses wore special masks and, as they worked, took regular swabs of the oily slime which were immediately sent for analysis.

Finally, just after 10 pm, Candy's whole body, with the exception of her eyes and hair, had been covered with a thick layer of Flamazine cream, and her hands and upper arms sealed in polythene wrappings. But still, after more than two hours, she showed no sign of consciousness, and her pulse rate on the monitor remained dangerously low.

At 10.10 pm a senior ophthalmic surgeon arrived to examine her eyes. His prognosis was not optimistic.

*

Attempts were being made to establish the child's identity and to inform her next-of-kin. Candy had not a scrap of identification on her. The one pocket in her lacerated track-suit bottoms contained a single crumpled dollar bill, two 'bits', a plastic model of a black kitten on a broken plastic chain, and a few coupons from a cereal packet promising a free trip to Disneyland. And one key clipped inside her T-shirt, which turned out to belong to a patent bicycle lock.

Meanwhile, in another part of the hospital, precious time was being wasted. Manuel and his companion – a tiny black girl called Simone with glistening plaits woven tight against her scalp – were taken into cubicles behind Casualty and examined by two doctors who tried without success to find out what had happened. But the children seemed too shocked and scared to make much sense. Nurses came in and washed them all over, dressed their hands and feet, and then made a series of tests, including blood and urine samples.

The doctors wanted them put in a private ward for observation. But the police now intervened. They wanted information. And the children, dressed in large dungarees which made them look like tiny clowns, were crowded into a tiny office where they were seated at a table and questioned by two officers from the Los Angeles Police Department.

At first this was not such a frightening experience as they'd expected. One of their interrogators was a dark, pretty girl in jeans and open sandals called Miranda who looked like the heroine of a children's soap opera – the one who always came to the rescue when the kids were in trouble. The other was a friendly-looking young man in uniform, with freckles and tousled blond hair, who asked them to call him Tommy. They sat, in mute fascination, staring at the gunbelt hanging over the back of his chair.

Both officers had already spent five dollars of L.A.P.D funds on fruit gum, *Chocababies* and Coke from the hospital dispensing machines; but progress was slow. When the children could be persuaded to talk at all, their versions of events were chaotic: by turns vague, over-elaborate and hopelessly contradictory. After getting a confused gist of a bicycle accident on some wasteland near the Freeway, the two officers concentrated on trying to extract Candy's identity from the kids.

This took even more time. After a lot of suspicious misunderstandings, they eventually established her name, and her mother's name; but neither of the kids seemed able to remember where Candy lived. Manuel did say that she had no daddy – her mom was divorced – as though it were the most natural thing in a child's young life.

After a few more attempts, Tommy hauled over a telephone, called the operator and asked for all Turners, particularly R.'s or Ritas, listed for the Inglewood area. He ended up with a list of several dozen numbers, which he now began to punch out on the handset. After the fourth call, Manuel said helpfully: 'Candy's mom's got no phone, Mister. She got no money.'

Tommy looked slowly at Miranda, then pressed down the bar on the phone and made another call, speaking this time in a rapid monotone: '. . . Mrs Rita Turner – husband unknown – one kid girl of nine answering to name of Candy – house somewhere off the San Diego Freeway on the Inglewood southside near Belmont. And shake it up, it's urgent!'

While he talked, Miranda began asking the two children where they lived. But they were suddenly hesitant, scared. Manuel tried to say he felt sick again. She ignored him. 'Don't you want to help your friend, Candy?' she asked them.

They did want to help her. But after more confusion,

more contradictions, broken by nervous silences, it turned out that only Manuel's mother had a telephone. No sooner had the child blurted this out than he began to beg Miranda not to tell his mother where he was or what had happened. He was close to tears. 'She'll whip me, ma'am – she'll whip me real bad!'

Miranda promised, called the mother, and said she was a friend of Candy's mother, Rita, and yes, she was fine, just fine! – she just wanted Candy's mother's address. After warding off a volley of questions, she scribbled down the information, thanked the woman several times; then hung up and passed the phone and the note to Tommy, who immediately called back to headquarters.

Manuel listened, his eyes wide with fear. Tommy was saying, 'Just tell her the kid's been hurt – that's all. Don't scare her too much – but get her over here to the Washington Hospital *prontissimo!*'

Manuel waited until Tommy had replaced the handset, then said quietly, 'She won't be home, Mister – she works nights.'

Tommy sighed. 'Do you know *where* she works, Manuel?'

There was a pause. Then Simone piped up: 'I think she works at the B-&-Q place, Mister . . .!'

Tommy lifted the phone again. When he'd finished talking, he stood up and smiled. 'Right, you guys. We gonna take a little ride in the squad-car and you're all gonna show me the place where it happened.' Then he put on his gunbelt.

It was already past ten o'clock.

Chapter Three

At 7.10 pm an alarm had flashed downtown, in an office on the ninth floor of a glass building on Sunset. The security guard immediately called his superior on the floor above: 'We got a flash on 57.' The other grunted and tapped the number into the computer. He didn't like what he saw; and a moment later decided to call his boss at home.

'Malley here, Sir. Sorry to disturb you, but we just got a flash on 57. Looks like the dump out on Belmont.'

'So? What's there?'

'Sixteen drums of D.X.P. Empty. But not cleared.'

There was a blunt expletive down the line, then a pause. 'Okay, Malley. Get a man right down there in an unmarked car to check. Call me straight back when you hear from him.'

Jim Malley called back thirty minutes later. When he had finished speaking there was silence at the other end of the line, then the same expletive, repeated several times.

'Right, Malley. This is what you do. Call Madison Security on the UHF link and tell 'em to get their best men down to the Belmont site to do a grand-slam Clearance Sale. *Everything Must Go!* Use recovery trucks – suction pumps – high pressure hoses, detergent – the works! And tell 'em to wear protective clothing. And, Malley – make it clear that this is *top classified.* Anyone blabs and he doesn't work again – for me or anyone else! And I want regular check calls. If the cops show, the men play dumb. But if it gets hot, call Lieutenant Erikson at the Ninth Precinct and get him to call me here. Now move your ass, Malley!'

At 10.20 pm the Chief Security Officer, responsible to the President of the Triton Corporation, received the final call. The 'sale' was complete. No wild cards. He could mix himself a stiff drink and watch the rerun of the ballgame from Minneapolis.

*

Tommy was driving, while Miranda worked the spotlight on the side of the squad-car roof, keeping the hard white beam trained along the edge of the embankment and the black void beyond.

Between them sat Manuel, next to Miranda, and the little black kid, Simone, squeezed up beside Tommy, her little legs tucked under her on the seat so as not to get them tangled with the gearshift.

The time was just 10.20. They'd been driving for nearly twenty minutes now. At first Manuel had given eager instructions – across Inglewood and on to the Freeway –

but once they'd passed near the giant billboard with the naked torso wearing only sunglasses, the boy became quiet, hesitant. It was Simone who directed them off the Freeway at the next exit; and the squad-car was soon bouncing along in bottom gear through the lunar landscape of the cratered ash-pit, with Miranda struggling to keep the spotlight trained on the treacherous contours of the track ahead.

Manuel was suddenly terrified, when Simone cried, 'It's right here, Mister!'

'Right?' said Tommy.

'No – left,' she said. 'Take a left – right here!'

Tommy swore silently, as he swung the big car off the dirt track, thinking it was like one of those old routines in the movies.

Manuel fell silent from then on. He was still terrified. For they were now deep in *La Caldera* – their very own No-Go Area where no grown-up was ever allowed. Yet here he was, brave Manuel Garcia, not only leading two grown-ups right into this sacred territory but leading two cops there in a squad-car! He felt sick – not only with fear but also with burning shame.

They had reached the cinder track, and Manuel sat crouched beside Miranda, trying hard not to move, not even breathe. Above all, he dared not glance over the edge of the track into the darkness. Simone suddenly shouted: 'There, Mister! Over there!'

The spotlight swivelled sideways, tracking over the blank emptiness; then suddenly lit up the white filigree of the fence, and the grey walls behind, with their small blind windows and metal doors.

Tommy slowed to a crawl. 'This the place?'

Manuel said nothing. Tommy glanced across at Miranda. 'Aren't those the old Triton buildings – the ones they closed down a few years back after that poison gas scare?'

'Oh Jesus,' said the girl. 'Maybe we should call back, then get the hell outta here?'

'This the place, Manuel?' Tommy said again, more sharply this time.

Simone answered, waving ahead. 'Further down, Mister!'

They crept forward again, holding the light on the high cantilevered fence until they came to the two broken stanchions, like a pair of thin fractured bones in the white glare of the spotlight. Simone waved excitedly; while the boy started to sob.

'What's the matter, Manuel?' said Miranda gently.

The boy jerked his head towards the broken fence, and shuddered. 'Down there, Miss! She fell off her bike. She fell in the mud!' He stared wildly at the woman, then at Tommy. 'It wasn't nobody's fault, really it wasn't!' He was shaking and gasping with sobs, filled now with the full shame of his treachery: '. . .Not . . . my . . . fault . . . Miss!'

'Sure it wasn't,' she said. 'Better hold it here,' she added, to Tommy. He pulled up, set the handbrake, then got out. He sniffed the air. Just the usual warm clammy smell of an L.A. summer night. He walked to the edge of the track and looked over. Miranda had the spotlight trained on the gap in the fence. It threw Tommy's long shadow far across the empty ash-pit below.

Then he walked slowly back to the car. 'Okay fellas. Show me just where it was.'

All three of them climbed out, Manuel hanging back to

the last. They crept up to the edge of the track and looked over. Then Manuel gave a shrill cry: 'It's gone!' He turned, his dark eyes round with horror. 'It's gone! — all, all gone . . .!'

'What's gone?' said Miranda.

'*Todos disparidos — o por el amor de Dios!*'

Both officers looked at the two children.

'What's gone?' But just then Manuel ducked down between the adults and ran off. Tommy only managed to catch him fifty yards further on, and brought him back kicking and howling like an animal.

Miranda slapped him twice, hard, then said something in Spanish. The kid seemed to quieten; he muttered something back, pointing down at the fence; then began talking fast, still in Spanish.

'He says the kid's bike's gone,' she said.

'*Si! Si!* Candy's bike! Candy's mountain bike worth hunnads o' dollars . . .!'

Then Simone spoke: 'The pirate picture's gone. And all them big yellah things gone, too!'

'What big yellow things? What picture?' said Tommy; there was an edge to his voice now.

Together the children began to describe the pile of drums and the sign with the skull-and-crossbones.

'You sure this is the right place?' asked Miranda. 'You sure you recognise it in the dark?'

'Sure we recognise it,' said Manuel, suddenly truculent. 'We come out here most nights!'

Tommy whispered something to Miranda and then said, 'Right, you guys. We're going back to the hospital.'

Chapter Four

Morning Conference at McKenzie Brackman and Partners, Attorneys-at-Law, began at 10 am sharp. The Venetian blinds were drawn, as usual, against the grey glare of the city and the air-conditioning was working smoothly. Brackman was in the Chair, while Leland was detained on a complicated case involving a shipping company registered in Hawaii which looked as though it was about to skip with a hundred million of Californian tax payers' money.

Grace Van Owen was the last to arrive, in her dark tailored suit, hands clutching a heap of files. 'Sorry, Douglas. I had calls to make.'

Douglas Brackman watched her, glaring under his biblical eyebrows and domed forehead. 'Hmmm.'

Her lovely straw-coloured hair looked as though it had been brushed too hastily, and there were those faint shadows under her eyes. Brackman glanced meaningfully at

Victor Sifuentes' empty place. He guessed that while Victor was away, Grace would act like a love-lorn schoolgirl. The best solution was to give her a big case to crack. She thrived on hard work.

Brackman shuffled some papers in front of him and began. 'Right. Two main items on the agenda. First – the Denver Boot Phantom. He's been caught. His father just called and asked us to take his case.' He looked at Kuzak. 'Mike, sounds like your baby.'

'Thanks, Douglas.' Kuzak grinned. 'I saw it on the late news last night. Seems he's a college boy? Should give an interesting social dimension. Nineteen squad-cars clamped in just nine days. Then the guy gets picked up in broad daylight outside the Beverly Precinct House. Sounds like he *wanted* to get caught.'

Brackman nodded. 'Get down there and see him. The Beverly cops don't think it's funny. They're refusing bail, claiming they've got more inquiries to make. Which is unreasonable – and probably malicious. Case of injured dignity to the Department, and so on. So threaten them with a writ of *habeus corpus*. Remind them that your boy's a public hero. Then, when you've got him out, get his story. And keep him away from the media – they'll only queer your pitch.'

Kuzak stood up, deliberately not looking at Grace. 'OK, boss!' He gave the gunman's two-fingered salute and left the room. Grace did not look at him as he went.

Brackman peered slowly down the table and paused at Arnie Becker. The firm's ace divorce practitioner – mature heart-throb and alimony-fixer to a thousand matrons and mothers, broads and bimbos – was now married himself: a wiser, humbler man, dressed this morning in a flawless English suit that was almost as smooth as himself.

'We're in a recession, Arnie,' said Brackman, with an obscure hint at Becker's out-of-office expenses. 'How's that affecting the divorce business?'

Arnie gave his best smile, something between a shark's and a kitten's. 'Makes 'em greedier, maybe. But it's like booze, Douglas. People find they can't live without it. So they go on getting hitched up and having babies – then they get bored and tear each other to pieces. Yeah, I guess business is okay.'

Brackman gave his executive grunt, which was his way of registering neutral agreement. His stare now moved to Stuart Markowitz. The little man sat baggy-eyed and crumpled in his $2,000 suit. 'You still on that grand-larceny case, Stuart?'

'Full house, aces up,' Markowitz said miserably. 'No recession ever affected the big-timers. If anything, they prossper.'

'Fine!'

At the end of the table Markowitz's wife, Ann Kelsey, sat marble-faced, staring ahead at the Venetian blinds. *Oh God!* thought Brackman. *Not more ructions in the marital bed?* Sometimes he wondered if the firm oughtn't to diversify and go into the marriage counselling business.

He shrugged, then studied his papers. 'Next – the Turner kid. The Welfare people have asked us to handle the case. You've seen the TV – read the papers. One blinded child, and her penniless mother, up against the mighty guns of the Triton Corporation.' He paused. 'Grace, I think this is for you. You might even get some *sub rosa* help from inside the D.A.'s office. Pollution of the environment is still Number One at City Hall. So it looks like being a big story. One that might run and run.'

'No it won't,' said Grace sharply. 'The child needs money – and plenty of it. And if Triton try to string this out, I'll break their balls – personally.'

Brackman chuckled. 'Well spoken, Grace! The D.A.'s office has all the papers – they're thinking of bringing their own action against the company for criminal negligence likely to endanger the public health. That can carry a stiff jail sentence, plus an unlimited fine.'

'Those people are bastards,' said Grace, with sudden venom. 'I'll see they get everything they deserve!'

'They're not guilty yet,' Brackman said quietly. 'Remember that. I don't want a grandstand performance on this, Grace. Just let the facts speak for themselves. But be careful. It looks like most of your witnesses are going to be kids.' He paused and drank some water. 'You think you can handle a lot of kids?'

'Sure. Every woman can handle kids.' Grace Van Owen's voice was smooth, her face impassive. She stood up. 'I'll get down to the D.A.'s office right away. Then I'll go see the mother. But I'll have to hurry – I also want to get in a few hours at the City Hall archives. When I go into court on this, I want to know everything there is about the Triton Corporation.'

'Fine. You're well on target, Grace.' He watched her leave, then added, 'Unlike some I know.' And he looked straight at the Englishwoman, who didn't even blush, 'What have you got today, C. J.?'

'One possible date-rape, which just *might* be interesting,'

C.J. Lamb began, in her perfectly modulated, Home County tones that so perplexed and delighted Douglas Brackman.

'Just *might!*' he exploded. 'We've been waiting for one of those for months!'

She smiled. 'I'll give it my best shot, Douglas,' she said, slipping easily into the American vernacular.

'Anything else?'

'Oh, just a couple of dreary arson cases at a school . . .'

They passed on to other business, before Brackman wound up with some minor items, then closed the Conference.

'Keep me posted on that rape-case, C. J.,' he said in a stage-whisper, as they were leaving. 'I've always wanted to know what's really supposed to happen – from the legal point of view, of course.'

'I certainly will. I'm just as curious to know as you are, Douglas!' Brackman paused outside and saw that Markowitz had stopped by the water cooler, his wife having already disappeared into her office.

'Everything all right, Stuart?'

Markowitz jerked his head up. 'Sure – fine!' He gulped some water, then wiped his mouth over a thin smile. 'Why do you ask, Douglas?'

'Just paternal interest. You look as though you slept in your clothes, that's all. Ann okay?'

'Sure she's okay. Why not?'

'I don't know, Stuart. I was just asking.'

Brackman moved away and this day in the life of McKenzie Brackman and Partners went on.

*

'Hi, Grace! Good to see you.' Sam Ohls was a tall man with a lined face and liver spots on the back of his hands. He waved her to a chair, then sat down at a desk under the furled Stars and Stripes. 'So what can I do for you?'

'The Turner case.'

He gave her a long, slow smile. 'Sure. If you were still with us, I'd have picked you myself. Instead, I recommended you to Welfare. That's why the mother must have called you.'

'She didn't call me. She called the firm. But thanks, anyway. Are you bringing charges yourself?'

'Maybe'. He spread his hands. 'Triton have been in trouble before. Last time cost 'em twenty million dollars against the City Health Department – leak of chlorine gas from their main Inglewood plant. Should make things easy.'

'I want to see all the papers.'

'Sure.' Ohls spoke into the intercom: 'Candy Turner case, Marsha. Right away.' He sat back and nodded. 'Basic facts are simple enough. Bunch o' kids playing out in an ash-pit near Belmont. Several of 'em come in with skin burns, and one of 'em – this Candy Turner – is admitted to hospital unconscious with third-degree burns to her face and hands. She's lucky to be alive. Only she's now blind. And she'll stay blind.'

'What's the catch, Sam?'

'Well, – he leaned back and spread his long arms above his head – 'the catch is, Grace, there ain't no evidence. Some of the kid's friends were taken out in a squad-car a few hours after the incident and identified the place where it's supposed to have happened. Trouble is, there wasn't anything there.'

'So how do Triton come into it?'

'Well, the kids identified the place as being near some disused buildings belonging to the Triton Corporation. Trouble is, they were all locked – no sign of a break-in – and bare as the proverbial cupboard.'

'You think the kids were lying? Trying to cover up something?'

Ohls shrugged. 'Maybe. You know what kids are like? They watch too many movies on video. They fantasise.'

'What else did they say?'

Ohls sat forward and frowned. 'The local cops who took them out there say their original story was pretty confused. Probably because they were scared of getting into trouble. That ash-pit where they were playing must contravene every child protection regulation in the book. But when they got out there, the cops say the kids were pretty convincing. Not only that – they stuck to their story. Said the place had been cleaned – and the Turner kid's mountain bike had gone. And so had a pile of yellow drums.'

'Yellow drums? Is that what the kids said?'

'Yeah. And not only that. They also described one of those poison warning signs – black skull-and-crossbones on a yellow triangle – the sort of thing kids remember. They referred to it as 'a pirate sign'. And said that had gone too.'

'Pirate sign,' Grace repeated, writing quickly in her book. 'Are you sure that's what they said?'

'It was the local cops said they said it. The sort of stuff kids do say.'

'Exactly. It's a nice touch. Should be useful in court.'

Ohls shrugged. 'It's all in the file.' Then he snapped on

the intercom: 'Marsha, where's that goddam stuff on the Turner kid?' He leaned back. 'Goddam secretaries.'

Grace was reading back what she'd written while Ohls chewed the knuckle of his thumb, when there was a tap on the door and a large, mulish woman came in, wearing a dress like a mauve tent, and carrying a pink folder which she put down in front of Ohls as though it were a plate of bad food. On the front was stamped: DISTRICT ATTORNEY'S OFFICE – CONFIDENTIAL, above the name *Candy Turner*, written in blue ballpoint.

Grace waited until the woman had gone; then looked at Ohls and said, 'Sam, you seemed to be suggesting just now that someone might have gone out there the other evening and *removed* the evidence?'

Ohls continued chewing his left thumb. He didn't say anything.

Grace went on: 'I mean, could they have had enough time? Enough warning?'

Sam Ohls spread his legs behind the desk and pulled a long wry face at the ceiling. It was as though this were no longer L.A. – city of mayhem and murder, the modern Babylon – but a sleepy one-horse town in the boondocks, and Sam Ohls was the Sheriff with all the time in the world. Grace almost expected him any moment to start chewing a plug of tobacco.

'Yeah. A guy like me's got to keep an open mind, kid. But there's one thing I didn't tell you. When I said the cupboard was bare the other evening, I forgot the alarm.'

'Alarm?'

'Yeah. Infra-red eye set in the walls of the building nearest the broken fence. Only it wasn't the fence that set it off

– that was damaged long ago.'

'Isn't that a pretty sophisticated device to keep on an empty site?' asked Grace.

'Who knows? Maybe it got forgotten after the place was closed down. There's no evidence it's been used for years.'

'Except the kids' word?'

'Check.'

Grace paused, then leaned towards the pink folder on the desk. 'Can I see this?'

'Be my guest. I'll have a photostat run off for you – if you promise not to leave it in a restaurant again.'

She smiled and took the file. 'You'll never let me forget that, will you?'

Ohls smiled back. 'Nor will 'Big Mac' Moses Arkwright. Losing that file, then having the contents turn up in the pages of the *Clarion* . . . getting it spread all over the papers saved that asshole five years minimum. I should've put you over my knee and given you a good spanking – only you might've enjoyed it too much.'

'Careful, Sam. A remark like that in California could constitute verbal sexual harassment. But thanks, anyway.' She paused. 'Sam – suppose they *did* get that warning – would they have had time to clear the site?'

Ohls stuck his little finger in his ear and wiggled it about like a cotton-bud. 'They had at least three hours – before the kids got back there in the squad-car. Triton's a big outfit which has already had at least one run-in with the authorities. So they'd be well prepared. Sure it's possible. – everything's possible in this city.'

'Thanks, Sam.' She went out, closing the door softly behind her.

Chapter Five

The cab dropped Mike Kuzak outside the Beverly Hills Precinct House. The sun was at its highest: that dead hour between the first chilled drink of the day and a light salad-lunch served on the poolside. Perhaps it was the abundance of shrubs and jacaranda trees and flowering cherries, or just the smell of money; but the air felt cool and fresh up here, and there was a nice breeze off the ocean.

The Precinct House was a low white building with shingled walls and green tiles, the windows had copper-tinted glass and white-slatted shutters. There was even a pair of artificial coaching lamps over the door. It might have been the home of some middle-executive with a TV company. But at least the money seemed to be rubbing off round here.

Inside, it was a different matter. Most people who called on the Beverly Hills police cold off the street were usually poor or in trouble, or both. The rich citizens got the local cops to visit them at home. Nor did lawyers rate much round here, unless they arrived in a gold plated Hispano Suiza with a Hungarian chauffeur in knee-breeches and a diamond pin at his throat.

The lobby was cool and neat, with a rubber plant in the corner and not even a trace of tobacco smoke, but with that special sense of hidden menace that lurks in every police station round the world – like a dentist's waiting-room, all nice and peaceful, while nasty things might be going on in the back rooms.

Kuzak gave his business-card to the sergeant at the desk, who told him to wait. A few minutes later a plain clothes man came in, snapping Kuzak's card between his finger and thumb. He was a big, heavy man with a lot of muscle running to fat, and his pale blue eyes held the dry glitter of the serious drinker. This diagnosis was confirmed by the split capillaries on his nose and cheeks, like nests of tiny crimson and purple worms.

'Yeah? Come for Nugent-Ross, I guess?'

Kuzak smiled. 'The "Phantom Boot"?'*

The big man stood rocking carefully on the balls of his feet. 'Huh-huh, smart guy, eh?' He suddenly snapped Kuzak's card out of his fingers so that it shot on to the floor at the lawyer's feet. Kuzak made no move to pick it up. Here was the kind of policeman who was supposed to be rare these days: the sort who still uses a blackjack on the right places, and doesn't even bother to ask questions afterwards.

'I've come to post bail for him,' Kuzak said tonelessly.

'He hasn't agreed to see you yet, Mister –' He broke off and looked slyly towards the card on the floor. 'What did

** Boot: wheel clamp in the U.S.*

you say your name was again?'

'Kuzak. And he's agreed to see a representative of my firm, McKenzie Brackman and Partners.'

'Never heard of them,' the man lied; then gave a slack grin. 'In any case, who said *I've agreed to let you see him?* We've still got questions to ask him.'

'What? – Is he denying the charges?'

The big man said nothing. Kuzak took a deep breath. 'Okay, Sergeant . . .'

'I'm not a Sergeant, Koo-sack. I'm a Lootenant. Lootenant Slazenger.'

'Like the rackets?'

The man grunted as though he'd been hit. 'What the hell's that supposed to mean?' he said, with a low hiss of breath.

Kuzak grinned, bending down to retrieve his card. 'Figure of speech, Lieutenant. Like in tennis rackets. Savvy?'

The man swayed back on his heels, the busted worms round his nose and cheeks growing into livid patches of scarlet. 'Be missing, lawyer-boy. Right now – before I sock you in the gut.'

Kuzak sighed. 'Okay, Lieutenant. But I'd still like to see my client first. Before I go downtown to see the judge.'

For a moment Kuzak thought he'd gone too far. He wasn't sure whether Slazenger was going to hit him or have a coronary, or both. The man stood breathing heavily, like a winded pig.

'This way,' he said at last. He jerked his thumb towards the door, then seemed to sag against the side of the desk. 'McPherson,' – the word came between pants of breath –

'take the lawyer down to see Harvard Boy. And if they give yer any crap, just call me.'

The desk-sergeant came round and nodded to Kuzak. He was a fresh-faced young man in a well-pressed uniform of Luftwaffe-blue and had a well-polished holster you could have seen yourself in. That's how it was in Beverly Hills: a team of bright young WASPs who looked like professional tennis-players and made a good impression during the house calls; while a brutalised, hard-drinking boss showed the honest citizens that the law still had a few teeth in these parts.

Slazenger stared at them both with his pale rheumy eyes. 'And one other thing – Mister Koo-sack – before you see your client down there. He took a swing at me yesterday. Used to be a boxer in College. He's been booked for assaulting a police officer in the line o' dooty.'

'Thanks. I'll look forward to defending him.' Kuzak followed McPherson down a whitewashed stairway to the cells. 'You like your Lieutenant?' he asked casually.

'He's a Lieutenant.'

'That all?'

'Why not?'

McPherson had paused by one of the battleship-grey doors. The place was very quiet. He turned to Kuzak. 'He's old and he's disappointed and he drinks too much. And he doesn't like rich young college boys who get kicks outta needling the cops and then getting cheered by the great American media-circus. Okay?'

'Okay. But just one thing. Was that assault yesterday kosher?'

'Why not?'

Because your Lieutenant looks about as much like a victim of assault as Sinatra looks like a virgin.'

The young man stared at the ceiling, then at his feet. 'You don't understand. The Lieutenant is a real gentleman – if they'd just give him a break. Like if my aunt had *cojones* she wouldn't be my aunt – she'd by my uncle.' He unlocked the door and swung it open. 'I'll have the bail papers ready for you upstairs.'

'Thanks.' Kuzak advanced into the cell. The prisoner was sprawled out on the bunk, his trainers, without their laces, tossed idly on the floor, his arms spread out behind his head. He yawned, then swung his long legs slowly to the floor.

'You a cop or a lawyer?'

'Which do I look like?'

'You're not a newspaperman, are you?'

'Why? Have you had many of them trying to see you?'

'A few. They want to buy my story.'

He was a good-looking, all-American hunk of home-wrecking beefcake, his pretty face only temporarily spoilt by a puffed, blackened eye and a bruised lip the size of a banana-split. His voice was muffled, as though he were talking with his mouth full.

'They don't seem to like you much upstairs,' said Kuzak. 'Maybe because they say you went to Harvard?'

'Nah, I flunked out o'Harvard. I went to the U.C.L.A. – where I was good at swimming.'

'Slazenger said boxing.'

'Slazenger's a lying asshole. Still, what the hell!' He shrugged. 'If I'd been black, he'd have most likely broken my legs, then shot me. And I wouldn't even have made the front page.' He gave a lopsided grin and waved to the single chair next to the lavatory. 'Sid yerself down, pard-ner! Name's James Stewart Nugent-Ross. But most people call me Stoo.'

Kuzak sat down. 'So. You are Phantom Boot? Meaning you've fully confessed to booting altogether nineteen L.A.P.D. vehicles in nine days?'

'I most certainly am, and I most certainly have! Think I'd do a thing like that, then try to wriggle out of it by denying the charge? The Californian public expect its heroes to come clean. People don't like a whimpering *kvetch*, for God's sake.'

'You Jewish?'

'With a name like mine? No, I'm a hundred percent Irish-American from the East Coast. Doesn't it show?'

'Not through that mouthful of marbles,' said Kuzak; then added, with his best bedside smile: 'So that just leaves the motive, Stoo. How would you call it? Provocation? Sense of injustice? Private campaign against City Hall and the Los Angeles Police Department?'

'The last. I'm leading a spontaneous crusade. Totally unpremeditated.'

'All right. Tell me what happened.'

James Stewart 'Stoo' Nugent-Ross settled back on the bunk and embarked on his defence: 'Ten days ago I was driving up to Pasadena for a date, and stopped at a drug-store on Beverly for a cold milk and a pee. I'm teetotal, by the way.'

'Great.'

'So – I came out exactly four minutes later and they were putting on the Boot.'

'What time of day was this?'

'Three-fifteen in the afternoon.'

'What sort of restrictions were in force? Beverly's not a good place to stop – even for a milk and the call of nature.'

'Ah, that's just the point! What made me stop at that particular drugstore was on account of an empty meter bay right outside!'

'Fine. So you had perfect cause for legal redress. Why didn't you go for it? Or had you forgotten to put any money in?'

'Better than that! I *couldn't* put any money in. The thing was out-of-order! But I only discovered that when I'd got out of the car. You know these new meters up here in Beverly Hills? – when they're out-of-order, the letters come up on the tiny computerised panel that marks the time elapsed. You have to have aviator-sight to read 'em by. And in the sun it's darned near impossible! They must have been laying in wait to sucker someone like me – because you can bet your sweet ass nobody cruising past could have spotted the thing was *kaput!* Don't you lawyers call that "entrapment"?'

Kuzak preferred to ignore this. 'Did you attempt to discuss it with them?' he said, writing busily as he spoke.

'I sure did. But they didn't listen. Told me to get a lawyer. And I don't like lawyers. Why throw good money after bad?'

'Damned right,' said Kuzak. 'So you got mad at them?'

'You bet I did. Mostly, at first, because they'd made me miss my date.'

'I think we'll forget about your date – for the moment,' said Kuzak. 'So what did you do next?'

'I brooded a bit, then I got this great idea. You know all those used car lots round the city? How they leave the merchandise outside and boot the back wheels so nobody tries to drive the stuff away? Well, most of 'em are standard issue, only without the L.A.P.D. logo. So I moseyed around a bit and got a salesman to let me have twenty for two-fifty in cash.'

'You only fixed nineteen squad-cars, before you got picked up?'

Stoo Nugent-Ross chuckled. 'I kept the last one as a badge of honour. But you already figured out I meant to get caught? Because I picked this place for my grand finale?' He was grinning like a schoolboy who's just had his head kicked in trying to make a twenty-yard touchdown.

'Well,' said Kuzak, 'it *does* figure, doesn't it?'

'Sure. Just my bad luck I drew Slazenger out of the pack. But there it is – you get good cards, you get bad cards. What's important is how you play 'em.'

'Okay,' said Kuzak, 'now let's figure how we can keep you a hero and out of jail at the same time. First, I'll make the preliminary moves towards summonsing that bastard of a Lieutenant up there for assault, battery and deprivation of your Constitutional rights. So we'll have to find you a good photographer, before the blood dries, and get you some really glamorous publicity pix.'

'Before and after, huh?' Stoo grinned. 'I got some great studio shots of myself earlier this year when *People* did a big spread on "L.A.'s most eligible bachelors"!'

Kuzak nodded. 'The eye will probably have cleared up before the preliminary hearing, but that kisser of yours should still look like a horror commercial when you go into court. We might even try getting a doctor to put some stitches in.'

'I won't be disfigured, will I?'

'No – but if you want to look your worst in court, you'll have to lay off the ladies for a bit, and not put too much dressing on your wounds. No raw steaks. Let your mouth *fester*, if necessary.'

'Oh God,' said James Stewart Nugent-Ross, confirming what Kuzak had always suspected: that martyrs to a cause were a vain bunch of bastards.

'The real decision we have to make is whether we want this settled at the preliminary hearing before a judge – or whether you want the case to go before a grand jury.' Kuzak paused. 'I advise the former – if you're pleading guilty. Strike while the iron's hot. The TV and newspapers are full of you, but if the case is delayed they might get bored.'

'No grand jury's going to convict the "Phantom Boot", Mr Kuzak!'

'They don't have to – if you plead guilty. It'll be down to the judge.'

'So? What'll he do?'

'You can never tell in cases like this. But I'd say you were in with a fair chance – of getting all the headlines, and ending up with a heavy fine and, at worst, a "suspended". After all, the only thing you really hurt was the Department's pride.' He paused. For all his injuries, his client seemed to be enjoying himself. 'The main thing is to keep you out of the slammer,' he added.

'I'm very happy to go to jail,' Stoo said calmly. 'But I won't pay any fine.'

'Okay – you want to be a martyr, I can't help you.'

Nugent-Ross thought about this, then laughed. 'I'm Irish, for Chrissake! We're a race of martyrs.'

'Okay, be a martyr.' Kuzak stood up. 'They're posting bail for you upstairs. Ready?'

Stoo shuffled after him in his laceless trainers. Upstairs the lobby was still cool and empty. No drunks, no derelicts, no screaming addicts and pushers with their guts full of buckshot. A nice neighbourhood.

McPherson said, 'Bail's fixed at five thousand dollars. We'll take a certified cheque witnessed by your lawyer.'

'That's twice as high as it should be,' said Kuzak. 'My client is a man of honourable character and the offence of which he is charged does not merit such a prohibitive sum.'

'You want to argue that with the Lieutenant, or you want to take your client downstairs again, then argue later with the judge?'

'The judge will fix bail at two to three grand,' said Kuzak.

'You want to argue with me, Mister Koo-sack?' Lieutentant Slazenger had appeared silently behind them in his big rubber-soled loafers. He still looked flushed and his breath smelt of sour peppermint. Kuzak wondered how much he'd put away in just over twenty minutes.

'I'm disputing the bail figure, Lieutenant.'

'Dispootin!' the man roared, his pale blue eyes bulging dangerously. 'You goddam little creep! I heard about you, Koo-sack! I read about you! I read about you goin' to jail for contempt! For dispootin' with judges – for insulting and abusing the law of this great land of ours, the U.S. of A!' He was hissing with anger, flecks of brown spittle appear-

ing on his lip and chin.

'Now take your goddam client downstairs again – then get outta here, before I book you for obstruction!'

'You're overreaching yourself, Lieutenant. You're way out of line.' Kuzak looked at young McPherson, as though to say *You're my witness, Sergeant, whether you like it or not*. It was a mistake.

Slazenger leant forward and breathed warm air against his cheek. This time Kuzak clearly smelt the whisky. 'You don't think I'm a nice guy, do you, Koo-sack?'

'Sure I do. You're about as nice as a cold sore on the mouth.'

Kuzak felt his arm grabbed from behind, then yanked up his back, as the steel of a handcuff snapped round his wrist. In almost the same instant the second cuff closed round Slazenger's own wrist. It was all done with the speed of a conjuror and Kuzak would probably have submitted, if Slazenger hadn't also stepped forward and trodden hard on his heel. The pain was excruciating. Kuzak went mad. He swung round a full half-circle, pulling the big man off balance, and with his free hand hit Lieutenant Slazenger low and hard in the solar plexus.

The Lieutenant must have seen the blow coming, but was impeded by the handcuffs, and by the time he'd regained his balance it was too late. The wind went out of him in a soft grunt, and he began to collapse at the knees, his blotched face draining to a dirty grey.

'Hold it!' a voice yelled. 'Hold it right there, Mister Kuzak!' Sergeant McPherson had come round the desk and was holding a .38 Police Special level with Kuzak's throat. 'Now just get moving towards those stairs. One bad move and I'll blow your neck off. You too, Harvard Boy. Get in front and walk slowly.'

They had to walk slowly, because Slazenger was only just getting the air back into his lungs. 'I won't forget this,' he said, in a small tight voice. 'Not ever!'

When they got to the cells, McPherson pushed Nugent-Ross into the one he'd just left, locked it, then opened the door next to it. Slazenger fumbled a key from his pocket and unlocked the handcuff on his own wrist; then followed Kuzak into the cell.

'Careful, Chief,' McPherson called quietly. 'Remember, he's a lawyer.'

'I'm not gonna forget,' Slazenger said. His face was still ashen and his eyes glassy with pain but he was smiling as he gestured Kuzak towards the bunk bed. It had a steel frame. The Lieutenant grabbed Kuzak by the neck and forced him on to his knees.

Until now Kuzak had been too angry to feel frightened. But now fear seized him, making the hair prickle on the back of his head, and his mouth feel cold and dry. This might be sweet Beverly Hills, home of the great and the glamorous. But it was still L.A. – city of random killings, serial murders, where the hard-pressed cops would rather shoot a man than risk trying to bring him in. And Kuzak had not merely assaulted a police officer — McKenzie Brackman or no McKenzie Brackman — but a police officer who was not only violent, but drunk and violent.

Slazenger pressed Kuzak's head down till it touched the floor, bounced it a couple of times, hard against the cold tiles, then snapped the empty handcuff on to the leg-frame of the bunk.

Kuzak cowered, waiting for the kick; but it didn't come. He watched Slazenger's rubber soles padding away. 'So long, lawyer-boy. But I'll be back.' And the door slammed shut. A bolt crashed. Then a deathly silence. Kuzak could feel, through his throbbing head, a small trickle of blood start up under his hairline and watched it drip, dark and star-shaped, on to the tiles. Then he lost consciousness.

It might have been five — or twenty-five — minutes later, when he heard the bolt crash again, the lock turn, and saw the knife-edge trousers of young McPherson approaching. He leant down and released the handcuff from Kuzak's numb wrist.

'You always do this when you visit a Precinct House?' McPherson asked, in a pleasant voice, as he helped Kuzak on to the bunk.

'Invariably — when I meet a mothering bastard like that.' Kuzak sat up, slowly massaging his wrist and the back of his foot.

'You're lucky. Last time the Lieutenant half killed a man down here.'

'What did the guy have to do to deserve that?' Kuzak asked weakly. 'Tried to sniff his breath?'

'Just spat at him. You want anything?'

'Yeah. Cup of coffee, and that phone call I'm allowed. Get McKenzie Brackman — say I want to speak to Douglas Brackman himself. And if that Lieutenant of yours tries to refuse me, tell him I'll have him on traffic roster for the next twelve months. And that I mean, Sergeant McPherson!'

The young man sighed. 'Okay. But I warn you, the coffee's not good here.'

Chapter Six

The Filipino maid glided in with a fresh cafetière of medium-roast breakfast coffee. It was Stuart Markowitz's third since getting back from the office, soon after Morning Conference. He still had a heap of, paperwork to get through, if he was to have any chance of getting his clients off this grand-larceny charge. But all morning he'd felt fidgety and nervous; he couldn't concentrate; and his mood had not been improved by Brackman's little intervention by the water cooler. What the hell had the man been getting at? Did it really show that bad?

Stuart felt like a man suddenly touched by the plague. All through Morning Conference he'd been light-headed with lack of sleep, pale and anxious after an exhausting night: and already the deadly buboes were beginning to show. Everyone at Conference must have noticed. The Markowitzes were having another bout of marital wobblies.

Stuart poured more coffee and stared vacantly at the ocean. It was only two months since he and Ann Kelsey had moved into their new home overlooking Pacific Palisades. They had needed a break – a physical change for both of them – and if their malaise wasn't to be permanent, it meant either a change of office or change of home. But Stuart, even in his glummest mood, could not believe that McKenzie Brackman could survive without him: while Ann Kelsey was *truly* invaluable – everyone knew that, even she. Besides, neither could face the idea of breaking the news to Leland – it might send him back to hospital with another coronary.

So they'd stayed with the firm and bought a brand new *adobe* house near Pacific Palisades, tucked away on a promontory overlooking a little bay called Sargasso, which had not yet been ruined by the jet set or the bikers. Ann had fallen in love with the place on sight. No matter that the pale-brown *adobe* mud had been plastered across a frame of breeze-block and reinforced steel girders. It looked fine. Above all, it *felt* fine.

Ann Kelsey was not a purist in these matters. She was a woman who liked what she liked. Besides, there were plenty of details that were genuine. The traditional jutting timbers round the outer wall had been plundered from a Spanish ruin near Santa Fe; the high wrought-iron gates at the entrance had come from a bishop's palace in Seville; and on the enclosed Moorish patio stood a green marble fountain which they'd found near Rome during their recent holiday.

Yet Stuart Markowitz was still not entirely happy. He chafed under that ancient biblical guilt-complex of having been born rich, without ever having to work for his money: from his earliest awareness of life, he had known he would one day be very rich. His grandfather had come from Poland and opened a jewellery business on New York's East Side. After he'd died, the whole business had gone to his only son – Stuart's father – who in the Twenties had moved to the West Coast and prospered mightily. But he'd made his real killing after Pearl Harbour, when he'd found himself cornering the market in industrial diamonds which were at a premium for the munitions industry. He had died just as Stuart graduated from college.

Stuart had inherited a fortune and had been feeling guilty ever since. He'd not been so much worried by taunts that his family had made their money out of the war – after all, his papa had been helping to win the Great Battle for Democracy, *for Chrissake*! No – what really troubled Stuart was the *money itself*. For he suffered the awful terrors of the rich – that without his money he'd be nothing. He was a moderately successful lawyer: but would that alone have been enough to win the charming Ann Kelsey? And poor, rich Stuart Markowitz – fifteen years Ann's senior – would lie awake in the small hours and worry about having *too much money*.

This latest crisis with his wife only compounded his sense of insecurity. He felt so useless, redundant to her needs since Matt Kelsey Sr.'s first telephone call ten days ago. And so alone. He was now left all on his own in this big luxurious house, brooding on what he might have done to help – if he'd only been allowed. It was all very puzzling and very painful.

Then, to cap it all, she'd announced to him today, after

Morning Conference, that she wouldn't be home that night and had arranged for their son, Matt, to stay with his regular baby-minder for a few days. Ann was flying up to the little town of Durango, in the foothills of the Colorado Rockies, where she was meeting her father face-to-face, determined to make him see sense, even if she had to bang his head against the floor.

When Stuart had protested that this was not just between father and daughter – but that a third party was involved, and this was just the sort of crisis where a lawyer would be needed, probably sooner rather than later – she'd told him bluntly, in that sterile jargon that lawyers prefer when things start getting nasty, that she did not 'think it appropriate for him to be involved at this stage.' She wanted to spare her old father any further anguish and embarrassment. Stuart wasn't sure he saw it quite like that: but didn't know what he could do, besides keeping them both awake all night, offering her endless advice and moral support.

But maybe she was right after all? For try as he might, Stuart was unable to feel unqualified sympathy for his father-in-law. He'd always got on well with the old man from the start, considering him to be built of the finest timbers in the American character – and had said so, more than once. For Matt Kelsey Sr. was a tough, down-to-earth, honest Joe, a good family man devoted to his daughter. Above all, he had not flickered an eyelid when Ann had first told him she was going to marry a Jew fifteen years her senior. All he'd said was: 'A race that's produced 85 percent of Nobel Prize winners and an Army that's won five wars in my own lifetime is good enough for my girl!'

Stuart, however, having spent most of the previous night

playing devil's advocate for the old man, was now, in the light of day, beginning to see Ann Kelsey's point of view. What her old man had done was so obviously selfish, irrational, even crazy. For if there ever was a marriage made in heaven, it was surely that of Matt and Eileen Kelsey!

Of course, it was the old story. What the Greeks called *Iistrus*, which is variously translated as 'a vehement bodily appetite, a gadfly that goads the loins; a senile lust for coitus.' (When Stuart had been at Law School he'd diverted himself by going to night-school once a week to study the Ancient Greeks: and there was nothing today's psychiatrists could teach these boys about errant sex!)

But the Ancient Greeks weren't around any more, or Stuart would have known what to do. It was all so unfair on his wife! He ought to be at her side now – an older, wiser counsel who could talk to her father as an equal, man-to-man, and maybe instill some sense into the old fool.

But Ann Kelsey had been adamant. This was strictly family, she'd said – at which Stuart had protested again that he *was* family. Then they'd stopped discussing the matter and had begun arguing instead. Stuart now felt rejected, unwanted.

The Filipino girl appeared and asked what he wanted for lunch. But Stuart wasn't hungry. Instead, he went for a swim, mindful of his doctor's advice not to exert himself too much. Afterwards, he was towelling himself down when the girl came out and told him his wife was on the phone.

'Darling, it's me! Douglas has been sweet – he's let me off early and I'm flying up on the afternoon plane. It'll give me more time to settle in.'

‘Won’t you be able to come back here and say goodbye?’ he asked miserably.

‘Oh darling, I’d love to! But I really don’t have time. I want to get up and see Daddy as soon as I can.’ There was a pause. ‘I’m sorry Stuart. But this *is* important to him.’

‘It’s important to me too,’ he said petulantly; and cursed himself as soon as he said it.

‘Stuart, please,’ – her voice had a sudden chill in it – ‘don’t start making things even more difficult for me.’

‘I’m sorry, Ann. But I’ll miss you.’

‘I’ll miss you too, Stuart. I’ll call you as soon as I get to Daddy’s. Must go down now. Bye, darling!’

‘Goodbye, Ann.’ He hung up and walked wearily back to his study.

Chapter Seven

Ann Kelsey was crying. Since speaking briefly with her husband earlier that evening, she had spent the last three hours talking and arguing with her father.

At sixty-five Matt Kelsey was a solid, handsome man with a shock of white hair and a weathered face, heavily tanned by the Colorado sun, who'd never quite recovered from being told at college that he was a dead-ringer for Spencer Tracy.

He was barefoot, wearing an old chequered shirt and Levis, and he was drinking Rye. His daughter, facing him across the wooden table on the deck of the Kelseys' ranch-house above Durango, Colorado, was starting on her second bottle of wine.

Ann Kelsey's mother was away with her sister on Cape Cod. She and Matt Kelsey had been married for exactly forty years, and Ann was their only child. They had spent their wedding anniversary this year – on Independence Day – apart for the first time in their entire married life, except for in their second year together, when her husband had been in an Army hospital in Japan. A Chinese anti-aircraft shell had burst inside his C46 in Korea, and the plane had crash-landed in flames. With his legs full of shrapnel, Matt had still managed to drag an unconscious buddy out of the burning wreck, for which he had been awarded the combined Silver Star and Purple Heart, and six months and three operations in hospital. He was still slightly lame in one leg.

During those forty years of marriage – despite his fine looks and a comfortable fortune as the recently retired founder of 'Kelsey High-Flyers', a crop spraying company in Wichita, Kansas – Matt Kelsey had boasted, quite truthfully, that he had never looked at another woman. His wife, Eileen – herself a retired and highly respected doctor in Durango, and the same age as her husband – was still a handsome woman with silver-grey hair and a pioneer profile that caused some folk to suspect she might have Indian blood.

Then, this Spring, the unthinkable had happened. Matt Kelsey had fallen in love. Blindly, pitifully, like an over-eager adolescent in the first flush of confused youth. The old adage, 'old enough to be her father', was a cruel understatement in this case.

The recipient of this feverish passion was all of 19 years old, with the improbable name of Daisy Trader. She was a local girl from a broken home in Durango. Matt Kelsey had met her at the end of March while she was working as a waitress in the local skiing resort, the aptly-named town of

Purgatory.

Matt and Eileen had been going up there for a month each year, from their retirement home in Durango. He went for the skiing, she for her health; and they always chose March, when the high season was over and the place wasn't too crowded. Also, it was sunnier.

But this year their last two weeks had been lousy, with rain and wet snow. The *pistes* were so bad that even the keen skiiers had spent most days hanging out in the two hotel bars, boozing and picking up girls to take dancing in the evening.

Then, in the last week, Eileen had had a bad attack of rheumatism, brought on by the damp weather, and had returned alone to Durango. Matt had insisted on going too, but she wouldn't hear of it. The weather might change any day, and she knew how much her husband loved his skiing. So Matt, against his better judgement, had stayed on. But the weather had not changed. It had rained for the next three days.

*

Matt's infatuation with Daisy Trader began as a mild, innocent flirtation. What great passions have not? They met while she was serving him brunch in the Purgatory Drugstore where she worked. '*Good day, Sir, I'm Daisy Trader and I'm your personal waitress! How can I help you*?' She was about to take her lunchbreak, when he asked her to join him. He drove her to a little diner well out of town: a haunt of the local 'art-set', mostly middle-aged hippies who'd moved down from California when the State got to expensive.

It was a good choice for their first date. The food was good, the ambiance relaxed, and, despite the phoney clientele, he saw she was impressed. But far more important, it was not the sort of place where he risked running into any of his buddies from Durango, all of whom would be as likely to be found in a local hippy-joint as in a gay bar.

Matt found her a spirited, gutsy little thing who was making the best of a life that had not so far treated her well. And he admired her for it. He also made the mistake of thinking Daisy a lonely, vulnerable creature who needed protecting. His second mistake was to fall in love with her.

*

Matt took Daisy to dinner the next evening, in the only good restaurant in town. It boasted traditional French *cuisine* and was called *L'Aiglon'* – known to the local wits as 'Leg-Loin'. Candles on the tables, Air France posters on the walls, canned Country-and-Western in the background. He had intended to look as unobtrusive as possible. He'd worn denims and collar-and-tie; but he might just as well have saved himself the trouble. Daisy Trader had arrived in white PVC boots, black, skin-tight leather trousers and a day-glo orange anorak which she took off to reveal a see-through chiffon blouse, with no bra. Little chance of their remaining inconspicuous, even in a crowded night-spot.

They had just started on their first course – tinned snails in garlic butter – when Matt experienced a moment of panic. A photographer had just come into the restaurant and was offering his services round the tables. Matt nearly made a scene, as he forced a reluctant Daisy Trader to put her anorak back on. The last thing he wanted was a front-page spread, with a two-column pic, in next week's *Rocky Mountain News:* DURANGO AVIATOR, 65, DATES WAITRESS, 19 . . . There seemed small hope that they would be mistaken here for father and daughter. Not if Eileen saw it – or worse, Ann. He suppressed a shudder.

Daisy Trader had noticed his anxiety and seemed annoyed. 'If you're ashamed being seen with me,' she said, with some dignity, 'I'll leave right now!'

He took her hand across the table and lowered his voice. 'It's just that there are people out East who aren't supposed to know where I am . . .'

She stared at him for a moment, wide-eyed: 'You mean – you're in hiding?'

He chuckled and patted her hand. 'Well – something like that.'

During the evening he noticed that she was drinking more than he'd have liked – she preferred beer to wine – and this time her conversation seemed to him coarser, more barbed. She talked about what assholes most of her customers were, especially in the high season: how the women argued about the check and didn't leave enough tips; while the men made offensive comments when she passed their tables. She told him her ambition was to get a job in Aspen – that had *real class*. But despite her jaundiced outlook on life, she was a flirt. Not a very subtle one, perhaps, but enough to flatter his ego.

Matt had no real knowledge of modern teenagers, and was at first a bit nervous of her. Afraid he might bore her, he said little, preferring the 'strong, silent' role. But she did enough talking for the two of them. Occasionally she would ask him the odd question about himself, but didn't seem very interested in the answers. He told her only what he considered he could decently disclose: that he was married and had a grown-up daughter who worked as an attorney in L.A. His only attempt to impress her was to say that he had been an U.S.A.F. pilot in Korea, and gone on flying for his own company in Kansas. He didn't play down the romantic, even dangerous side to his life. He did not volunteer the information that he was retired; and didn't even state openly that he was still living with his wife. Nor did he conceal the fact that he was wealthy.

Yet by the end of the evening he was feeling a little foolish, as well as slightly anxious. Although the girl had stuck to beer all evening, she'd taken to the Cointreau he'd offered her like a wasp to jam; and was suddenly, noticeably drunk as he hurried her out of the restaurant. For a moment, standing outside in the wet snow, Matt did not know what to do next. He did not want to offend her by dropping her cold at the door, wherever that was; while the thought of inviting her back to his hotel room had, quite honestly, never entered his head.

In the event, she solved his dilemma for him. She wanted to go dancing, and made him drive to the noisy shack on the edge of town where, she now told him, she'd already agreed to meet friends later that night. He drew up outside, gave her a quick peck on the cheek, then turned the car round and headed back towards his hotel.

As he drove carefully through the sodden streets, he could imagine how Daisy Trader would even now be describing him to her friends – hunks of golden youth in designer *après-ski*, who'd be crowding round her to hear how she'd met 'this real sweet old guy who used to be a pilot and has a stash of money. A real nice sugar-daddy . . .!' And Matt felt a qualm of sadness. He was an old man with a sick wife, and he was driving home alone to an empty bed, with nothing to look forward to except the rest of his comfortable retirement, and then, sometime, death.

Before turning in, he called his wife in Durango. Thinking about it afterwards, he realised it must have been a pretty downbeat conversation. The weather wasn't much better in Durango, she said; and he hadn't got in more than a couple of hours' skiing since she'd left. They both sounded depressed. He said he hoped to see her in about three days, and she said she was looking forward to it.

*

That night Matt did not sleep well. He lay awake for a long time, vaguely troubled by thoughts of Daisy Trader. Sometime, around midnight, he'd had the crazy idea of getting dressed and going down to the disco, like an ancient latter-day knight in armour, where he'd challenge the local studs on their own turf and bear away the lovely Daisy Trader on his white charger – or at least, in his white Toyota GT convertible. Twenty years ago – perhaps even ten – he'd have done just that. And the girl wouldn't have even protested.

Instead, he got out of bed and drank half a pint of whisky, growing maudlin and reflective, before falling into a restless sleep.

Chapter Eight

Grace knew that if she went to visit Candy's mother dressed as she was – an attractive blonde in a smart business suit – she'd never get out of the neighbourhood alive.

She put on some old overalls she'd worn to paint the porch last summer, a pair of sneakers, scarf over her hair and big sunglasses to hide her face. Then she fetched the car from the parking lot. Few taxi drivers were prepared to venture where she was headed; and those that were would be likely to rape her. She might be exaggerating, of course – but probably not by much.

Grace got the car out and headed east, to Mar Vista District, where she joined the San Diego Freeway south towards Inglewood and the International Airport. Was it only yesterday she had driven on the same road with Victor?

The tract-house was on a dirt road below the Freeway.

Grace passed the occasional rusted jalopy, most with flat tyres, others with no wheels at all. The few trees along the road were stunted and shrivelled by the baking smog. Bursts of salsa and rap sounded above the hum of traffic from the Freeway and the howl of jets from the airport. Otherwise, it wasn't much noisier than any other neighbourhood of Los Angeles. And a good deal less crowded.

Grace went through the broken picket fence, up some wooden steps to a flimsy frame door and tapped on the wire mesh. There was a movement inside; then a stout dark woman in a flowered dress, with a bandana over her scraped-back hair, pulled the door open without unlocking it. It snagged on the jamb and she said something in Spanish. She was smoking a cheap filter-tip stuck to her lower lip. She peered out at Grace, sucking smoke up her broad nostrils. 'Yeah?'

'I've come to see Mrs Rita Turner.'

The woman stood studying Grace carefully, still without removing the cigarette. From behind her came the inane chatter of a TV gameshow, with the volume turned up too loud. 'Who wanna see her?' she said at last, narrowing her eyes.

Grace hesitated. 'Are you Mrs Turner?'

'No. Mrs Turner she sleep. She stay all night in the hospital.' The woman spoke with a thick Hispanic accent. 'That your automobile?' she added, frowning past Grace, at the blue sedan parked outside the picket fence below the steps. Grace nodded.

'You leave it there, lady, you got no more automobile.'

'Thanks. But I must see Mrs Turner. It's very important. Can she be disturbed?'

'No, she sleep, she very tired – her kid very sick in the hospital.'

'Yes I know, that's why I'm here,' said Grace. 'May I come in, please?'

The woman went on staring suspiciously at her, the cigarette still stuck to her lip. 'You from the *polizia?*' she said finally.

'No. I'm a lawyer. I've come to help Mrs Turner and her child.'

A voice suddenly called out from inside the house: '*Maria – who is it*?' A woman's voice, at once harsh and feeble, as though enervated with fatigue:

'Who is it, for Chrissake!'

The woman turned and shouted something in an Hispanic patois which Grace didn't follow; and the voice inside called something back, none of which Grace could understand. Maria turned to her, seemed to hesitate, then stepped back and opened the door. *'Entrada, por favor!'* She led Grace down a short dingy passage cluttered with piles of children's clothes and old shoes, black plastic garbage bags, a broken skateboard, a ghetto-blaster without a plug, a rusted kettle, rows of empty liquor bottles, and a jumbo carton of potato crisps. The only touch of charm was a small, crudely-fashioned bow-and-arrow hung above the door next to a child's plastic Navajo mask.

Grace caught a glimpse of a narrow kitchenette, stacked and filthy, before Maria led her through a bead curtain, into what Grace took to be the living room. It filled her with instant claustrophobia. The curtains were drawn, the windows shut, sealing in a warm stench of stale cigarettes and the bitter-sweet smell of rancid cooking, decaying fruit, damp washing, and a few other things that didn't bear thinking about.

The one light, apart from what seeped through the thin curtains, was the glow from the 24-inch television set in the middle of the room. It was the one concession to luxury. Otherwise, the few decorations looked as though they were rejects from a car boot sale; a cracked mirror framed in plastic 'mother-of-pearl'; a fake *art-deco* table-lamp, without its glass shade; a poster for a 'Doors' concert; and bizarrely, a discoloured bumper-sticker with the message, *NIXON FOR 72*!

On a side table Grace could just make out the shape of a half-eaten hamburger on a disposable plate. The whole scene, with the exception of the bumper-sticker, reminded her of one of those 'amateur' TV documentaries from the Sixties – filmed in coarse monochrome with a hand-held camera, depicting life among the new American underclasses. Still, Grace thought, there were worse places. Rita Turner at least had four walls and a roof, even a certain degree of privacy. As good a place as any in which to grieve briefly, and then to die.

The woman's voice called out from a sofa in front of the TV. 'Who is it, Maria?'

'Mrs Rita Turner?' Grace asked, having to raise her voice against the din from the TV.

'Yeah? Whatya want?'

'I'm a lawyer, Mrs Turner' – she had to speak up, against the cackling applause from the gameshow – 'My firm was recommended through the Welfare people at the hospital. I'm Grace Van Owen, from McKenzie Brackman and Partners.'

'So whatd'ya want with me?' the voice rasped. 'I don'need no lawyers, lady. It wasn't my Candy's fault. She was just playing' – the words caught in a low, wheezing sob – 'I just want my baby back!' she wailed. 'My poor Candy baby . . .!'

Grace suppressed a slight shudder. She could just make out a puffed, shapeless face, reflected in the jumping pink lights from the TV, peering out from under a halo of dirty blonde hair like a fright-wig. The rest of Mrs Turner lay wrapped in a dingy nightgown.

The sobs had become short, gasping hiccups. Then suddenly she shouted across the room, *'My baby's blind!* She can't see. She'll never see anything ever again. Never see any TV again! You understan' that, lady? *Do you?'*

The last two words were hurled across the floor with such fury that Grace thought the woman might leap off the sofa and attack her. She was filled with pity and terror – those ancient ingredients of true tragedy – and knew it was time to get out. To flee back to the city in her Ford sedan, listening to the soothing tape of Monteverdi on the car stereo.

She felt instantly ashamed. 'Please believe me, Mrs Turner – I'm not here to blame you for anything. I'm here to help you – protect you – to get you some money, lots of money, from the people who did this to your daughter – to Candy.'

At the sound of her child's name, the woman uttered a terrible cry, like a tortured animal. 'I don'wan' no money! What good is money when my baby's blind? *Oh God!*' – and the sobbing began again, with mounting hysteria. Maria walked over to her and turned down the TV, though not enough. She stood over Mrs Turner, whispering softly, soothingly to her; while Grace watched helplessly. After some time the mother seemed to collect herself. She lit a cigarette from a packet on the floor, next to a coffee cup full of dead stubs smoked down to the filters; then reached down beside the sofa and hauled up a half-bottle of Smirnoff vodka, which Grace had not noticed before.

The TV host was yapping quietly, *'And now, ladies, for the twenty-one thousand dollar prize – the complete de luxe Renaissance bathroom, modelled on the exact replica of a sixteenth-century Venetian room – round sunken bath with gold-plated fittings . . .'*

Rita Turner unscrewed the bottle and drank thirstily; then belched genteelly, and said, 'How much money you say it was, lady?'

'It'll be a lot of money, Mrs Turner. The people who did this to your daughter have been in trouble before. But this time they're going to pay for it.'

'Yeah. Lawyers! She leant out and spat into the coffee cup, then leant back, eyes closed, pulling deeply on her cigarette. 'You find out who did this to Candy and I'll kill 'em. With my own hands. I'll get a gun and blow 'em away!'

'I don't think that would help, Mrs Turner. Much better to let the law take care of things.'

'Screw the law. Screw you all. I'm tired. I wanna sleep. I wanna die.' She seemed to consider this last proposition for a few seconds, then reached down again for the bottle.

'I'd like to talk to you again, Mrs Turner. When you're feeling a little stronger. Then we can decide what we're going to do.' But Grace knew the woman wasn't listening;

her cigarette had gone out, but she was holding the bottle like a baby. It was almost empty now, and her eyes were closed. Maria came up to Grace and nodded towards the door. '*La Senora* – she sick very sad. *La nina chica* – so sad, so terrible.'

'Yes. Terrible. I'm really so sorry. I want to thank you, Mrs – I'm sorry, I don't even know your name?

'I am Senora Garcia. My boy Manuel, he was a very good friend to Candy. He found her – went with her to the hospital.'

'Thank you, Mrs Garcia. Maybe I can speak with you again sometime? And perhaps meet your son? All I want to do is help Mrs Turner – and Candy, of course.'

Outside, Grace suppressed a terrible urge to run. She gave a last wave to Mrs Maria Garcia, then pulled away and drove fast back down the dirt track, towards the Freeway and the reassuring smog-laden blue of the city. She realised that, for the first time in many weeks, she'd spent at least half-an-hour without once thinking of her own emotional problems – her tangled relations first with Mike Kuzak, now with Victor Sifuentes.

She felt a curious elation, a release from her own pain as she experienced another, more tangible misery – this time not her own. She could not get out of her mind the sight of that stricken, powerless woman, with her vodka bottle in front of the ghastly gameshow, telling Grace in her tear-sodden voice how her little girl *would never watch television again.*

And by the time Grace reached the big metropolis her mind was fixed with a grim, absolute determination. She knew what she had to do, and she was going to do it.

Chapter Nine

Grace spent the rest of the day at the City Hall Library, poring through back-numbers in the newspaper archives. She first looked up all the contemporaneous reports on the giant law suit five years ago, brought by the County of Los Angeles against the Triton Corporation and its newly appointed Executive President, Randolph D. Miller Jr. – known, according to the various feature-writers of the day, as 'Randy' to friends, colleagues, and intimates alike. Randy Miller, despite being well the wrong side of fifty, was obviously one of the boys.

The accompanying photographs showed a handsome, middle-aged face with a tight smile and the brutal eyes of a man who's got to the top and isn't too worried about how he's done it. *'Certainly not just by being nice to his mother,'* as one newspaper columnist wrote after the case: *'In another age, a more decent age, he might have been hanged as a pirate. Today, in the America of the late Eighties, he's rich, he's respectable, he gets to shake the Governor's hand, and he does for the image of U.S. Capitalism what Robespierre did for the slogan,* 'Liberté, Egalité, Fraternité'. *In short, any common dunghill would smell sweeter.'*

At the time of the case, the Triton Corporation – headquarters Pasadena, L.A. – dealt primarily in chemical products – mostly industrial fertilizers, detergents and designer pesticides. And Grace gathered, reading between the lines, that most of the scientists and experts employed with the company were big names in the academic world, who were more interested in making a splash in the scientific journals – with at least one eye on a Nobel Prize – than in such mundane chores as bothering about safety regulations. Nor did Randy Miller sound the sort of man who'd lie awake chewing his fingernails worrying about it.

Grace read that the L.A. District Court had found against Triton, and fined the Corporation a total of twenty million dollars on six counts of damaging the environment and endangering the public health of Los Angeles and its surrounding counties. But the Judge had stopped short of closing the Corporation down, which led to a furious outcry and almost cost the Governor the ensuing election.

Miller was also fined half a million dollars for 'gross and willful neglect of his executive responsibilities', and the Board of Triton had decided to bite on the bullet and pay. But to save his own job, Miller had taken his conviction to the Supreme Court, where he won because of the relatively short period he'd been in charge of the Corporation at the time the offences occurred. The Court had then ruled, by a majority verdict, that blame should rest with his predecessor – who was beyond the jurisdiction of the U.S. courts, for the good reason that he was dead.

Later, Grace read, Miller had himself sued a number of newspaper and TV stations for libel. Most had preferred to settle out of court; while the outstanding cases Miller prudently decided to drop. But that was not the end of it. Reading on towards the present day, Grace came across cases of other kids, some quite recently, in both the Pasadena and Inglewood areas, suffering from various complaints – skin rashes, vomiting, respiratory problems. The rumours and accusations had become so bad that eventually, last year, an official inquiry had been held; but while several fingers seemed to point towards the Triton Corporation, nothing was proved.

By the time she'd finished the last file and returned it to the desk, the library was getting ready to close. Grace had already made up her mind that she did not like Mr Randolph D. Miller Jnr., or the lazy, greedy, glory-seeking empire he presided over.

When she got back that evening to her comfortable, chaste apartment in Santa Monica, she took a long cool shower, then fixed herself a stiff drink – the first of the day – determined to make it last until it was time to cook dinner. She had no date, no engagement for the evening. She nursed her drink and played back the messages on her answering-machine; her heart pounding with each fresh voice.

But Victor hadn't called from Las Vegas. Maybe he was too busy? Maybe out playing the tables and making them both a fortune? Maybe . . .?

She thought of ringing Mike Kuzak – or just walking round to his beach house at the edge of the ocean. It was barely five hundred yards away.

Instead, she turned the radio on to the music station – '*For your very own favourites through the night*' – sat down on the Chesterfield divan and set to work condensing her mass of notes into a coherent mini-chronicle of the life and times of an American success story.

She began in her neat hand writing:

RANDOLPH DAVID MILLER, Jnr.

Born 1932. Father discharged bankrupt from St Louis, Missouri. Mother, nothing known. Graduated from High School 1949; good grades, chemistry and science. Enrolled same year at Madison University, Michigan but left after two months – reason unknown. (Here Grace made a brief note GIRL IN TROUBLE???)

Joined Marine Corps 1950. Served with distinction in Korea. Invalided out 1951 with Purple Heart. A year in hospital, underwent extensive plastic surgery. Returned Stateside 1952 and joined Parlane Plastics, San Diego, as a trainee industrial chemist.

Married 1958 Pauline Skarden; two kids, one boy, one girl. 1964 made Corporate Overseas Director at Parlane. Moved to Paris, France, 1966. Divorced same year. 1968 married Anne-Marie de la Molinard, French citizen. Family believed v. wealthy. 1970 wife killed in car smash – Miller driving. No further details. Returned Stateside 1972, made Corporate Vice-President at Parlane. 1975 convicted of serious assault against husband of local woman.

Claimed self-defence, given two years suspended. Fired by Parlane.

1976 started his own pharmaceutical company. 1980 married Dawn Smithson-Lund, Texan heiress to a cattle fortune. Three kids, all girls. (POOR LITTLE BITCHES, Grace wrote in the margin.)

1982 head-hunted by Triton. 1984 made Executive Vice-President of Triton, 1986 President.

Then followed the dates of the law suit against Triton, and Miller's counteractions for libel. But at this point Grace became too upset to go on until she'd had just one more drink, only slightly milder than the first. The radio was playing Tchaikovsky's Fifth, 'La Pathetique'. It seemed peculiarly apt. And when she began writing again, it was as though she were penning a death sentence:

Miller still married – though Press rumours abound. Believed to be worth upwards of 100 million. Keeps race horses, plays polo. Also keen yachtsman. Competed 1989 in the Americas Cup. Owns property in: Bel Air, L.A., Tucson, French Riviera. Apartment in Paris 16th, and East 35th St., N.Y.C. Member of the Harvard Club, New York. Jockey Club, Paris. Royal Yacht Squadron, Cowes, England.

Politics: Strictly Rep. And how! Grace commented.

Finally, in an angry scribble at the bottom of the page: WHAT A SHIT.

By the time she'd finished, it was past nine o'clock and she was no longer hungry. She was mixing a final drink, when the telephone rang. She grabbed at it, almost dropping it in her haste, and held the handset upside down.

'Grace?'

Oh God. She sat gripping the phone with both hands,

trying hard to control her breathing.

'Grace – is that you? It's Mike!'

She took several long, slow breaths.

'Grace! I don't hear you.'

'What do you want, Michael?' But even as she spoke she was aware that her voice sounded funny, as though her jaw muscles were slightly paralysed.

There was a pause. 'Grace – are you okay? You haven't been drinking, have you?'

'Listen, Michael. I've had a hard day and I'm very tired. What do you want?'

'I've been hurt, Grace. I was on a case and I got beaten up by some lousy cop in Beverly Hills. I was in the slammer till Brackman bailed me. But I had a suspected concussion, and I only just got out of Casualty.'

She felt a warm liquid glow begin in her belly and spread upwards until her scalp tingled. 'But are you all right, Michael? Where are you?'

'In a drugstore on Sunset, trying to keep some coffee down. Are you alone?'

'What do you think?' She waited, screwing up courage; then said: 'Have you eaten yet?'

'No. But I don't think I feel like it. They gave me a shot of something at the hospital and I feel kinda drowsy.'

It seemed another long time before Grace answered. 'You'd better come round. I'll fix you something light – you got to eat *something*, Michael. Can you get a taxi?

'I'm on my way, Grace. And thanks.' The line went dead. Grace went into the kitchen, threw away her last drink, and began to prepare an omelette for two.

Chapter Ten

Matt Kelsey's little adventure might have ended the morning after – a brief, silly flirtation at the end of an abortive skiing holiday – but for one trivial factor. Next morning Matt Kelsey had a hangover. Although he'd been a tough drinker most of his life, he usually recovered quickly. Perhaps this time the effect was more psychological; or maybe he was just getting old.

Pain slammed round the steel walls of his skull, and he had difficulty focusing in the mirror to shave. He went down to breakfast, but could only manage coffee. He tried going for a walk, but instead of bracing mountain air, there was a damp blanket of fog which made his headache worse. It was then that he decided to jack it in and drive back to Durango. He'd ask for his bill, and ring Eileen from the hotel. But first he needed a pick-me-up. Not the hair of the dog – that was strictly for novices. If he wanted to enjoy his next drink, he needed to clear his head first.

He decided – fatally, as it turned out – to try that old trick he'd learnt in the Air Force: a lungful of pure oxygen before the dawn take-off. Civilised drugstores still kept a cylinder in the back parlour, supposedly for just such emergencies.

The Purgatory drugstore was crowded for the early lunch hour. The first thing Matt noticed as he came in was a beefy, white-aproned woman behind the counter, standing with her back to the customers, in a posture that gave off waves of female aggression like Gamma rays. Her voice carried even above the hubbub of the diners, in a coarse bellow: *'I told you once, sister, and I ain't telling you again! One more time, I said, and you're out on yer pretty ass . . .!'*

In front of her stood Daisy Trader, her arms stiff at her sides, her face flushed and streaked with tears. Most of the customers seemed amused by the scene. The girl didn't notice Matt at first. She started yelling at the woman, incoherent and foul-mouthed: '*. . . Just because you can't make it, you fat fag-hag . . .!*'

The woman made a lunge at the girl. Matt, even with his stiff leg, dashed round the counter and had grabbed the woman from behind, just as she was about to seize Daisy Trader's hair. *'Hey, lady, you hold it!'*

The woman, who was obviously the manageress, swung round and jabbed him hard in the side with her elbow. 'Drop dead, buddy, or I calls the cops!'

The blow in his side had made him momentarily loosen his grip on her, and this time she was able to grab a fistful of Daisy Trader's hair. The girl screamed and Matt stepped round and gave a short chopping blow to the woman's upper arm that was still dragging at Daisy Trader's hair. She let go and the arm fell limp.

The last time Matt had done this was to a drunk in a bar in Denver who had called Eileen 'a cheap broad'. That had been twenty years ago. Part of him was gratified that he still hadn't lost his touch. At the same time he realised he was close to the Rubicon – if he hadn't already crossed it. In safe Middle-America a woman like this would readily bring a charge of battery. He thought of what his daughter, a respectable attorney, would think . . .

They'd better get out of here – quick! The customers were already crowding closer, taking his and Daisy Trader's side, some cheering: *'C'mon, fella, give 'em hell! – go kick ass, boy*!' This was better than a day on the slopes.

Matt had grabbed Daisy Trader round the midriff and began half-carrying her out from behind the counter, when the girl suddenly wheeled round and gave the manageress a sharp kick to the kneecap. She gave a squeal of agony and crumpled half to the floor. Matt was trying to keep his head, aware of someone moving in with a camera a few feet away. He got Daisy Trader outside and began to run with her, dragging his bad leg through the slush. She was still wearing her thin working shoes.

'The f . . . bitch! I should sue her . . .! *Did you hear . . .?* She called me a whore!' Breathlessly, Matt reached his hotel with her and told her to tidy herself up in the ladies room; then, hoping no-one had noticed them both coming in together, went to the desk and asked for his bill. Upstairs he packed, quickly and efficiently. His headache had gone.

*

That evening Matt called his wife from a motel beyond Cortez, on the highway to Four Corners – the only place in the Union where four Statelines intersect, between Colorado, Utah, Arizona and New Mexico. John Wayne country. He told Eileen that he'd decided to spend the last two days of his vacation driving up into the mountains, north of Purgatory – in the very opposite direction to where they were now – and that he wanted to try and get as far as Black Canyon, if the roads were clear. She told him to be careful and have lots of fun. She knew his life was a little dull these days.

His wife's tolerance and selflessness made him feel even more guilty. He told her he didn't know how far he'd travel that night, but that he'd call again tomorrow and let her know how he was getting on. She said the Weather Bureau reports for the Rockies were not good, and told him again, '*Do be careful, Matt*!' He promised her he would.

Daisy Trader had gone to use the motel's indoor pool and jacuzzi, both free, courtesy of the Cortez Inn. The place suited Matt because most of the guests would be long distance one night stopovers, bound for such dispersed destinations as Phoenix, Salt Lake City, Las Vegas, even Monterey and the Central American Isthmus. Again, little chance of running into one of his and Eileen's friends. Still, he'd like to have got a lot further that night.

He went to the ice box and fixed himself a drink from a miniature Jack Daniels; then removed his shoes and stretched out on the generous bed. He glanced at the closed door, and felt a lump in his gut. He was in so deep now . . . Was it too late to pull back? Or was there still time to check out? Leave a note with the desk, enclosing a couple of C's and a blunt message, saying it was all a terrible mistake? After all, he hadn't committed himself yet. He hadn't even touched her, beyond the odd formal kiss. She could probably get some job in Cortez, maybe even here in the motel.

But he was too close to Durango. The odds were too short on Daisy gossipping, and the word might get back to Eileen and her knitting circle. A girl of nineteen who'd just had the sack, being picked up by an old roué and dumped without warning in the middle of the empty flatlands between the Rockies and the Grand Canyon. The story might even make the local papers. Daisy Trader didn't seem the sort of girl who'd be reticent in telling her story.

She appeared in the room a moment later. She was barefoot, wearing only a motel bathrobe. She slipped it off as she came in and started towards the bathroom. She smiled at him, briefly, almost as though he were a stranger – which, in a way, he was.

He watched her from the bed, experiencing a warm, melting sensation, a racing of the pulse, knowing that that glimpse of her would remain with him until he died. From behind, she reminded him of a Venus he'd once seen on a trip to Europe, in an art gallery in Spain. He'd thought at the time, *God, if I ever had a girl with a body like that . . .* That had been nearly thirty years ago, and he'd remembered that picture ever since. Now he'd go on remembering them both – the painted image and the real thing – until there was nothing else to remember.

Matt Kelsey had never thought of himself as a particularly romantic or emotional person; and he was certainly not morbid. But then you never knew. And by the time you did, it was usually too late.

It seemed an age before Daisy Trader came out of the bathroom. However vividly, furtively, Matt had imagined this moment, he was unprepared for the reality. All doubts were vividly dispelled. Venus stood before him, arisen fresh and warm from the sea, her body without a blemish.

He didn't move. The girl reached the bed. She leaned forward and unbuckled his belt. He could smell her body, warm and faintly scented. A cheap scent, maybe, but the rest was genuine – her body rich, tangy and intoxicating, as he felt her beginning to peel his Levis down over his thighs. She looked into his face and smiled – a bright artless smile – *'My name's Daisy Trader and I'm your personal whore for the evening . . .'*

He noticed that she had perfect white teeth. A healthy all-American girl. He lay back on the bed and closed his eyes.

*

They had an early breakfast in their room, shortly after sunrise. Once again he was anxious – even more since last night – to get moving, to put as many miles as he could between himself and Eileen.

Daisy didn't say much during the meal. She'd drunk several beers last night, before they eventually went to sleep, and now looked tired and slightly hungover. But he was relieved to see that she ate with her usual good appetite. At 6.30, while she was still eating, he checked out and asked for their bags to be put in the car. Then, for a last brief moment, he thought of making a run for it – leave her big case on the forecourt and not stop driving until he reached Durango. He tried to remember if he'd ever mentioned that he lived in Durango? He didn't think so – all he'd told her was that he was a pilot from Kansas.

Then she joined him at the desk. The moment was past. He had signed them in the evening before as Mr and Mrs Harcourt, of Albuquerque, New Mexico; and he'd paid cash, so the trail would be cold from the moment they left.

In the car she slept for the first two hours, until they were well inside Arizona. He wondered if, in these enlightened times, the Mann Act still applied: transporting a female across a Stateline for immoral purposes. He thought probably not – unless his daughter found out, in which case the Act would be just for starters.

They stopped for gas at a little place near Tuba City, on the Highway 85 down to Flagstaff and Phoenix. It was in a Navajo Reservation, and an old man in a shapeless hat, with a face like a pickled scrotum, begged a dollar off him.

Daisy Trader disappeared 'to freshen up'. When she returned she was scowling: 'They don't even have real coffee. God, I hate these Indian places. They give me the creeps! They don't even look at you – even the women.'

'They consider it rude to look at anyone, even if they're talking to you.' Matt grinned. 'It's a whole different way of life, Daisy!'

'Well, I prefer to stick to my own way of life,' she said sullenly, getting in beside him. 'They still give me the creeps. C'mon, let's go!' Yet she showed no real interest in where they were going. Perhaps one corner of God's Own Land was the same to her as another. Maybe she just didn't care – as long as she had the car, and Matt to pick up the bills as they went. The idea that he meant nothing to her, except as a casual sugar daddy, began to depress him profoundly. Yet, on reflection, he should have been relieved. It would become intolerably complicated if she came to rely on him totally. Worse, if she were to fall in love with him.

As they approached Flagstaff, under the lowering dormant volcano of Mount Humphrey, he picked up on the car radio a Public Service station that played only classical music, without commercials. (Who said Middle America wasn't civilised?) After a few minutes Daisy Trader yawned and said, 'Let's get somethin' else. Somethin' with a bit of pep in it!' She pressed the buttons until she found some caterwauling local pop station, and rested her head back, keeping time by tapping her bare knees.

'This looks a dump,' she said, looking out at the railroad-tracks and the low, nondescript houses, as they drove into the centre of Flagstaff. He said it would do for lunch. They stopped at the main hotel, The Garsen – a square, solid building, built at the beginning of the century, with its famous Zane Grey Suite on the third floor where the master had lived for many years, churning out his tales of the Old West.

During lunch in the hotel restaurant, she began worrying about not having any decent clothes. She still wore the *après-ski* slacks and black sweater she'd been wearing yesterday, after changing from her work clothes. Matt agreed at once to get her a whole new wardrobe, and blow the expense! The idea of her turning up somewhere for dinner, wearing that leather and bare-boob outfit filled him with dismay.

After lunch they took a walk down Main Street and looked at the shops, but Daisy Trader didn't see anything she much liked. 'Phoenix next stop!' she said, hugging his arm as they returned to the car. 'I've always wanted to go there! You're a very wonderful man, Matt!'

He put his arm round her shoulder and pulled her to him. Her kiss was again warm and soft. He was happy.

*

It was 7.30 pm local time when they drove up the steep winding roadway to the Inn-in-the-Buttes, just outside Phoenix on the road south to Tucson and the Mexican border. A Category 'A' hotel, real executive class, he assured Daisy Trader in case she wanted to go to some glass tombstone downtown. She seemed to think that Phoenix was full of young millionaires all lolling around looking for a pretty wife.

They checked in at a green marble desk, against the sound of designer waterfalls splashing down naked rock hewn out of the original Butte – those massive slabs of volcanic basalt that litter the landscape in every respectable Western. He saw with relief that she was impressed. At the same time Matt knew that it was the sort of place where he'd have to pay by credit card. Cash would be considered suspicious.

'For the one night?' said the elegant young man at the desk. 'You haven't booked?' He studied the big desk ledger through very long dark eyelashes: while Daisy Trader studied him, as she waited dutifully at Matt's side.

'A single room for yourself, Mr Kelsey?' he said at last.

‘And a separate one for your daughter?’

Daisy Trader threw back her head and gave a loud throaty laugh. The young man looked at her, then laughed too. He had very fine dark eyes. ‘I’m sorry, Mr Kelsey – I’ll just make that the one room.’ Daisy Trader watched the young man, while Matt signed them both in as Mr and Mrs Kelsey, of Sacramento, Northern California. Misleading, perhaps – but still, the first written evidence on the mystery trail.

After they’d unpacked and taken a shower, separately, Daisy went down to the hotel boutiques, which were still open. When he got back to their room, he found Daisy sitting in the lotus position on the floor, surrounded by half-opened parcels and boxes, arranging them as though for an exhibition. Matt didn’t know much about clothes, but he recognised several famous logos from houses in New York and Paris, and at least three boxes of shoes from Rome. As he came in she scrambled up and flung her arms round him, kissed him passionately, then broke away and handed him the receipt, as though it were for groceries. ‘I’ve been a bit naughty, Matt . . .’

He gave her a hangdog smile. ‘That’s all right, honey. We’re only young once!’ The bottom line, added to the hotel bill, came to a total of $21,136 33c., including State Tax. *But what the hell!* he thought. What else could he spend his money on – except for subscriptions to exclusive golf clubs, charity dinners, and presents for his daughter, who was married to a rich man, anyway.

Chapter Eleven

Grace Van Owen lost no time in filing a suit for damages totalling $8 million, on behalf of Candice Amy Turner, against the Triton Corporation and its President, Randolph David Miller, of Oakhill Rd., Pasadena, in the county of Los Angeles. She then spent the rest of the day at the L.A. Headquarters of the Securities and Exchange Commission.

She arrived armed with a signed authorisation from Sam Ohls, entitling her to examine all Form 10-K's for the Triton Corporation over the last five years – that is, the annual files required under S.E.C. regulations for every publicly-quoted company in the U.S.A.

Grace had not majored in Business Studies, and at first found the task both tedious and daunting – reams of figures, dates, computer-speak, making her head ache, her eyes begin to glaze over. And she wondered how accountants and auditors, who spent their lives in this work, did not go mad with boredom or frustration. Perhaps it was like being an archaeologist or code-breaker? But you had to be a professional – which, in this field at least, Grace Van Owen was not.

She decided to pass over Parlane Industries – Randy Miller's first step up his slippery ladder – which appeared to be a routine company, with a record no different from a thousand other moderately successful hi-tech industries along the West Coast. At first the Triton Corporation appeared to have the same profile, though on a much larger scale. Up until the big law suit brought by the L.A. health authorities five years ago – just after Randolph Miller Jr. had taken over as President – Triton's turnover and profits had been impressive.

Then, gradually, Grace began to notice something odd. During and immediately after the law suit, the Corporation's value on the American Stock Exchange had fluttered only slightly; then seemed to recover remarkably well. In fact, during the first three years of Miller's stewardship, the company's turnover had increased thirty percent. According to one set of figures, the audited ones, Triton remained extraordinarily robust during those first years after Miller had taken over. The Corporation had survived a nasty scandal, having its name and reputation systematically trashed by the media over many months; yet it had come out the other end virtually unscathed.

But, as Grace persevered with her digging, she discovered something even more paradoxical. Normal business logic should have shown Triton, with the scandal well behind them, thriving in the new boom economy of the late Eighties. Instead, quite the opposite had happened. Over the past two years its profits – though not its turnover – had begun to slide, slowly but steadily at first; then, in the last nine months, to slump dramatically.

Grace searched vainly for some explanation – either concealed in the plethora of statistics on the print-out; or in some random outside factor, like an unwise investment or a huge loan which could no longer be serviced. But here Grace ran into those sands and reefs which betray the financial amateur. There were certainly a lot of loans showing, particularly over the last year, but they did not seem big enough to wreck an outfit on Triton's scale – unless, of course, they'd been so arranged as not to benefit the company one cent.

But Grace was feeling tired, stymied by her own ignorance. To relieve her frustration, she began to write on a separate page of her notebook:

IS MILLER A CROOK? IF SO, HOW?

She paused, wondering if she should commit such vague, unlegalistic rhetoric to paper – even if only to keep her thoughts on track. Brackman would call it 'tentative and prejudicial'. Besides, Grace was already committing that cardinal sin among lawyers. She had already found Miller guilty on all counts, and that was before she'd even started to probe the facts behind Candy Turner's terrible accident.

She decided to press on, writing on the same sheet of paper:

1. External factors, plus scandal of law suit, must be discounted after five years.

2. No attempt to unseat Miller or any others from the

Executive Board.

3. No evidence of any outside takeover bid – despite fall in value of Triton stocks on the A.S.E. – from $5.65 in Jan 1988 to $2.70 in Jan. 1991.

4. Are any investigations pending re Triton's affairs?

5. What is – unofficially – Miller's personal standing in financial circles? viz: Wall Street, American Stock Exchange, Federal Control Commission, L.A. Chamber of Commerce etc.?

Grace broke off here, staring at the page, wondering what damned use any of this could possibly be to that poor child, lying burned and blinded in the Washington Children's Ward? Would a bit of extra dirt on Randolph D. Miller Jr. make any difference at all – after he'd already walked away free from a half-million dollar fine for gross negligence and abuse of public health regulations?

Anyway, this was surely a case more for ambitious politicians and pressure-groups than a humble attorney. For Grace's job was to present conclusive evidence that Triton's negligence, already established in the earlier case, had this time led directly to a terrible human tragedy. She wasn't a one-woman crusader, a zealot. The words made her flinch, feel ashamed.

For a brief moment she allowed herself to wonder if she wasn't immersing herself in this ferocious examination of Randy Miller's life and career merely as a means of distracting herself from her own emotional confusion and the ties that hopelessly bound her to both Kuzak and Victor Sifuentes?

Yet however much she kept to her professional scruples, she still had a public duty to see justice done. For how many other little kids were at risk, and would go on being at risk, innocent and unknowing, because of an incompetent and probably corrupt poison factory? For Grace was by now convinced there was something very wrong with the Triton Corporation – something that went beyond its safety record.

The trouble remained, however: she felt she did not have the competence to sift through the maze of information and extract enough to unearth some major fraud; but she also saw no clear way that such a discovery could help little Candy Turner.

Grace tore off a sheaf of print-outs, almost as thick as a toilet roll, and took them to the photocopying room to have them run off, in duplicate. She was told the work would take some time. While she waited, she took her notes to the building's cafeteria where she ordered a coffee, without sugar or sweetener, and a BLT. But she wasn't hungry. Only last week Victor had told Grace that she was losing too much weight. But Victor was a Latin – he liked his women on the plump side, 'something to get hold of', as he'd indelicately put it. She'd told him angrily that most women in L.A. would be proud to have a figure like hers – which was probably true, despite the ferocious competition in this City of Dreams. Victor had just smiled and said, 'Maybe . . .'

It was then that Grace noticed the man sitting a couple of tables away, pretending to read *The Christian Science Monitor*. It was mid-afternoon and the cafeteria was almost empty. The man gave her a sidelong glance, then looked quickly away. He had just ordered a cheesecake and what looked to Grace like a bottle of rootbeer.

She returned to her notes, frowning, deciding they were an exercise in futility. Half the corporations in America could probably produce such figures, at one time or another. Miller wasn't a Jimmy Hoffa, or even a Michael Miken. She was in danger of becoming obsessed.

She glanced up and saw the man at the other table looking at her again. This time he smiled – a faint uneasy smirk, the hallmark of the nervous lech. He was a smallish man in a light-blue seersucker suit, with an uninteresting face and a thin pale moustache that was trying hard to make him look like David Niven, and failing utterly. She gave him a cold stare, then looked at her watch. 3.20. They'd said the photocopies wouldn't be ready much before four o'clock.

She left some money on the table and walked out. Down in the marble vestibule the security guard checked her pass, and nodded her through. She went out into the muggy afternoon. Los Angeles is not a good city for walking in, especially if you're an attractive young woman in a business-suit, and alone. But half a block away she found a bookshop, a branch of one of the big New York publishing houses.

It was spacious, cool, and full of the murmur of Vivaldi from speakers high up near the ceiling. She chose the latest Kurt Vonnegut novel, and a fat paperback entitled "*The American Leviathan: A Study of the Practices and Malpractices of American Big Business*". She looked up the index, but there was no mention of Triton or any R. D. Miller. She settled for the novel. She reached the desk and had just got out her card, when she saw the man from the cafeteria watching her from only a few feet away.

Grace shivered, and when she reached for her receipt,

found her hand was shaking so violently she could hardly hold the slip of paper. The man had given a little smile of recognition – neither intimate nor neutral. And she noticed that he had slight psoriasis showing under his thinning sandy hair. She looked at him as though he were a dog's mess on the pavement; then walked out into the warm smog. Only then did she realise she was scared.

She thought she'd lived too long in Los Angeles to be upset by clumsy pick-ups in the street. But then you could never be too sure – American cities were full of serial killers and sex maniacs who appeared to be mousy, harmless-looking creatures, until you saw their mugshots in the papers next day.

She reached the S.E.C. Building without once looking back; and once inside, past the security guard, found she was trembling uncontrollably. Then she realised it wasn't the fear of being attacked, even raped, that had seized her. It was more an instinct – an intuitive certainty that the man was following her for a quite different reason. Supposing Triton had got wind that she was working on the Turner case? There were all kinds of ways they could have found out – through someone in the D.A.'s office; even somebody keeping watch on Rita Turner's shack, who might have taken Grace's licence-number and traced her back to McKenzie Brackman.

They'd have had to work quickly, of course; but then, if Sam Ohls and the local police report were correct, she was up against people who had moved fast the other night – fast enough to clear that whole site of the drums of chemicals, spillage, warning signs, even Candy's bike – all in less than three hours, before the incriminating evidence could be found. And who was to say they wouldn't go to similar lengths with her?

Grace tried reassuring herself with the hope that where destroying the evidence on the poisoned site was one thing, putting a clumsy 'tail' on a hostile attorney was quite another. Anyway, what purpose would it serve? To scare her off – with that little runt in his cheap suit and nasty little ginger moustache? The question would be senseless – unless, of course, they were working in pairs and wanted to steal something from her? But what . . .?

She hurried back up to the Inquiries desk, in the big Archive Reading Room. There was a new clerk at the desk – a smart young black man who hadn't been here when she'd arrived earlier. She said breathlessly, 'Was anyone in here today asking if somebody had been in,' – she paused, trying to unscramble her words – 'anybody asking for a Form 10-K on the Triton Corporation . . .?'

'I'll check it out, ma'am, right away.' The man turned to a computer screen and began to tap in the information.

'Thanks,' said Grace absently, her eyes straying around her, looking out for the man with the moustache.

'Form 10-K, was it?' The man looked up from the screen. 'For the Triton Corporation, Pasadena, Los Angeles County . . .?'

'That's the one!' Grace cried, feeling her heart thumping painfully against her ribs. 'Do you know who it was?'

'Well, ma'am, I only came on duty at lunchtime. But somebody else might know.' He turned and called out, 'Rick! You remember who came in this morning asking for a 10-K on the Triton Corporation?'

A bald man along the desk turned and said sleepily,

'Yeah – how could I forget? A young blonde – real good-looker! I processed her security card.' He paused and checked a ledger. 'Name of Van Owen, attorney-at-law . . .' He looked back at her. 'Hey – it was you!' And he gave her a bright, toothy grin.

'Thank you,' she said, wondering why he hadn't recognised her at once. Was it because she was now drained and tense with fear? Had the sight of the man with psoriasis changed her that much? 'There was no-one else?' she asked. 'Not a little guy in a blue suit with a moustache?'

'I didn't see nobody. But we get a lot of people through in the day. I only remember the special ones.' The man leered, cocking his head on one side. He must have noticed the look of relief in Grace's face. 'Your husband been checking up on you, lady?'

Grace gave him a thin smile. 'Well, yeah, that's about it. Thanks, anyway.'

'Any time, lady. I'm off in an hour. How 'bout a nice chilled gimlet at Donahue's – it's just across the street in the next block?'

'Some other time,' she said wearily; smiled at the young black clerk, then walked swiftly away, feeling the bald man's stare trained on her lovely behind like a ray-gun.

In the photocopying room they told her they had the material almost ready. Another five minutes. She felt restless, trapped, longing to get out of there. She started pacing the room, glancing every few seconds through the glass connecting door, expecting to see her pursuer at any moment. *God!* she thought, *I'm getting paranoid. First Miller, now this little creep . . .*

Then she had an inspiration. A means of killing two

birds with one stone. And she wondered why she hadn't thought of it at once. She started looking for a public phone. If she were to establish anything from her day's work, she'd need an expert to examine the stuff. Stuart Markowitz! Not only was he a financial ace –scourge of the IRS, and friend alike to many a bigtime fraudster and petty crook. But Stuart was also a pillar of McKenzie Brackman. And McKenzie Brackmen meant friends, refuge, security.

She found an empty booth and called the office. The firm's new switchboard operator put her through to Roxanne, who said that Stuart was working from home today. Grace thanked her, and was about to hang up, when a demon of masochism seized her. 'Oh, Rox – has Victor called?'

'N-no. Not yet. But we're expecting him to . . .'

Grace could hear the tone of pity in Roxanne's voice, and cursed herself. Then she rang Stuart's home number. She knew he wouldn't mind being disturbed – might even welcome it. He was always ready with a favour. Above all, he knew everything there was to know about financial scams.

He answered on the second ring, 'Ann!?' But was quick to conceal his disappointment when he heard Grace's voice. 'Hello! What a pleasant surprise, Grace! So what can I do for you?'

'Stuart'– her voice was brittle – 'can I draw on your wisdom?'

'Me – I got no wisdom,' Stuart chuckled. 'And I got two marriages to prove it!' He paused, sounding suddenly wary. 'Business or pleasure, Grace?'

'Strictly business. And it may even be urgent.'

'Try me.'

'I'm on a public phone in the S.E.C. Building, Stuart. I'd rather talk in private.' There was an empty pause. 'Also, I think somebody may be following me.'

'Do you want me to come and get you?'

'No. It'll be quicker if I call a cab. Okay if I come straightaway?'

'Sure. Ann's not here, by the way. She's up visiting her father in the Rockies. So we'll be alone.' He spoke the words without the least insinuation. 'When do I expect you?'

'Give me half-an-hour. You're a darling, Stuart!' She hung up, called a cab, collected her photocopying and then went down to wait inside the big well-guarded doors. There was no sign of the blue seersucker suit.

Chapter Twelve

Meanwhile, while Grace was labouring in the S.E.C. Building, Brackman was cracking the whip over the Morning Conference table.

'I said I expected eighteen hundred hours' work from each of you. Per annum – absolute minimum,' he was saying. 'And what do I get? Half the team don't even show! And most of the others are walking wounded. Mike – how's the head?'

'The head's fine, Douglas. I got raindrops falling on it.' Kuzak looked truly awful. He had two black eyes and a thin white bandage round his hairline, and was scowling like John McEnroe after a bad skirmish with a linesman.

Brackman turned now to the new English woman. 'How's the date-rape coming, C.J?'

'It isn't, I'm afraid.'

'So – how come?' Brackman sounded disappointed.

C. J. Lamb squared her padded shoulders. The others were watching her eagerly. 'It's turned out to be a bit of a – how would you say? – a busted flush. I called on the girl yesterday, straight after Conference. She had a hangover, and got quite shirty when I told her who I was and what I was doing there. She said she'd had another visit from the police the night before – two women police – and they'd tried to pressure her. The upshot was, she'd told them to kiss off – then gone out to a disco and got drunk with some friends. Then she cut short the interview, saying she was expecting an important visitor.

'So I went out and tried my hand at a little P.I. work. I drove round the block, then stopped a little way up from her apartment where I could get a good view of whoever came in and out. About twenty minutes later a young chap rolled up in a white convertible, carrying two bottles of champagne. I left them together, then rang her bell. I had a hunch, you see. And it paid off.

'When she opened the door, she almost threw a fit. But her boyfriend seemed quite amused by the whole business. He even offered me a glass of champagne. You see, he was the guy who's supposed to have date-raped her.'

'The same guy? said Brackman, unbelieving.

'The same guy. He was even quite happy to admit it.'

'What about the girl? What was her attitude?'

C.J. Lamb smiled. 'Actually, I think she couldn't wait for me to leave. So they could both hit the sack.'

'So now we at last know what 'date-rape' is!' said Arnie Becker, his shoulders heaving with laughter. 'Crazy! In the old days she'd have been given a sharp talking-to, told to stay on the Pill, then sent her home to Mommy.'

'And that's what you'd have done, is it?' Abby said, eyes flashing.

'Me?' said Becker. 'I'll tell you what I'd have done, Abby. I'd have lifted the girl upside-down and shaken her till whatever she's got inside her head fell out, then put her in a taxi.'

'Arnold Becker, you're a chauvinist!' Abby snapped, without a trace of irony. 'I should have expected a man of your experience to be more sensitive.'

Becker held up both hands in mock innocence.

'Now come on, guys,' Brackman cut in. 'Fun's over. Let's do some lawyering.' He turned to his notes, ticking off the names of his flock. 'Victor's still in Vegas, and hasn't even called in yet. Anyone heard anything from him? Mike?'

'Not a whisper,' said Kuzak, more or less truthfully.

'Hmmm. Grace is on the Turner case. Stuart's working from home on the Hawaiian shipping scam. His wife's gone to visit her father in Colorado . . . Hey, what is this I'm running – a vacation camp? What about you, Abby?'

Abby crossed her hands on the table. 'I've got an appointment this afternoon with the supervisor of the Glenmead Beauty Clinic in Bel Air. The actress, Liz Dawn-Chetwynd, had her varicose veins fixed there six months ago, and now her insurance won't pay. Say she lied about her age on the application form.'

'And what is her age?' asked Brackman. 'Her real age?'

'Forty-two,' said Abby. 'She told the insurance people it was thirty-eight. But after forty – under her particular policy – they don't pay for what they call 'vanity' surgery. So she's stuck with a medical bill for seven thousand dollars, which she doesn't have.'

'All right for a *kid* with varicose veins,' Becker said irreverently.

Abby ignored him. 'The trouble is, she's broke. She hasn't worked in six months and says she's being treated for high blood pressure and depression.'

'I saw her last picture,' Arnie said. 'Real back-lot cheapie about a circus dwarf with the IQ of Einstein who meets a nurse in the hospital where he's recovering after falling off a high wire. The twist is, it's the girl who falls for the dwarf, instead of the other way round. They finish up going to Africa together to help the starving. It's beautiful!'

'You may think it very funny,' said Abby furiously. 'But have you ever thought what it must be like for a professional actress to be not only out-of-work, but ill and unable to pay her medical bills, in a city like this?'

'So? She should have stayed home and married the local gas pump attendant.' Becker was beginning to enjoy himself.

'You're vicious!' Abby cried.

'Nothing wrong with gas pump attendants,' Becker said airily. 'They oil the wheels of our great American way of life.'

Abby Perkins looked at him with narrowed eyes. 'My God, if I was ever married to a man like you, Arnold Becker, I'd put cyanide in your food!'

Becker gave a sarcastic bow. The opportunity was too good to miss. 'And if I was married to a girl like you, Abby dear, I'd eat it!' he said, taking a chance she'd never heard the old Churchillian saw. She obviously hadn't.

There was laughter round the table. Abby flushed down

to her neck line, trembling on the brink of tears.

'All right – that's enough,' said Brackman, swallowing back a smile. 'We're wasting time, and time's money.' It was one of his ritual refrains which he trotted out at least five times a week. No Morning Conference was complete without it. 'Now – where were we . . .?' He looked up, as Roxanne put her head round the door.

'It's the Captain of the Beverly Hills Cops' – she made it sound like the movie – 'wants to speak to you personally, Douglas. Do you want to speak to *him*?'

Brackman glanced briefly across at Kuzak's bruised, bandaged face. He remembered the trip yesterday out to the Precinct House, to bail Kuzak and his client; then the trip to the hospital to get Kuzak checked for concussion. And all in the Partnership's valuable time. Brackman was going to make sure the Department paid for it.

'Thanks, Roxanne. I'll take it in my office.' He stood up. 'Right, get to work. And remember, from now on I'm clocking you all in – every hour – and anyone who falls short of that eighteen-hundred-hour norm forfeits a corresponding percentage of his – or her – total annual salary.'

When he'd gone, C. J. Lamb said, 'Has he always been like this?'

'Since he got his basic training in the Gulag,' Kuzak said, touching the bandage above his eye. 'But it gets worse when Leland's away.'

'Are we now supposed to start informing on each other?' said Arnie.

'Sure, why not?' said Abby, under her breath. 'I'm sure you'd be good at it.'

*

'Don't pull rank on me, Captain,' said Brackman, in his most overbearing voice: 'I don't care if you're the Commissioner's twin brother, or the Governor's pet cat! I'm not impressed – okay?'

The man at the other end was also used to abject deference. He was now getting angry. 'I got one of the toughest cities to police in the world, Brackman. My men get assaulted, shot at, burned, beaten – most days of the week. Then some arrogant, punk city lawyer comes in and slugs my Lieutenant in the guts . . .'

'Not before your Lieutenant put the cuffs on him, without any good cause.'

'Lieutenant Slazenger was trying to restrain him. He'd become abusive.'

'You were violating his rights, Captain.'

'*Rights, my ass*! People like you, Brackman, you know nothin' about this city! Nothin' about the way people live here. What their lives are like – what this city does to people – *real people*!'

'I know, it's tough,' Brackman said. 'I live here too.'

'*Horseshit*! You work in a sassy office at the top of the Delmonico Building, you eat in restaurants on fat expense accounts, then back to some mansion in Brentwood or Bel Air, with an English butler to bring you a fresh towel every time you get out of the pool. Wise up, lawyer! We're talking about another city, another country. Further from where you live than Fairbanks, Alaska!'

'I'm not talking about Alaska, Captain. I'm talking about Beverly Hills, which is down the road from Brentwood and Bel Air. So don't give me all that wind and water about the Great Social Divide, and how the L.A. cops have to hold the line. It doesn't wash with me. Unless I get a positive response from you before the end of this conversation, I'm going to put this phone down and talk to the Mayor's office. Then I call the TV networks . . .'

'Now hold it Brackman! I haven't said anything negative. All I been doing is standing by my man. Like they stand by people like you and protect you from a Lebanon situation. Or perhaps you don't care? Just as long as your own little neighbourhood gets its streets cleaned and the garbage collected and your wives can go shopping at De Lory's without getting mugged in the middle of the afternoon . . .'

Brackman was growing tired of this. He placed the handpiece on the desk and called Roxanne. He could still hear the Captain's voice buzzing like an angry wasp trapped in the handset. 'Rox, get me a nice strong coffee, will you? Black with two sugars.' He picked up the phone again. The snarling, go-boil-your-head voice had lost none of its steam:

'. . . You hear me, Brackman? I was talking to you, for Chrissake!'

'I'm still here, Captain.'

There was a thick pause down the line. Brackman could almost hear the officer at the other end knitting his brows and thinking, in tight circles of frustration. Roxanne came in with the coffee. She put it down on Brackman's desk, and whispered, 'I gave you just one sugar.'

'One? I said two!'

She stood shaking her head. 'Now remember what happened to Leland – we don't want you getting sick, do we?' She blew him a chaste kiss and withdrew.

Brackman scowled after her, then turned back to the phone. 'Captain – you still there . . .?'

'Damned right I'm still here! You think I went to powder my nose? This call's costing the city time and money.'

'It's costing my firm time and money, too,' Brackman said evenly.

'Okay. What's your bottom line on this one, Brackman?'

'Twelve thousand dollars' *ex gratia* payment to Michael Kuzak. Two thousand for wasting his valuable time – at four-fifty an hour. And ten thousand for physical and mental battery. We shall also require a full apology in the Press. But most important, I want your Lieutenant Slazenger moved some place where he can no longer shake hands with the public.'

There was a grim pause. When the Captain spoke again, he sounded almost sentimental. 'Slazenger used to be a good officer. Seven Police Commendations. Saved five patrolmen from almost certain death in the Watts Riots. Drove in there alone and rammed his car through a burning barricade, and got all five out, just as the mob was going in with machetes to chop them up for a barbecue feast. Beyond the call of duty, they said, in the Commendation – because the order had already been given to pull back, so technically Slazenger was going against orders. He didn't have to stay.' The Captain sighed down the phone. 'As I said, Slazenger used to be a damned fine officer.'

Brackman let this pass. He said, 'Captain, do I take it you accept our demands – unconditionally?'

'I'll have to discuss it with our legal department.'

'They'll advise you to accept. You won't get a better deal. If it goes to court, it could cost you five times that figure – not counting legal fees.'

Another pause. 'I don't like the media clause, Brackman. It's demeaning and vindictive.'

'I said "unconditionally", Captain.'

'I'll talk to the lawyers. Then get back to you.'

'The offer's open till ten o'clock tomorrow morning. If I don't hear from you by then, I'll file the papers and we go to court.'

'Okay, Brackman. Have your pound of flesh. I'll see Slazenger gets early retirement on grounds of ill-health – with full pension rights.'

'Sounds as though you like the guy?'

'I do, Brackman. I was one of the five guys he saved in Watts.'

*

For some time Douglas Brackman sat staring at the blank wall of his office. Then he buzzed Kuzak's office: 'Mike – could you come in and see me, please?'

Kuzak appeared a moment later, without knocking. 'Hello Douglas.'

'Hello Mike. Sit down. I've just been talking with the Beverly Hills Precinct.'

'Oh yeah? Are they going to send me some roses and a get well card?' He sat down in the clients' chair opposite Brackman. 'So what did they have to say?'

Brackman took his time answering. He placed both hands on the desk and leaned slightly forward, looking directly at Kuzak's midriff.

'Mike – I want you to drop this thing.'

'*What?*' Kuzak sat gaping at Brackman.

'It's my considered judgement, Mike, that to bring a case against this Lieutenant Slazenger runs a serious risk of showing up McKenzie Brackman in a bad light.'

'*Bad light!* What the hell is that supposed to mean? You think we might lose the case – is that it? In other words, you think I was lying about yesterday!'

'No, Mike, I don't. But a jury might see it differently. Let's face it, Mike – as a lawyer, you've got yourself something of a reputation in this city. An attorney who goes to jail for contempt, rather than submit to some lousy ruling – well, most people admire that. I admire it. What they call the "Don Quixote Syndrome". Only that kind of reputation can cut two ways. I'll be frank with you, Mike. Attorneys don't normally get themselves into fights with policemen – even in this city. And remember – Slazenger claims you assaulted him. He's talking of bringing his *own* charge of assault.'

Kuzak's tiredness was seeping over into anger. 'Damn it, Douglas! I told you what happened! It was self-defence – after he put the cuffs on, for no good cause.'

'You were still way out of line there, Mike. He claims you called him a "cold sore". Did you?'

'Maybe I did. But was I supposed to roll over and let him tickle my belly?'

'Oh for Chrissake, Mike. You know how to deal with cops.'

'Slazenger's different. He's a psycho. A man who hates real good.'

'No, Mike. Slazenger's like most tough cops in most tough cities all over the world. The difference is, he probably cracked a long time ago, only he doesn't know it. And those who do know, haven't so far had the nerve to tell him.'

Kuzak sat very still. 'You get all that out of a book, Douglas, or by talking with Slazenger's buddies in the Precinct House?'

'Don't be impertinent, Mike! You know my primary interest is to protect the Partnership. That also means protecting you – even against yourself.'

'You're treating me like a kid, Douglas! Just tell me – what happened on the phone just now?'

'Now keep calm, Mike –'

'The hell I will! You don't want to go up against the L.A.P.D., because you don't trust me to take the stand – that's it, isn't it?'

'I don't want you exposed to hostile cross-examination in what might prove a doubtful contest.'

'Shit, Douglas! Do you know what you've just said? I'm a lawyer, not a nervous old woman who's never been in a courtroom before!' He stood up suddenly, sending the chair rolling back on its castors. 'I've had enough of this crap! If a senior partner of McKenzie Brackman doesn't trust me in court, then I don't trust McKenzie Brackman. Over and out!' And he swung round and marched to the door.

'Hey, now wait a minute, Michael, don't start taking this –'

'Go stick your head up a dead bear's ass!' Kuzak went out, slamming the door behind him.

Chapter Thirteen

Mike Kuzak had grabbed up a handful of things from his desk, stuffed them in his briefcase, and stormed out, pausing only to tell a bewildered Roxanne that he wouldn't be back. She asked him where he was going, and he yelled at her: 'I'm going to see a lawyer!' He didn't even say goodbye.

She caught him up at the lifts. '*Michael*! Michael – where are you going? What's happened?'

'I've resigned, that's what's happened.'

'*Your job*?'

'Yeah, my job! What else is there to resign from – my manhood?' She looked aghast. Kuzak added, 'I told Brackman to stuff it . . .' The elevator had stopped at their floor. Roxanne stuck her foot out to stop the door from closing.

'But why? Is it because of Grace?'

'Grace?' Kuzak was growling with rage, looking round for someone suitable to hit. 'Why should it have anything to do with Grace?'

'Well, I was just thinking . . . Her being with us as a Partner – and now Victor . . .'

'Stand back, Rox. I've got to get out of here!'

'Would you like to talk about it? Have a coffee somewhere? I'll pay.'

He relented; he had nowehere else to go. 'Okay. If you don't mind being bored.'

'I'm never bored by you, Michael.' She released her foot and they rode down together, Kuzak already venting his wrath on the duplicity, the kowtowing, the downright *treachery*, of that two-faced asshole, Douglas Brackman.

Half an hour later he was still at it, scowling and raging, between cups of black coffee, in a brave effort to get on top of his lingering hangover, as well as to release his boiling resentment against McKenzie B. and its bastard of a Senior Partner.

'I'm sure Douglas didn't mean it,' Roxanne was saying, for about the fifth time.

'Of course he meant it! Douglas is about the most literal-minded man in America! He's also pompous, he's got no imagination, and he's a hypocrite . . .!'

They were in the nearest watering-hole to the office – a place called the The 'Moviedrome Leisure Lounge, that tried hard to re-create the atmosphere of old Hollywood, with a white piano to match the curving white bar, and blown-up prints round the walls of Bogart, Bacall, John Gilbert, Garbo and their ilk. None of your fancy young modern stars, wearing their causes on their sleeve, Kuzak thought savagely: This place was strictly for dreams.

'A policeman assaulted me, Rox. In the line of duty! He assaulted my client, then he attacked me. I was treated for concussion, for Chrissake!' Several people round them were beginning to sit up and listen. One of them was a very pretty young woman in a sweeping flounced skirt and wide sombrero hat. Roxanne thought there was something familiar about her. She was looking intently at Kuzak; but he didn't seem to have noticed her. He was still too busy raging against how he'd been treated.

'. . . I was even taken to hospital, and bandaged up like a goddam medivac case. Then, instead of taking the day off, like a normal person, I actually drag myself to the office today, feeling like a dog's dinner, and the first thing Douglas does – after he's disposed of all his more important work – is call me in and tell me to drop any charges against the L.A.P.D.! Drop any charges! My God, do the police have to murder one of us before Brackman stirs his ass!'

'He probably just wants to avoid any scandal, Mike. You know how Douglas is . . .'

'I know damn well how Douglas is! He's a Goddam ass-licker! And I'll tell you something else, Rox. He's *disloyal!* – and in my book that's the pits! The man's got the moral fibre of a butterfly! I tell you something, Rox – a commanding officer who won't stand by his own men, just to avoid a bit of potentially awkward publicity – that makes me want to stick my fingers down my throat!'

'But a big court case, Michael . . .' she began. 'I mean, you know what these L.A. cops can be like in court? They'd try to make out it was your fault. And it isn't as though . . . I mean . . .'

'Yeah? What *do* you mean?'

She was looking flustered, terrified of saying the wrong thing again, yet aware that with every word she was only making things worse. 'Well, Michael, you know how hot-headed – how *impetuous* – you can be . . .?'

Kuzak had sprung to his feet, fists clenched. 'Dammit, Rox! Who's side are you on?' With the bandage round his head and his blackened eyes, he looked wild and dangerous. The other customers were beginning to grow uneasy; and a couple of tough-looking waiters were watching him carefully. The girl in the wide hat and sweeping skirt was also watching him; and again, distractedly, Roxanne was sure she'd seen her somewhere before.

Kuzak still hadn't noticed the woman – although she was striking enough to turn most heads in the room. He stood glowering down at Roxanne, who now seemed on the edge of tears. 'If you want to take Douglas' side against me – okay, fine!'

'I didn't say that! Please, Michael, just stay . . .'

But he'd already turned and was storming out of the room. On the sidewalk outside he stopped for a moment, blinking and moving his head about like a bull entering the ring. He was trying to work out what to do next. Where to go? He started down the sidewalk, in no definite direction – worried that Roxanne might try to follow. He felt vaguely ashamed of taking it out on her. The poor girl was only trying to help.

He heard a light footstep behind him. He kept on, quickening his pace. Someone drew abreast of him – a girl, slimmer than Roxanne, wearing a big dark blue hat. He turned his puffed eyes to her and saw her give him a faint smile. His heart leapt against his ribs. No – it couldn't be!

'Michael . . . Kuzak?'

It was the voice he remembered, more than the face. Soft and deliciously husky. A wonderful voice. The sort of voice you fall in love with on the telephone. He stared at her. It was a lovely face, long and classical, with clear grey-green eyes and a small pale mouth – not the sort of face you see much in California these days, among the hordes of young hopefuls – tanned and leggy and half-naked along the sidewalk. But this girl was different. She was a dream. And Kuzak was angry he had to meet her looking as he did. But she didn't seem to mind. She gave a faint, tentative smile – not a Hollywood smile at all.

'You are Michael Kuzak? I'm Francine Faber. Remember me?'

He remembered her. He stood rooted to the concrete, mouth open, gaping. Oh yes, he remembered her all right – but only dimly, as though from the fragment of a bad dream. The last time he'd seen her had been about a year ago. She'd been crouching barefoot and white-faced – her lovely coppery hair filthy and dishevelled, eyes staring, her emaciated body hidden under a plain grey smock – in a little white cell in the private Lady of Mercy Clinic, in Bel Air, about four miles from where they were now standing.

Kuzak hadn't signed the papers – he'd left that to Leland McKenzie, who'd been unhappy about it but insistent, claiming that the firm was now responsible, and they were only doing it for their client's own good. Kuzak had hated Leland for that, but there was nothing he could do. A judge had backed Leland, with an order to confine 'one Francine

Delacroix Faber, until further notice, to a mental institution for her own safety, care and protection.'

After the initial sense of shock, Kuzak now felt thoroughly confused and embarrassed; but not without a faint *frisson* of excitement and morbid curiosity.

What had happened to her? How long had she been free? Was she now recovered?

He said, 'Of course I remember you. But only just! My God, Francine, you're looking *wonderful!* I mean it. You look a million dollars.'

She smiled sweetly. 'Same old Mike Kuzak! By the way, what have you been doing to yourself? You've been in a fight.'

'Yeah, a police lieutenant in Beverly Hills beat me up.'

Her lips parted and she gave a little silvery laugh. 'Oh my! Can they do that?'

'Sure they can! This is L.A., remember?' He took her arm. 'Listen, we can't hang around here on the sidewalk. Shall we go somewhere and talk?'

'I've got my car just one block away, in the Niemann-Marcus lot. Shall we go?'

Kuzak didn't argue. Clutching his briefcase, containing the papers he had originally swept off his desk, he set off with her towards the most expensive shop in the world. Her arm felt of cool dry silk and he thought he could smell money. A lot of it.

*

As they walked, Kuzak remembered how he had first met Francine about eighteen months ago. She had been introduced to him in Leland McKenzie's office where he remembered her as a thin, waif-like creature, dressed like an undernourished nun, with a vegan pallor and the limp, exhausted look of someone who didn't want to go on living but was too scared to do anything about it.

Leland McKenzie had entrusted her case to him. He'd thought at the time that an older, more mature man – Leland himself, no doubt – would have been a better choice. But perhaps Leland had felt that a more modern, streetwise approach was needed. Or maybe the old man had thought a good-looking young lawyer might help to raise the girl's spirits. Anyway, for better or worse, Kuzak had been offered the case and he had accepted. For the next six months he had been landed with Francine Faber.

It was a sad, nasty case, and one which had aroused all Kuzak's rage and indignation at a cruel injustice, wilfully perpetrated by two powerful individuals against a third, helpless one.

Francine Faber had been born into an old Huguenot family which had settled in California around the turn of the century. Her father, until his marriage to the heiress of a big bakery business, had been a penniless drifter. Francine's parents had never got on. Her mother had shared none of her husband's bizarre enthusiasms; she'd been neither pretty nor amusing; and, always eager to please, had lived in a state of permanent anxiety.

But from her husband's point of view, his wife had one supreme virtue. She was enormously rich. And Claude Faber, from the first day, had dipped his hand deeper and deeper into the honey pot. For the first few years of marriage, he had spent money like a steel worker on

Saturday night. He bought a *hacienda* near Santa Fe; and a small ranch-house on the beach at Oceanside, north of San Diego, costing a cool million. And he bought many fast and flashy automobiles, some of which he never even drove.

Kuzak stole a glance at Francine's elegant figure as they walked and found it hard to believe she was the same 'poor little rich girl' he had known. She had been brought up in the only way her mother knew – in the lap of sterile luxury, with a string of governesses and private schools; and during vacations, packed off to summer camp. But at times she would have to stay with her father's brother and his wife, Amos and Arlene Faber, who were the proverbial poor relations – envious and embittered – who'd treated their niece badly.

Francine had told Kuzak, in the various conversations he had had with her in the early days of the case, how she used to return home in tears, telling her mother how she hated her uncle and aunt, and beg not to be sent there again. But her mother had explained feebly that it was her father's decision. But whenever the little girl had tried to talk to him, he'd always expostulated that a child shouldn't have too much of the soft life. She had to get used to the world outside – not all kids could have it rich, and she must not despise her uncle and aunt for being poor.

During all this time Claude Faber had also been flamboyantly unfaithful. Little Francine couldn't remember how many strange young women she'd bumped into, in dark corners of their various houses – usually when her mother was in some clinic – who'd stop and say, '*Gee, what a cute little kid you are*!' or, sometimes: 'What a lucky daddy you got!' The memory had seared into her young soul like a branding iron.

Francine Faber had been a bitterly unhappy child. She'd become a loner; first talking to her dolls, taking them for walks, having most of her meals with them. Until, at the age of eleven, after she'd been expelled from her third school for setting fire to a piano, she had been taken to see a child psychologist – an old crow of a woman, who'd reminded Francine of the witch in *Snow White*, and who'd spoken with such a thick Viennese accent that Francine, terrifed, had been unable to understand most of the questions the woman asked her.

Later, many years later, she learnt that she'd been diagnosed as having marked schizophrenic tendencies. In despair, perhaps tempered with indifference, her parents had dispatched their daughter to a special school in Oregon, long since closed down, where they handled 'difficult children'.

In her second month there, for no evident reason, 12-year-old Francine had flown into an uncontrollable rage during School Assembly and had called the Principal names that even some of the other inmates had not heard before – certainly not in such surroundings. Francine had been sentenced to a caning in front of the whole school. She'd managed to run away before this could be carried out.

They reached Francine's car: a white Alfa Romeo convertible, the very latest model of Italian chic. Kuzak helped her in, folding the long skirt around her legs.

Chapter Fourteen

Grace Van Owen climbed slowly out of the pool at Sargasso Heights, the Markowitz mansion above Pacific Palisades. She had just completed her second six lengths of the evening. She now stood exhausted and refreshed, wearing Ann Kelsey's swimsuit which was slightly too big for her, scooping up her wet, tawny hair and watching the sun lowering itself behind the distant rim of the Pacific.

Stuart Markowitz was still ensconced in his study, wading through the thick sheaf of photostats which Grace had brought with her from S.E.C. Archives. He'd already been at it for more than an hour, and Grace did not want to disturb him. When Stuart became engrossed in a case, it was best to leave him to it. In the meantime, she was left to swim, to try and forget her problems, and enjoy the view.

She was enchanted by Sargasso Heights, and envious of Ann Kelsey for being able to live in such a fabulous house.

She wondered if she and Victor would be happy in such a place – if they could ever afford it, even with their new combined salaries as full Partners of McKenzie Brackman? But would Victor be happy with her? Happy with any woman? Would *she* be happy? – anywhere, with Victor or Michael or anybody? Ann Kelsey was a lucky woman!

Grace just hoped, rather cattily, that her colleague appreciated it all – appreciated her husband, who was so gentle, so kind, so cuddly. But it seemed that even a Spanish palace with a poolside view over the Pacific didn't mean instant happiness. And the proof was right here in the city, where more dreams were broken every day than there were smashed glasses after a Dean Martin house party.

It was getting a little chilly now the sun was down. Grace went inside and showered in the downstairs cloakroom, then dressed and went into the long high drawing room to wait for her host to appear. Stuart had told her to make herself at home, showing her the silver drinks tray on a heavy, pitch-pine chest against the brilliant white wall; and the hi-fi, with his large collection of classical records concealed in a huge cabinet covered with elaborate, dark-stained carvings which Grace guessed was genuine Spanish Empire, sixteenth-century. She wondered again if Victor would feel at home here, or whether the place would remind him of his ancestors' oppressors? Probably the latter. He'd sell all the antiques and do the place up in L.A. *Bauhaus* – all leather and chrome, with hidden lighting behind a jungle of well-manicured plants.

Hell! What was she thinking about? This was Stuart and Ann Kelsey's place! And they were happy, more or less – if any married couple was ever happy. And they had one other advantage which Grace did not yet have. They had a beautiful little baby son. Grace forced herself not to think any more along these lines: it was both futile and dispiriting.

With a twinge of guilt she mixed herself a long pale drink from the only whisky on the tray – from a decanter marked 'Glenfiddich 1972' – diluting it irreverently from a bottle of English spring water – and carried it over to the hi-fi cabinet where she selected Bach's Harpsichord Concerto No.5. As the music swelled through the room, she sank into a deep Chesterfield, eyes closed, her mind temporarily at ease.

'Grace, honey! I'm sorry, I just got lost in that stuff of yours. *Fascinating!*' Stuart was still wearing his white tennis shorts and Hawaiian shirt open half-way to the navel, showing the tiny gold Star of David nestling in his chest hairs. 'And you got all this from the S.E.C. files here in L.A.?' he added, fixing himself a Campari-and-soda.

Grace said modestly, 'I got an old friend in the D.A.'s office to help with the 10-Ks.'

Stuart Markowitz nodded. 'Smart work, Grace! Those things don't grow on trees.' He popped a slice of lemon peel into his glass. 'Can I freshen up your drink?'

'I'm fine,' she said, wondering if her choice of whisky might be too much too early. 'You think the stuff might come in useful, Stuart?'

'Well,' he said, carrying his drink back to the armchair opposite the sofa. 'I'd certainly say it might be useful to the I.R.S. – even maybe to your old friends in the D.A.'s office. Whether it helps the Turner kid is another matter.' Stuart stretched his legs, wriggling his toes in their doe skin sandals. His short bare legs were well-muscled and very hairy.

'Of course, I've only skimmed the surface so far,' he went on, sipping his Campari. 'Reading a Form 10-K properly is rather like breaking a code. At first you're looking at a string of figures and entries that don't make much sense, until you marry them up with a lot of other figures, and then, maybe, if you're lucky, they'll give you the key – at least, part of the key to part of the solution. But to get a solution, you first need a problem.'

'The problem is Randolph Miller,' she said, taking a sip of malt whisky and water. Grace knew from many a Morning Conference that there was nothing Stuart Markowitz enjoyed more than pontificating before a captive audience. Sometimes, she thought meanly, he could even be a tiny bit boring. Patiently she waited for him to complete his disquisition on problems and solutions, and the dialectic that joined them, before interrupting him:

'Is Miller a crook, Stuart?'

He paused judiciously. 'That's a big word – even in the United States. And, of course, there are crooks and crooks. I'd call most politicians – on the Hill and in most of the country's City Halls – crooks. As well as a helluva lot of admen and P.R. people – in the sense that the last thing they want to do, unless they're forced to, is tell the whole truth.'

Grace nodded patiently. 'Is Miller the sort of crook who could be indicted?'

'On the evidence I've seen so far? N-no. But as I said, I'm still only on the surface. However, there are a couple of things I've spotted that don't look quite right.'

'For instance?'

'Well – you know that S.E.C.'s regulations require every Form 10-K to include not only all company reports, but – and I quote – any relevant information required under the Securities and Exchange Commission Act of 1934. And it's there, if you look hard enough and are lucky enough, that you'll find the skeletons in the cupboard.'

He paused, sipping his drink, enjoying the luxury of having Grace as his captive audience. 'Only in the case of the Triton cupboard, I've only been able to find, so far, a couple of bones.'

'Meaning?' Grace waited, her eyes fixed on his hairy legs. Her drink was almost finished.

Stuart pressed his hands together, like an indulgent professor with his favourite student. 'Well, I've already found two very interesting items. Both are contained in Triton's Annual Financial Statements for last year. They refer to company loans of no less than five million to two of Triton's company directors, in each case giving as reason for the loans, 'purchase of real estate' – with the money deposited in off-shore banks in the Caribbean.' Stuart smiled, proud of his renowned memory.

'Is that illegal?' Grace said.

'No. Technically it isn't. But I've been in this game a long time, Grace. Longer than I care to admit, sometimes. And I'll let you into a little secret. In my experience, you get a big company like Triton which has been losing a lot of money – apparently for no good reason – then you find tucked away on its Form 10-K that the company has a)' – he counted the items on his fingers – 'been making huge loans to certain of its directors, and b) that these loans are for buying real estate – and I begin to smell something wrong about that company. And when c), I find these loans have been deposited in accounts well outside U.S. jurisdiction – well, that smell starts to get pretty bad!

'I'd say yes, Grace. Your Mr Miller probably is a crook. And from what I've managed to get through so far, a pretty big crook. He's also arrogant. If my hunch is right, I'd say he's working a big-time scam and thinks he's so smart he can tell the rest of us to go climb a juniper tree.'

Grace swallowed hard, beginning to wish she could have a second drink. 'But this information isn't secret, or even restricted,' she said at last. 'Almost anyone, providing they give a valid enough reason, can apply to see it. I mean, assuming what you've found is only the tip of an iceberg – one part of a gigantic scam – wouldn't the S.E.C. have got on to it as well by now?'

'Not necessarily. Not unless someone's already looking for a scam. You see, my guess is, the inclusion of that Note in the Account was quite simply a mistake. Miller and his boys were getting over-confident. And in my experience, the bigger the scam, the more confident they get – until they go one mistake too far. In other words, it looks like our Mr Miller's got careless.'

'We know that already – from little Candy Turner,' said Grace. 'I just hope this information helps to hang him!'

Stuart Markowitz started to chuckle. 'It might do just that . . .' he began, then started upright. He could hear a telephone ringing. The Filipino maid appeared a moment later. 'The Senora is calling, Sir.'

Stuart grabbed the phone beside him, its buzzer switched off. '*Ann darling*! Yes – yes fine!' He hesitated just a fraction of a second. 'Grace is with me. I'm helping her with some work . . . How's Matt . . .? Yeah – well, I guess he must be glad you're there, darling . . .'

As Grace eavesdropped, she noticed how happy and relieved Stuart looked, and she thought again of Victor, and wondered why her handsome, bloody lover couldn't have the decency to call *her*.

Stuart was still talking as though Grace wasn't there. '. . . Yeah, well you mustn't worry, honey. And remember, if you want me to come up and talk to him . . . Well, just to hold your hand and help see you through it . . . Okay, darling . . . *But just don't worry*! And Ann – I love you!' These last words were spoken with such quiet passion that Grace found herself blushing. Ann Kelsey sure was a lucky lady.

'I must be going soon,' Grace said, when Stuart had finally replaced the phone. She put down her empty glass.

'Tell you what,' Stuart said suddenly. 'Why don't you stay and eat? Maria can get us something light – one of her fish specialities. They're pretty damned good! That is, if you're not already busy, of course?'

'I don't know – I'll have to phone home first for my messages.'

'Ah, yes. Victor's still in Las Vegas, is he?'

'I hope so,' she said, trying to smile.

Stuart stood up. 'You go ahead. I'll just put some clothes on. You don't want to be found dining with some ageing beach boy!'

'Thank you, Stuart. You're very sweet!'

She waited till he was gone, then dialled her own number and listened. Most of the calls were to do with business, and could wait until tomorrow. Some could wait even longer – like the woman psychiatrist who was questioning her bill. Then she heard Roxanne's voice. It sounded tense:

'Grace? It's Rox. I'm worried about Mike. Have you seen him or heard from him? He's had the most dreadful row with Douglas and he's resigned. I think he may even mean it. I'm so worried – I've tried his number all evening, so he must be out. And his answerphone's turned off.' She paused. *'Sorry to bother you. Perhaps, later, you can try him . . . 'Bye . . .'*

The tape ended here. Still nothing from Victor. And she realised, miserably, that she didn't give a damn any more about Kuzak and his latest tantrum.

She sat for what seemed a long time. The Bach Harpsichord Concerto was long finished and the house seemed very still. She could hear the distant swish of the Ocean. She hesitated only one brief moment, then decided she'd leave Michael Kuzak and his trouble till tomorrow. She felt deflated, depressed. At last she got up and poured herself that second drink – the pale fluid, golden and friendly, without any water this time. At least, it would help get her through the evening. She had nothing else to do, after all.

*

They had fried oysters and lobster thermidor with a light cream sauce, and drank a chilled Muscadet. With their dessert – a delicious concoction of flaky pastry, fresh raspberries and peaches – Stuart served a Chateau d'Yquem '64. Grace was feeling relaxed, even happy. She sensed that

Stuart wanted to talk about his wife, and Grace rather hoped he would. But he must have felt that the subject would bore her, and instead talked about the price of real estate and how the Recession might be affecting McKenzie Brackman. Not once did he mention Victor, or even Randolph Miller, during the whole meal.

Then they returned to the big Spanish sitting room for balloon glasses of antique French brandy, with almost the colour and texture of maple syrup, and Stuart put on Mozart's Symphony No. 31, The Paris Symphony. Music to dream by.

Suddenly he said, 'Grace – you got to be careful. This Triton business. That guy you said might have been following you this afternoon . . .'

She stirred sleepily on the sofa. 'Careful? Who got anywhere being careful . . .?'

Stuart was pouring them both more brandies. 'You don't know these people, Grace. Not like I do. They can get very mean . . .' He suddenly reminded her of Edward G. Robinson talking about the Mob. She laughed. What did she care?

'Remember – I used to be a judge,' she said.

'These people don't play by the McKenzie Brackman rules, Grace. They're *dangerous.*' She leaned back and closed her eyes. She wondered if Edward G. Robinson had hairy legs too.

Chapter Fifteen

'It was stiflingly hot. Matt Kelsey and Daisy Trader had spent most of the morning by the pool. But by lunchtime she was getting restless. She made him drive her the twenty miles into the downtown shopping area where she at once homed in, like a guided missile, on the Phoenix branch of Cartier's. It wasn't the firm's most prestigious outlet – there were finer offerings in New York, London and Paris – but Daisy Trader wasn't to know that.

She spent nearly twenty minutes wandering slowly, wistfully among the maze of display cabinets, her fingers trailing along the glass-topped trays, at first without uttering a word, like some bemused child on its first visit to a toyshop. Matt watched and waited, with stoic resignation, until she had made her final choice.

A handsome power-dressed woman, like a de luxe wardress, ceremoniously unlocked one of the glass cases and picked out the tiny item. It lay in its black velvet box, giving off flashes of fierce blue flame, even in the twilight from the impending storm outside.

She presented it first to Daisy Trader, so she could touch it, then, almost as an afterthought, showed it to Matt Kelsey. It was a platinum ring with a large unflawed sapphire set in a bed of twelve 3-carat diamonds. The price tag, according to the woman, was a mere $52,700. Daisy Trader stood looking expectantly at Matt. 'Isn't it just beautiful, Matt darling!'

He nodded thoughtfully. It wasn't the price that worried him but the means of paying. A cheque drawn on his personal account in the Durango branch of the First City Bank, Denver, was too close to home. His accountant would have to see it, at least, perhaps also the financial secretary of 'Kelsey High-Flyers', in which, even as the sleeping partner, Matt still had a controlling interest. No – it had to be the other account. A banker's draft made out to 'Blue Max Enterprises', in that nice little offshore storehouse he kept for a long rainy day.

'Yes, honey. It certainly is beautiful,' he said at last. 'It perfectly matches your eyes.'

'That's why I chose it!' she cried, bouncing up on her toes. 'You'll get it for me?'

'I guess I will,' he said grimly, bracing himself for the wild embrace, the warm kisses, while the wardress stood discreetly aside. Then Matt asked to speak to the manager and explain his method of payment. It would necessitate two phone calls and a delay of twenty-four hours. The manager seemed quite content. Such a dealing was nothing unusual in Arizona.

*

On the drive back she was excited and affectionate. The rain started as soon as they were out of the city, and during the last five minutes back to the Inn-on-the-Buttes the noise on the roof and windscreen was so loud that conversation became impossible. Daisy Trader caressed him instead, forcing him to slow right down.

Back in their room he took advantage of her expansive good will, and made love to her with the sound of wind and rain lashing the palms outside. For the first time she showed real passion – but whether towards him as a man, or as a rich provider, was something he couldn't quite fathom. Perhaps she couldn't either. Afterwards he encouraged her to go for a swim. He told her he had some calls to make.

As soon as she'd gone, he got himself a stiff drink from the restocked ice-box; then, steadying his nerves, he called Durango. As he listened to the first dialling tones, he wondered if the sound of the storm would sound odd the other end? He was supposed to be somewhere in the frozen Rockies, for Chrissake!

'Yes?'

'Eileen, honey!'

'Matt. Hello.' Her voice was suddenly very clear, and cold as ice.

'Darling, I couldn't call you before. We've had terrible storms up here – power lines down, God knows what . . .'

'Matt. You're not alone, are you?'

'Well, not totally.' He felt a tightening in his gut. 'There are a few grisly bears up here, I guess. And maybe some wolves . . .' The joke died on his lips, as he reached out and slurped down some whisky.

'You can stop trying to fool me, Matt. I don't know where you are, and frankly I don't want to know. But I *do know* you're not alone.'

For a time the roaring, slashing of the palms outside seemed to grow silent. He had experienced this moment once before, many years ago; the steady, deafening roar of the engines; the vague sense of sustained fear and boredom; then the sudden ear-cracking explosion as the shell ripped through the skin of the aircraft, metal white with heat, all sound blasted into a deep, dreadful silence; then the wait for the crash, mercifully short . . . Oh God, he thought.

He sat rigid, the handset growing damp in his hand. He found he could even hear his heart beating. Then for a moment he thought it had stopped.

'Eileen? Honey . . .?' His voice was a croak, joined with a whining sound from deep inside his head. 'I don't understand. *What's happened*?'

There was a long pause, until he thought she had hung up. 'Eileen . . .?'

'It's in the local paper, Matt. With a damned great photo of you both, brawling with the manageress of some drugstore.'

He let out a muted expletive, and swallowed the rest of his drink.

'It seems you left the reporters a paperchase all over town,' she went on, her voice stiffening with anger. 'What sort of damned fools do you think everyone is down here? You really thought you could get away with it? Or perhaps you just didn't give a damn?'

'But how – I mean – how . . .? I just took her to a restaurant. And one other place. Hell, it's not a crime . . .!'

'Matt – don't pretend I'm stupid. She called half-a-dozen friends before she left. She must have been awfully impressed by you. The paper describes you as a war hero. Silver Star for dragging your pal out of a burning plane – then in you go like John Wayne, to protect some poor little waitress who's just been fired.' Her voice broke. 'Matt, what sort of bastard are you? Waiting till your wife's ill and out of the way, then running off with some cheap teenage bimbo!'

He heard a sob, and didn't say anything. The room was filled again with the roar of the storm, the rain thundering against the sealed windows.

'Go boil your head,' his wife said, and he heard the line go dead.

For a long time he didn't move. His knuckles were turning white around the handset, when he heard the squeaky voice saying, '*Will you please replace your handset and try again.*' He hauled himself to his feet, steadied himself, then ran into the bathroom and was violently sick.

Daisy Trader found him lying on the bed. 'Hi!' She smiled and started towards the bathroom for her shower; then paused. 'Are you okay, Matt? You look awful pale!'

'I'll be all right, honey. A touch of sunstroke, maybe.'

This time when she emerged naked from the shower, he hardly glanced at her. He lay listening to the rustle of clothes as she quickly dressed. 'I'm just gonna take a walk, darling, and leave you to rest.' She came over and kissed him on the forehead. 'Matt, your head's awful clammy. You want me to get you a doctor or something?'

'I'll be all right. Just leave me a little.'

She went out, wearing a red flared dress with a matching shawl of heavy red silk. He thought she looked a million dollars.

Matt slept for about an hour. Then he felt better; he got up, ran a cold shower, then went down to look for Daisy. He found her in a corner of the lobby, chatting to the dark young reception clerk with the fine eyes. Daisy was laughing, and did not see Matt until he was almost standing beside her.

The young man fell silent. Daisy turned and her face clouded with faint but unmistakable annoyance. 'Hi Matt! You feeling better?'

'A little.' He ignored the young man. 'But I think I'll turn in early. You'd better dine by yourself. I'm not hungry.' He turned abruptly and walked away. He thought he heard her call something after him, but he kept walking, like a sailor on a heaving deck. There was no sign of the storm letting up.

Chapter Sixteen

'Oh you poor dumb fool, Daddy! How could anyone be such a fool?' Ann Kelsey lifted her head and wiped her eyes. Her cheeks felt rough with dried salt tears. 'Didn't you see what was happening? Why so blind, Daddy? *Blind, blind, blind . . .!*'

They had gone through it all, over and over as the evening got longer: and they were getting nowhere. Repetition only made the wounds more raw. They were now both quite drunk: the daughter by turns maudlin and frantic, often close to hysterics; her father grown monosyllabic, sunk in a black depression.

'Do you know absolutely nothing about women?'

'Absolutely nothing,' he answered thickly.

There was a long, morose pause. 'In six weeks,' she went on at last, 'in just six goddam weeks you give the bitch over *two hundred thousand dollars*. And in gifts alone! Holy Mother of Jesus . . .!'

'Don't go on,' he growled. 'Please, Ann don't go on.'

'And I'm not counting the fifty grand pay-off,' she went on, relentlessly. 'Oh what *generosity*! How everyone must love you – the great Matt Kelsey, holder of the Silver Star for gallantry, the great family man . . .'

'Stop it,' he said.

'The wonderful husband and loving father. The great war hero. The great lover. The great *breeder*!'

'Stop it, please.'

She sat shaking her head, beginning to cry again. 'And so generous. While Mom's sick in Boston General. Sick with a broken heart, Daddy. She said at first she wouldn't have minded if you'd told her yourself. Even better, if she hadn't had to know at all. She always said you were too good to be true – and too handsome and charming for your own damned good.'

The tears were flowing again down her face and she made no effort to wipe them away. 'But to have to read about it in the local paper – and with that awful photo! Knowing all her friends had seen it, and were too polite, too embarrassed to mention it . . . Can you understand what that must have done to her?'

'*Stop it, for God's sake, girl!*' Her father's eyes were wild and bloodshot.

She stopped. There was another angry silence. Ann sniffed, poured herself more wine, then got a tissue out of her bag on the floor. 'Quarter of a million bucks,' she said slowly. 'And what for? So she can run off with some hotel receptionist and have his child? Or maybe *your* child?'

'It isn't my child,' he said, thick-tongued and weary

now. 'I've already told you – the times weren't right.'

'Oh sure, I forgot. It couldn't be yours, could it? Because when she missed her first period, you were already holed up in that hotel in Douglas, right on the border, all ready to vamoose down Mexico-way and get nice and truly lost. Only you didn't, because you were getting so smashed you couldn't even remember your own name. Till the hotel calls some nice local head-doctor who gives you the needle treatment, so you can just about manage to shave and use the telephone.'

She paused. Her father said nothing.

'So what went wrong? I've only seen you get drunk to enjoy yourself, Daddy. Never to black-out and forget – like a man drifting out to sea and hoping the tide doesn't wash him back in again.'

She waited for him to answer; but he just sat staring at the backs of his hands, pressed hard down on the table.

'Too proud to come home and face the the music?' she went on in a brutal, automatic voice, picking its way emphatically through the drink-sodden vowels. 'Only not too proud, maybe, to ask your daughter to defend you against a paternity suit brought by this Miss Trader-bitch, when her gigolo-guy gets bored with her and pushes off, leaving her holding the baby?' She smiled bleakly at the unintended play on words. 'Should make an amusing case for McKenzie Brackman!

'By the way,' she added, 'is this pretty-boy receptionist in Phoenix *sure* it's his kid? Or is that one of the reasons for the fifty grand? So the poor little bastard doesn't have to starve on Welfare?'

'I told you, daughter. *It isn't mine*. Anyway, does it

matter?'

'I guess it matters to you. Or you wouldn't have given her the fifty thousand kiss-off in the first place.'

'We've been through this before, Godammit! The money's not important.'

'Maybe not to you. Or not anymore. Where did you get it, anyway?'

'*Huh?*'

'A quarter of a million, Daddy.' She was beginning to slur her words. 'Mom says you're both well-off – but not that well-off. I mean who can go round spending quarter of a million in six bloody weeks and not have it show? How much have you got left in your Denver account, anyway?'

Matt tried to focus across the table, his daughter's face swimming around in a watery blur. 'I didn't touch the Denver account, I took it outta the Cayman set-up. It's all secret.'

'Oh God,' she said, 'you really have gone apeshit, Daddy! You draw any of that money in the States and they'll get on to you, they'll stamp on your balls. Still – maybe better the I.R.S. do it then that little whore!'

Ann Kelsey gulped and took a long breath. 'You go to Boston, Daddy, and buy Mom the biggest bunch of flowers you can find' – she spoke carefully, ponderously, trying to make sure he fully understood – 'then you tell her you're sorry – and I mean really sorry, for her, not just for your poor damn self – and then promise her the best holiday she's ever had. Costing fifty grand, like you paid the bimbo to clear your conscience, or whatever. And then you buy her a present costing at least as much as the most expensive thing you gave the bitch.'

Matt splashed some more Jack Daniels into his glass, slopping half of it on the table, and swallowed it neat. 'You think your Mom can be bought off that easy?'

'I dunno. It's worth trying. She's worth a million of that Trader-bitch. So give her a break, Daddy.'

'And if I don't?'

She leant forward, her tired red eyes suddenly alive, her voice clear again. 'Now you just listen here, Daddyo! If you're not on that plane tomorrow' – she squinted at her watch – 'today, I mean – I'm going myself, alone, and I'm gonna help Mom file the divorce papers. Then I'm going back to L.A. to get our best man to take the case. Name of Arnie Becker. He's a real bastard. He'll not only skin you alive, Daddy. He'll scrape the flesh off and chew the bones, then give what's left to the I.R.S. . . .

'Come to think of it,' she added, with a leer of pure malice that would have been faintly shocking, had her father been able to recognise it. 'If you don't play right by Mom – you just try to duck out and screw her up again – and I might just have a word in my husband's ear about that scam on Grand Cayman. He usually defends people like you. This time I'll make sure he defends my mother!' She grinned. 'It's a longish stretch, I believe, if they find you guilty. There won't be much left of you when you come out . . .'

Matt slowly lifted both hands and let them fall palms down with a smack on the wooden table. For a few moments he sat quite still, his Adams's apple jumping like a yoyo in his throat. Then he finally climbed to his feet. ''Night, baby daughter! I'm going to bed.'

Chapter Seventeen

'I'm sure we'd all like to congratulate Leland on his great success and welcome him back to the office!' This little speech was delivered by Douglas Brackman, as Morning Conference began.

Leland McKenzie cringed slightly as he heard the murmur of assent from round the table – in agreement, at least, with the second proposition. Leland's return would at least mean that future conferences would no longer be presided over by the funereal Brackman, whose pomposity had recently been growing more fatuous and unbearable by the day.

On the first count, however, the communal agreement was less than sincere. For they all knew – not least Leland McKenzie himself – that his latest clients, tucked away in Hawaii, had been as innocent as Al Capone, with the combined moral virtues of the late J. Edgar Hoover and

Ivan Boesky combined. Still, the firm's Senior Partner had won the case, and his bill would more than compensate for any ethical misgivings.

Leland acknowledged their congratulations with the same agonised smirk that he displayed once every year when they started singing, '*Happy birthday to you, dear Lee-land . . .!*'

'Right, let's get down to work,' he said calmly, adjusting his bifocals. In spite of having been engrossed for many weeks now in one of the biggest fraud and larceny cases the State had seen in a decade, he had kept himself well-informed about what had been happening in the office.

'Grace, I hear you're making progress with Turner-versus-Triton? Douglas here tells me we may be able to settle out of court? Good!'

'I'm not so sure,' she said. 'In the short term, yes. It would relieve the financial pressure on the mother, certainly. But in the long term, she might lose out. Also,' she added po-faced, 'since costs will surely be awarded against Triton, a quick settlement is certainly *not* in the best interests of the Partnership.'

'That's heresy!' Leland snapped. 'And you know it, Grace! My maxim is, and always has been, that the law's a mug's game. If you absolutely have to resort to it, it should be done with as little pain, time and expense as possible. Justice is the bottom line, in this firm. And I say that with my hand on my heart – as one who has just had to get up on the stand and plead successfully for a bunch of greedy, unscrupulous assholes who've taken the taxpayers of this State for the equivalent of the G.N.P. of half a dozen Third World countries put together! Still, somebody has to keep the humble firm of McKenzie Brackman in business, so it can continue to fight for the little guy!' He seemed pleased with his little speech.

'I agree with Leland,' Brackman said predictably. 'A court case might drag on a whole year – two years, if Triton take it to appeal – and at the end of it maybe the mother gets a million, two million, maybe more. And what's she going to do with it? You know what those broken families from the *Barrio* are like? Half the sharks and pimps in the city would hustle in on her. Within a year she'd be cleaned out. And then where would your Candy Turner be?'

Grace felt she ought to respond to this patronising little sermon; but Leland's next words reduced her to cold silence.

'And Victor's due back from Las Vegas tomorrow, I gather?'

'He is,' said Brackman. 'He tells me he's also fixed his case. He's got the White Magic Casino to agree either to rehire the Mexican croupier, or pay him $100,000 compensation. According to Victor, the guy looks like accepting the latter – which isn't quite what Victor had been going for. He told me he thinks it makes the guy look cheap. But at least the costs will be up to the casino owners, some of whom, according to Victor, belong to a syndicate that doesn't bear too much looking into.'

'We don't want the Partnership getting mixed up in that kind of game,' said Leland gravely. 'Victor's done well to get a settlement. Why isn't he flying back today?'

'I told him to,' said Brackman. 'But we all know how Victor is. He said he had some business to tie up before he pulls out.'

Grace had listened to all this with a face of stone. *Thanks, Victor! Your client comes first, of course – but just Hello and Goodbye would have been better than nothing.* Leland now looked at her uneasily. He was more concerned with her new relationship with Victor, than with Victor's welfare in that desert-jungle of crooks and contract killers. For Leland McKenzie regarded sex within the Partnership as a fly in the ointment – or like a bad summer cold – highly undesirable, a darned nuisance, and usually quite unavoidable.

Leland's benign eyes now turned to Stuart Markovitz. He and Ann Kelseys's personal travails, which he'd been hearing piecemeal along the firm's grapevine, were also a great nuisance; but this latest trouble in their neurotic marriage now looked – thank God! – to be close to a happy solution.

'Everything okay, Stuart?'

'Fine!'

'That little personal matter with Ann's family all sorted out?'

'I think so, Leland – thanks!'

'Good. I gather,' Leland added, half turning to Brackman, 'that Douglas here has given her leave-of-absence till the end of the month?'

'That's mightly kind!' Stuart agreed eagerly. 'And I think Ann's managed to fix for my father and mother-in-law to go on their second honeymoon round the world – Hawaii, Hong Kong, the South Seas . . .' The little man would have gone on forever, if Leland hadn't cut him short:

'I'm very happy for you all, Stuart. We'll all be glad to see Ann back.'

Stuart sat hunched in his chair, as anxious and guilt-ridden as ever. For guilt and *angst*, Leland had long decided, were to Stuart Markovitz what death was to Keats.

That just left Michael Kuzak. *Damn Kuzak*! Leland didn't mind the odd hasty resignation – which was usually withdrawn next day, after a few quiet words. But this time things seemed to have gone too far. Kuzak was a hothead who needed to be treated at times like a prima donna. Altogether Leland McKenzie was pretty annoyed with the way the whole business had been handled. Kuzak should at least have been informed of the reasons why Brackman had decided to go soft and back down in what was a pretty clear case of police brutality. Douglas was a foolish sentimentalist! Leland would have demanded, at the very least, an official reprimand against this Lieutenant Slazenger. As it was, his action – or rather, lack of action – had effectively isolated Kuzak's rights to bring his own civil action against the L.A.P.D.

But what really upset Leland was that Mike Kuzak had now disappeared. His phone rang unanswered – he even seemed to have switched off his answering machine; and above all, he'd made no effort to contact Leland personally. From what Roxanne said, it sounded as though young Michael Kuzak was going to need a lot of tea and sympathy before he came to his senses. But Leland McKenzie was certainly not going to bribe him back with a hike in his salary, and certainly not by offering him a Partnership. He felt personally slighted by his young protégé's behaviour. Above all, he didn't like one of his flock quitting in the middle of a case.

He said finally, 'Then we have this so-called "Phantom

Boot" case.' He paused, looking down at his notes. 'The "L.A.P.D. versus Nugent-Ross".' He glanced up. 'Mike's case, I think?' He glanced at Brackman. 'And we have a little trouble with Mike on this one?'

'A lot of trouble,' Brackman said stonily.

Leland McKenzie's eyes travelled down the table, mentally ticking off each member of the firm. 'This one looks as though it's up for grabs. Who wants it? C.J.?'

C. J. Lamb squared her shoulders and smiled. 'I hear this Nugent-Ross character is a real handsome playboy bastard,' she said, her English accent again slipping easily into the local vernacular. 'He's apparently got most of the girls from Malibu and Santa Monica swooning for his favours!'

'You should have fun,' Leland said drily. 'You want him?'

'I'll give it a whirl,' she said, smiling.

Leland nodded, then frowned. 'One last item on the agenda.' He glared for a moment at Arnie Becker, casually draped across his chair and looking as though he were about to pare his fingernails. 'Arnold, I've warned you before about your conduct and general attitude to the female members of this Partnership –'

Arnie Becker had sat up straight, looking startled. Leland was deliberately ignoring Abby Perkins. Before Becker could comment, he went on:

'If you have any wisecracks to make to your peers, you'll kindly make them well outside this office, and certainly not in Conference time! Is that understood?'

Becker started to bluster about some people not being able to take a joke, but Leland cut him off in mid-sentence: 'From what I hear, Arnold, it was a series of not very funny jokes. Rape, in any form, is *not* a joke! Keep that kind of talk for the locker-room.'

'But this rapist was a phoney, Leland! He was dating the girl next day – even *sleeping* with her, for Chrissake! With her full consent!'

'I should hope so,' said Leland, suppressing a certain inner mirth.

'That's right,' said C.J. Lamb. 'It was the most barefaced fraud I ever saw – with my own eyes too!'

Leland sensed that Abby was about to intervene and start the whole thing off again. He cut them all short with a slight chopping motion of his hand. 'That's enough! All of you! Arnold, you owe Abby an apology, which I shall leave you to make in your inimitable way.' He stood up and sighed.

It was all rather ridiculous, he thought. Forty years ago, when he'd started in this racket, Abby would have been a harassed, housebound mother enjoying the tribulations of a second unhappy marriage. But times had changed. As Leland knew only too well, all McKenzie Brackman needed for its corporate image was a noisy, internal case alleging 'verbal harassment against a female member of the firm'. *Still, I mustn't become a cynic*, he thought.

As Conference ended, Roxanne came in. 'Grace, there's a call for you from the D.A.'s office!'

'No consorting with the enemy, Grace!' Brackman said, only half-jokingly. 'Even if they *are* on our side in this Triton case. Keeping too friendly with the D.A. people loads the dice.'

Grace ignored him. She took the call in her office. It was Sam Ohls. 'Grace honey! *Howaya*? Still shakin' the tree?'

'I'm making progress, of a sort, Sam,' she said neutrally.

'Yeah, well I could have something for you. It may not help you directly, but it helps to colour the picture – of our friend Randy Miller, in particular.'

Grace felt relieved to be back on track – doing what she was best at doing, which was fighting her and her client's corner. 'Let's have it, Sam.'

'Well, after I fixed for you to see that Form 10-K, I decided to have a look at Triton myself. And at its President, Mr Miller. Just an idle moment, you understand, sweetheart! No prejudice involved.'

'Get to the point, Sam. I'm a busy girl.'

Sam Ohls chuckled down the phone. 'Aren't we all? Keeping America safe and clean for our children.' He paused, sensing that this was not quite what he should have said. 'Anyway, I got a look at Miller's record, then did some checking of my own. That's to say, I got one of our bright college trainees to do it – run a trace on Miller's banking arrangements, his associates, and so on . . .

'Well, this morning I got the results. Want to hear 'em?'

'Go on.' Grace sat holding the handset, a heavy weariness creeping over her. It was one thing having Stuart Markovitz crawling all over Randy Miller's affairs – that was at least within the firm, it was almost family – but the D.A.'s people were altogether something else. She wasn't employed any longer by the D.A.'s Office. In fact, this was just why she'd quit – to be her own boss, and choose her own cases, instead of having to do the State's dirty work – even if there was no-one dirtier than the likes of Randolph D. Miller.

Grace felt slightly grubby as she listened to Ohls's cheerful drawling tones:

'As I said, I don't know how it'll help your case – but I think Miller's contravening at least three S.E.C. regulations. One of them also infringes U.S. laws – at least as far as the I.R.S. is concerned. If I'm right, Randy Miller and at least one of his associates at Triton could be looking at a three-to-five in the State Penitentiary.'

'And how's this going to help me?' she said woodenly. 'Or my clients? You send him down, and the I.R.S. take his money? So where's the compensation coming from to look after the Turner kid?'

'I thought you wanted Miller strung up by his balls?'

'I want justice for Candy Turner, Sam. And that's all I want!'

'Okay, okay. I know you lawyers always like to claim the high moral ground!' He chuckled again. 'At least in this office we go for the jugular, and if someone knocks the knife out of our hands, well, to hell with it! – there's always plenty more out there where that one came from! No moral ambiguities here, Grace.'

She paused. 'What else did you find out, Sam?'

Ohls sounded disappointed: his call was not being greeted with the enthusiasm he'd expected. 'Quite simply, it looks like Randy Miller and at least one of his fellow directors have been soaking Triton for their own personal gain.'

'I know all that, Sam,' Grace said, not wanting to pass up the chance to claim equal expertise in these arcane affairs – though without giving poor Stuart a grain of credit. She felt mean as soon as she'd done it. 'Have you got enough to prove it?' she added.

'Ah, that's goin' to be more difficult. The sort o'banks

Miller and his pal have been using keep their records buried like in the Pharaohs' tombs.'

'So how do Miller and his friend stand with the law? U.S. Federal Law, I mean?'

'Well, what we have so far – that's to say, what Miller's chosen to admit to the S.E.C. – is not necessarily against the law. But it's not necessarily legal, either. It all depends on the circumstances, of course.'

'And the circumstances in this case?' Grace asked.

'Well, it's not of course illegal for U.S. companies to move money around outside the jurisdiction, *providing* it's fully declared – not used for purchasing drugs or for laundering the proceeds. And providing nobody contravenes the restrictions on strategic exports to countries on the State Department's blacklist. Like arms and certain advanced technology, usually in the nuclear field. And, of course, certain substances that can be used in the manufacture of chemical and biological weapons.

'We've checked with the D.E.A. and they have no record of anyone at Triton being involved – or even suspected of being involved – with drugs. That doesn't prove a darned thing one way or the other, of course – it's just for the record. All we've got to go on are a load of possibles and probables. Goddam, guesswork! Let's take illegal arms dealing. Possible – *sure*! But not probable. It would have to be pretty small potatoes. The most likely racket for Triton to be mixed up in – and for which they're best placed to operate – would be chemical warfare. The money involved is relatively modest – which is why all these Third World countries are trying to get hold of the stuff.'

'How much money is involved?' Grace asked.

'In this case' – Sam Ohls paused – 'from what I've seen of Triton's records, I reckon at least five million *plus* – most of it going into a couple of those Caribbean outfits which are so offshore they're practically at the bottom of the Ocean! One's a French set-up called *"La Banque Creole et Occidentale"* – his accent was comically grotesque – 'based in Martinique. The other's an affiliated outfit on Grand Cayman which I hear is about as well-regarded by Treasury as the late and unlamented B.C.C.I.'

'Five million plus, you say?' Grace shrugged at the phone. Two and a half million dollars each? It probably wasn't a great deal, she thought – not for people like Miller, who, according to the files, might be worth anything up to $100 million. But you could never tell with such people. (What was it F. Scott Fitzgerald once said? – '*The rich are not like you and I*' to which Hemingway is supposed to have replied, '*No – they got more money.*')

Of course, there might be another explanation. Randy Miller might know he'd been rumbled – at least, that the Feds were already snooping about – and know he'd have to cash in his chips and get out. The incident with Candy Turner had just speeded up the process. Perhaps $2.5 million was all he'd been able to get his hands on in the time available? The rest he'd have to leave to the creditors. If so, Grace was mightily glad she wasn't a Triton stockholder. She said to Sam Ohls, 'Do you have any line on who his buddy is? His fellow director?'

'N-n-no. Not yet. That is, we don't have a name. Or rather, we have six names – for the six full directors on the Triton board.'

'Could it be a phoney director? A sort of sleeping partner

who doesn't exist?'

Ohls considered this. 'Possible again, but not probable. Much easier to prove a director doesn't exist, than find a crooked one who does. You've got to understand, Grace, this is a pretty routine scam, as these things go – at least, in this State. A guy like Miller doesn't run much of a risk as long as he don't get too greedy, and nobody gets suspicious. But once they do, it's like a piece of knitting – you pick one tiny bit loose and the whole darned thing starts to unravel.'

Ohls paused. 'I'll tell you something, Grace. Randy Miller's been a very unlucky guy. If that kid of yours hadn't got blinded out on that Triton site, Miller and his friend might have gone on skimming the cream off the com-pany until the cows came home, or the brokers moved in. Over a few years a sum like five million just gets mixed up in the shuffle. As long as Miller ran the whole show, and could keep a strict eye on the accounts, he'd be in the clear. Until that kid came along.'

'Can you let me have a list of those six directors?' asked Grace.

'Sure thing. I got 'em right here in the file – ' He paused again, while Grace got her notebook out.

'Ready when you are, Sam.'

Ohls began to read out the list of six names. When he reached the fourth, Grace uttered an audible gasp.

'You okay, sweetheart?'

'It's okay, Sam. I just sneezed.' And she made him repeat the name, then spell it. The last two names on Ohls's list, like the first three, meant nothing to her. Of course, it was a coincidence. There'd be plenty of good WASP names like that, even in California. She only had to look in the phone book.

'Thanks, Sam,' she said, trying to breathe calmly. 'By the way, are these accounts in Martinique and the Caymans registered in the directors' own names?'

'No. According to the books, the loans were all made to a holding company called "Blue Max Enterprises". Neither of those schyster banks will give out any names at all – even aliases. Any ideas?' he added. 'Besides Miller?'

She hesitated. 'I'm not sure, Sam. But thanks, anyway! I'll be seeing you around.'

'*Here's looking at you, kid . . .!*'

Grace hung up and sat for a long time staring at the wall in front of her. It couldn't be? *It – just – could – not – be!* Then she reached for the four directories covering L.A. County – just to see how common the name really was.

Chapter Eighteen

Mort Carne was immensely fat, like a Sumo wrestler dressed in English plus fours of tweed check, white silk cravat, white socks and brown suede shoes. His hair was sleek and black, lying flat against his scalp like a bathing cap. A white silk handkerchief sprouted like a lily from his breast pocket.

He greeted Grace with an oily smile. 'Miss Van Owen – delighted! I'm Mort Carne, in charge of Triton Public Relations, and I also handle the company's legal problems. We do have legal problems, do we not?'

'We certainly do, Mr Carne.'

He gave a small, top-heavy bow and showed her across the outer office into a main room that looked like Mussollini's private parlour. Grace almost expected the fat man to add, '*Said the spider to the fly . . .*' Her appointment at the Corporation had been for eleven o'clock. It was now 11.42.

Mort Carne led the way across a green marble floor to a desk the size of a pool table which was supported by four stone lions. At the far end of the room, about the length of an Olympic swimming pool away, was the boardroom table, no bigger than the deck of a small aircraft carrier; and behind it, a long shallow chromium stairway, looking like the running board of a pre-war limousine, leading up to a wrought-iron gallery reaching round three sides of the room. From the high ceiling hung several *art-deco* chandeliers with white globes suspended from stainless steel frames.

Carne had settled his great bulk behind the desk, in what looked like an archbishop's throne. The desk in front of him was empty, except for a row of telephones – one, a repro-antique was a gilt stand and detachable earpiece. All that was missing was a portrait of *Il Duce* himself. Instead, high above Carne's head, was a gilt-framed photograph of the President of Triton, Randolph D. Miller Jr.

Grace sat down in a more modest chair of soft black leather, its padded arms fitted with silver ashtray and coaster, and studied the photograph of Miller. The hard regular features, posed against a neutral background, would no doubt appeal to the sort of person who didn't mind being kicked around and kept waiting a couple of hours.

Mort Carne shuffled his huge buttocks to get comfortable, then leant forward. He spoke in the best honey-smooth P.R. tones, with an oily charm to match – layers of it – and he was as tough as a Tiger tank. 'I understand you are representing a member of the public' – he opened a drawer in front of him and produced a slim file, as though he'd only just remembered it – 'with a view to lodging a complaint against this Corporation?'

Grace had been prepared for this approach, but when it came she could only barely control her temper. 'My client, Mr Carne,' she said, speaking slowly and deliberately, 'is a nine-year-old girl who has been blinded by chemical refuse dumped on open ground by this company.'

Carne gave a fat patronising smile. 'Forgive me, Miss Van Owen, but where and when is this incident alleged to have occurred?'

'At a disused site of yours on the Belmont Road, off the San Diego Freeway, last Thursday evening.' She laid her Samsonite case across her knees and took out a file that was much thicker than Carne's. 'But you know all about it, don't you? The Inglewood police have already talked to you.'

'They talked to one of my assistants, Miss Van Owen.' Carne had peeled off several layers of charm and his cherry lips were set firm. 'But I'm afraid you are mistaken. The police have been shown the site you mention, and there is no sign of any chemical refuse. The place has not been used for a long time.'

'We will be establishing, Mr Carne, that that is not entirely true.' Grace was partially bluffing but her words had the desired effect. The last layers of honey peeled off: the soft fat contours of Mort Carne's face had firmed up and his small eyes took on a cold glitter.

'Are you calling me a liar, Miss Van Owen?'

'No – just an average public relations man trying to clean up after his master.'

Mort Carne nodded. 'I see. I find your manner, Miss Van

Owen, both offensive and highly unprofessional. Who did you say you worked for?' he added, although he knew perfectly well.

Grace didn't bother to answer this. Instead, she said, 'Mr Carne, you say this site of yours – on the Belmont Rd, Inglewood – hasn't been used for a long time?'

He nodded. 'That is correct' – and looked at his watch.

'How long is long, Mr Carne?'

He shrugged. 'I don't think it's been used for at least three years.'

'Then why is it fitted with an active infra-red alarm system?'

For a second she saw a flicker of anxiety cross the smooth, fat face. 'What alarm system?'

'There's an alarm fitted at the site – a modern infra-red device, placed just inside the wire a few feet from where the accident occurred. Your boys must have missed it last Thursday evening.'

'What the hell's that supposed to mean?' It looked for a moment as though he might lunge at her, except for his huge weight and the distance across the desk.

'Just what I said, Mr Carne. And we know that alarm went off just after seven last Thursday evening – at exactly the time my client was blinded.' Grace was still bluffing; but the shots were hitting home. The fat man had begun, very slightly, to sweat.

When he spoke next, he said the wrong thing. He showed his hand: 'How do you know all this?'

'Those alarms all have a link to the local police. As soon as the one at your site went off last week, your security people called the Inglewood Precinct and told them it was a false alarm. The police accepted that – they shouldn't have, but they did. Then a bunch of your detox' boys drove out there and cleaned up all the evidence. They even stole the child's bicycle.'

'Ah, larceny, now, huh?'

'Yeah, larceny, Mr Carne – along with some rather more serious charges.'

The fat man sat looking at her, like a giant toad contemplating a particularly delicious insect. Then he said what he should have said earlier: 'Look, Miss Van Owen, let's be sensible about this. I know that area off the Freeway – it's a derelict ash-pit. The local kids regularly go out there to play. Their mothers shouldn't let them, but they do. The place is damned dangerous! Some of those crazy kids are bound to get hurt sooner or later.

'Of course,' he went on: 'Now that one of them has been hurt, it's pretty damned convenient to pin it on a big company like Triton. Damned convenient! What can we do to defend ourselves against one blind child and the mighty media-circus?' He raised his pudgy hands in a gesture of fake despair. 'I'm very sorry for the kid, but I do not accept that this company can be held in any way responsible. There's not a shred of evidence. Nothing but a kid's word. Sorry – but a good try, Miss Van Owen!'

Grace just managed to control her temper; she wanted to get the fat man angry first. 'Supposing we can prove this kid *was* on your disused site out at Belmont last Thursday evening? What would you say then, Mr Carne?'

Carne gave a fleshy smirk. 'Then I'd say she was trespassing. It's private property out there – or were you and your clients not aware of that?' he added, relieved to be back on what he thought was safe legal ground. Grace, however, felt a surge of triumph, and made a quick note in her book. *A few answers like that in court and she'd be home and dry!*

For a moment she let the fat man drone on: 'So what have you got? I'll tell you what you got, lady – a woman comes to you from the *barrio* with a story about how her kid's been blinded playing out on that ash-pit near Belmont . . .'

Grace had opened the file on her knees, turned a couple of pages, then interrupted. 'Where does Triton usually store its supplies of *Dioxypretalyn*, Mr Carne?'

The fat man answered too quickly: 'I'm not a scientist, Miss Van Owen. I don't even know what it is.'

'Then let me tell you. It's a product of Dioxyn, which is one of the most lethal chemical agents devised by man. It was used in "Agent Orange" in Vietnam, and it's still used today in powerful pesticides. *Dioxypretalyn*, commonly known as D.X.P., is a refined and superior version. It was developed by Triton, under its R & D programme, and is patented and widely marketed under the Triton name. So don't say you've never heard of it – unless you want me to think you don't know your job, Carne.'

The man's face reddened at the deadly familiarity. 'So what's the stuff got to do with this case?' he growled.

'Traces of the chemical were found all over my client's face and hands, and her clothes was saturated with it. The lab tests are quite definite. They can't be challenged.'

'Dioxyn, you say?' Carne asked cunningly.

'No. Dioxyn would have killed the girl outright, and probably most of the kids with her. What the lab found was

Dioxypretalyn – the Triton tradename.'

'That doesn't prove a damned thing! Our stuff's marketed under licence all over the States – you said so yourself! It could have come from any number of sources. Have you bothered to check that?'

'Yes I have, Mr Carne. There *are* other chemical plants in the L.A. region. But you ignore two things. One, the place where this particular stuff was found belonged to your company. And second, none of these other companies has a track record like yours.'

'Meaning?'

'Meaning, Mr Carne, that this isn't the first time your company's been in the doghouse. Remember that big law suit five years ago? . . .'

'I wasn't with the company five years ago!' Carne sounded slightly desperate now. 'Anyway, that suit doesn't prove a damned thing. Any more than this cock-and-bull story cooked up by a bunch of kids who were in a place they shouldn't have been!'

'Sure, Mr Carne. And those barrels of *Dioxypretalyn* were in a place *they shouldn't have been*. Only those poor kids didn't know that.'

'Those sort of kids aren't dumb!' Carne said savagely. 'I should know – I was brought up in the old Bronx,' he added, letting his accent slip, as though to prove his point. 'Anyway, I already told you once! If what you say's true, they were goddam trespassing!'

'So you admit they were on your site last Thursday evening?'

'I did not say that, Miss Van Owen! Stop trying to railroad me! I admit nothing! And you can prove nothing . . .'

'Oh I don't know about that, Mort. Maybe she can!' The voice came from the far balcony high above them. Carne and Grace turned at once.

A man was walking slowly down the chromium stairway. He was tall and casually dressed, in a white Fairisle sweater, grey slacks and black moccasins. He strolled towards them both, smiling slightly, as though they were all meeting at a country club.

Mort Carne had lumbered to his feet. Grace just sat looking at the man, thinking that he seemed much younger than in his photographs. His face was rather pale, without the usual executive tan that is *de rigeur* among the West Coast big-business set, and his expression was much more relaxed, more human that he'd appeared in any of the pictures Grace had seen of him. When he was only a couple of feet from her chair, she noticed that the photographer must have touched up the big portrait on the wall. She also knew why the man avoided getting a suntan.

One side of his face and necky had a glossy texture, a whitish-grey sheen puckered at the edges with tiny white scars; and as soon as he spoke, she noticed that his face had a frozen, slightly lopsided look. She found it made him oddly attractive, even vulnerable.

'Miss Van Owen – Randolph Miller. I've heard a lot about you.' He gave a stiff smile, without opening his mouth. 'I always let Mort here go in first to absorb the flak. I just hope you haven't been giving him too hard a time?' As he spoke, he glanced at the fat man as though he were a piece of furniture.

'Let's go to my office, Miss Van Owen. We obviously have things to talk about.' He turned and indicated the stairway at the far end of the room. Grace stood up and followed him, wondering if Miller had been listening upstairs on an intercom. It was what she would have done, if – God forbid! – she'd been running the Triton Corporation.

She reached the balcony and looked down. Carne was still standing behind the desk, staring straight ahead of him, like the head eunuch on guard. Randy Miller stopped at a couple of swingdoors of smoked glass framed in platinum. He held one of them open for Grace, and she entered what she took to be Miller's inner sanctum. It was comfortable and not too large. Pale oriental rugs were strewn casually about the parquet floor, the walls were matt copper and most of the fittings were copper. Copper and chrome safe, small built-in bar with copper-coloured glass top and matching leather stools, copper lamp on the desk, copper ashtrays, copper pen set and letter-opener, copper corners of the blotter pad.

He waved her to a leather Chesterfield and walked over to the bar. 'Can I tempt you with something to drink, Miss Van Owen?' He glanced at a copper clock with Roman numerals. It was just 12.15.

'I'll just have water,' Grace said, determined not to fall in with his easy manner. She waited, not watching, while Miller poured a glass of still Evian water and a dry Amontillado for himself, drawn from a miniature cask on the bar. He handed her the Evian, then carried his sherry over to the padded desk chair.

So, mud in your eye, as the British say!' Miller took a sip of the Amontillado, seemed to wash it round his mouth, then leaned back and gave her his frozen smile. 'I'm going to be absolutely honest with you, Miss Van Owen' – the smile turned into a stiff grin – 'or as a lawyer, do you find honesty a rather suspicious commodity?'

'It depends who the person is who's being honest.' Her voice was deadpan, determined not to return his smile. And she wondered how Victor would have reacted to Randy Miller? Knowing Victor, he'd probably have got on with him, man-to-man, like Reagan and Gorbachev – two fading lights on a distant horizon.

'Well, let me say at once that I've obviously read about this case and I think it a terrible tragedy. Quite awful. Not only for the poor child, but also the mother. I know some of the newspapers have been saying that the mother's partly to blame. But these people are poor, they've got no home help, and most don't even have husbands. So their kids play wild, and sometimes they play dangerously. Perhaps we should blame the city and the politicians for not providing –'

Grace cut in sharply. 'You haven't thought of blaming yourself, or your company, Mr Miller?'

'Well, I certainly would, if I could be sure that this company was at fault. But I'm sorry, Miss Van Owen' – Miller's voice was heavy with sincerity – 'you have said nothing so far that convinces me that it was.'

He shrugged. 'The secret of good management is to know everything that's happening, particularly when it's right under your own nose. I run a tight ship, Miss Van Owen – 'he broke off, with a slight frown, and added: 'Do you have any other name? I mean, this Van Owen stuff is a little formal.'

Grace ignored this. 'You're in this business to make money, aren't you, Mr Miller?'

'I won't argue with that. Triton is certainly not a charity.'

'And you accept that many of your products are inherently damaging, even dangerous? That sooner of later there are going to be accidents and people are going to get hurt?'

He gave a weary sigh. 'Accidents happen every day. People drown, they fall off ladders, they smash up their cars, and their kids stick nail clippers into wall sockets. On that line of argument, we'd better start by locking our kids away in padded rooms – then close down General Motors, and we can all go back to using the horse. Maybe that last one wouldn't be such a bad idea!' He leant back in his chair, enjoying his little soliloquy:

'Personally, I've thought for a long time that this country relies too much on chemicals, drugs, phoney hi-tech solutions – just as we have too many psychiatrists, too many doctors, too many lawyers. No offence!' he added; then paused, looking at the ceiling.

'Sometimes I think I might just jack it all in and go live on an island in the South Seas.'

'Then why don't you?'

He gave his stiff grin. 'Because I don't like the sun! Anyway, we're all creatures of habit – or we wouldn't go on living in this hell-hole of a city, poisoning our lungs and driving ourselves apeshit with neurosis masquerading as energy.'

Grace could not decide whether he was a genuine cynic trying to soft-soap her, or just another hard-faced Californian businessman weeping all the way to the bank, and spouting crackle-barrel philosophy all the way back? Or whether there really was a soul inside the man – a disappointed idealist who'd given up trying to get out?

'You ought to get into politics,' she said drily.

He chuckled. 'On my record? With people like you on my tail, I wouldn't get to first base! Would I, Miss Van . . .?' He paused. 'Hell, do we have to continue on this last name basis? It makes me feel like I'm already in court!'

'*Grace*,' she said quietly, trying to keep any hint of intimacy out of her voice. 'Grace Van Owen.'

'Miss Grace Van Owen?'

'I'm not married, Mr Miller.'

'Call me Randy.' He sat for a moment looking at her. It was not an unpleasant look – neither hostile nor friendly, nor even lecherous. It was the look of a man who's used always to winning, yet doesn't mind if he occasionally misses a trick. Grace thought she understood what the various Mrs Millers had been up against.

'You know, of course, that you're an extremely attractive woman, Grace?'

She drew in her breath with an inward groan. Surely he could do better than *that*? It was the sort of line they used to put in cheap B-movies when they were behind schedule and the scriptwriter had a hangover. She looked pointedly at the clock.

'I'm also a lawyer, Mr Miller. And the taxi meter's ticking – either for my client, or for you. I think it's going to be for you. So let's not horse around, okay?'

'Okay.' His expression was wistful, almost sad. 'You made a lot of allegations downstairs, so I'll save time by answering them right now.' He stabbed at a tape recorder on the desk, and the conversation downstairs began to play back to them. With skilful use of the fast forward button, and the help of some recently scribbled notes taken from the time-counter, Miller was able to edit out everything except the end of Grace's questions and statements. It was the kind of trick that any schoolkid could master, but it would still take a lot of practice. Grace guessed that Randy Miller had had such practice, many times before.

As her voice finished each sentence, Miller put the machine on hold, then answered each point raised. Grace felt as though she were taking part in some strange experimental film, as she sat listening to her own disembodied voice filling the room:

'. . . *Then why is it fitted with an active infra-red alarm system*?'

Miller touched the 'pause' button. 'Routine,' he said. 'Our corporate insurance policy requires a specified alarm system on all our properties.' He snapped the machine back on. It was a truly weird experience:

'. . . *modern infra-red device, placed just inside the wire a few feet from where the accident occurred. Your boys must have missed it last Thursday evening.*'

'You're right – the alarm did sound that evening. It's logged on the computer. And we did send a couple of men out there. But there was nothing – just a bit of broken wire that looked as though it had been down for a long time.' Miller switched on again, not giving Grace time to interrupt. Instead, she began taking notes.

'. . . *We know that alarm went off just after seven last Thursday evening – at exactly the time my client was blinded.*'

The machine paused again, while Miller took a sip of sherry. 'A coincidence, I'd say – even assuming these kids were right about the time. And that's a big assumption –

given that kids in that neighbourhood don't wear watches. And even if they did, kids have a lousy sense of time.' He flicked the switch again:

'. . . *Then a bunch of your detox' boys drove out there and cleaned up all the evidence. They even stole the child's bicycle.*'

That's just not true, Grace. None of our emergency teams was called out on Thursday night – except for the initial reconnoitre. You can check the computer. As for the kid's bike – well' – he gave a faint shrug of contempt – 'we just don't employ people like that, Grace.' He returned to the machine:

'. . . *Where does Triton usually store its supplies of* Dioxypretalyn, *Mr Carne?*'

'We store it at a special depot out in the desert. It's fully registered – a long way from where anyone lives.'

'It's as dangerous as that, is it?' Grace managed to break in "live", feeling she was in the presence of her own invisible *doppelganger.*

'Sure it's dangerous. If it's handled by the wrong people.' He spoke with a smooth, persuasive self-confidence, and his timing was brilliant. He'd have made a good lawyer, Grace thought.

'Can you tell me the location of this depot?' she asked.

'I'm sorry, I'd rather not. Company policy. If some outside pressure-group – and God knows, this State's got enough of them! – somehow came by the information, it would only cause trouble.'

'Very convenient.'

Miller ignored this, as he reached for the button:

'. . . *the place where this particular stuff was found*

belonged to your company. And second, none of these other companies has a track record like yours.'

Miller pursed his lips. 'For the record, I categorically deny that any *Dioxypretalyn* was stored anywhere in this city, last Thursday or at any other time. And any further allegations to that effect will be treated as libellous. As for the law suit five years back' – he shook his head sorrowfully – 'as a lawyer, you know that that is *not* evidence. It is simply a device by which to blacken your opponents, and would be ruled inadmissable by any judge. You ought to know that.' He paused, then smiled. 'Nothing personal, you understand.'

Grace nodded, and waited for the last of her disembodied voice:

'*. . . I'd say she was trespassing . . .*' – the voice of Mort Carne had slipped in, sounding both oily and coarse – '*It's private property out there – or were you and your client not aware of that . . .?*'

Miller shut the voice off, then sat shaking his head: 'I'm sorry, that crack of Mort's was right out of order. Although I guess,' he added, draining his sherry, 'that if people *didn't* trespass, most of you lawyers would be out of a job! This has never been a law-abiding country, you know It was built by pioneers who were mostly no better than bandits. *They* didn't respect frontiers, and they didn't teach their children to either. Maybe it's better that way.' He gave Grace his frozen grin and for the first time a doubt began to creep into her mind.

Randy Miller had switched off the machine and stood up. 'I know you've got a job to do, Grace. But I have too.' He paused. 'I suppose the Welfare people put you on to this?'

'Yes – through Washington General.'

He nodded. 'A tragic business. And very, very sad. But sorry, this is one they can't put on me – not this time.' He gestured towards the bar. 'Sure you wouldn't like something – a bit more lively?'

'No.' She swallowed hard; her throat was dry and desperate for a drink. A proper drink. Worse, the doubt in her mind was getting stronger.

'How about lunch then?'

She stared at him. He smiled back – his funny, half-sad, frozen smile that must itself, she thought, be the result of some horrible accident. 'All right,' she said, quite spontaneously, and regretted it at once.

As they got outside, she said, 'By the way, do you have a man working for you who's got a little ginger moustache, going bald, and wears a blue seersucker suit?'

Miller hesitated on the sidewalk, frowning slightly. 'N-no. Doesn't sound like a Triton man. Why?'

'Oh nothing, Mr Miller. I thought he followed me from the S.E.C. Building the other day.' She shrugged and went on walking. 'Probably just a friendly neighbourhood rapist.'

'Call me Randy,' he said. 'You can't go making out you're some bimbo secretary having a free lunch off me!' Then he seemed to remember what she'd just said. 'But how awful,' he added. 'Have you told the police?'

Chapter Nineteen

In 1983, a few months before Francine escaped her public thrashing at school, Claude Faber had bought a boat. A handsome forty foot cabin cruiser which had cost him – or rather, his wife – a quarter of a million dollars.

It was on the same night that his daughter had managed to get home to the ranch-house in Desert Hot Springs – mostly by Greyhound bus, though God knows where she'd got the money! Her parents had been about to leave for Oceanside, just north of San Diego. Here the cabin cruiser was moored at the jetty, ready to host a big party to celebrate their thirteenth wedding anniversary.

Both had been put out by Francine's appearance, though not for the normal reasons. They had been merely worried about what to do with her, on this night of all nights. They hadn't wanted to leave her alone in the house – there were already a lot of nasty rumours in the neighbourhood, about how they had a crazy daughter who was totally out of control, and besides, they couldn't be sure she wouldn't do something awful, either to herself or to their valuable property. Besides, it had been far too late to get a babysitter.

Instead they'd taken Francine along with them, on the hour's drive to Oceanside. Once on board the boat she'd been given a shower, some food, and told to keep to one of the cabins. There had been more than a hundred guests, and a great deal to drink. Some of those present were famous, but most were the usual riff-raff from the movie scene – small-time agents, PR and press people, a lot of aspiring or disappointed actors and what might politely be called 'actresses'.

Francine had obeyed her father and kept to her cabin; but could not sleep because of the noise. At 2 a.m. the guests began to leave. Most of them sounded pretty drunk. The incessant baying of laughter and excited party-jabber had become punctuated by arguments, and there had been at least one fight. Then the boat became silent.

At some time just before dawn Francine was woken by voices. They came from the next cabin, and she soon realised that her parents were having one of their interminable rows. Her father was very drunk, and had done most of the talking, or yelling: while her mother's voice could occasionally be made out whimpering and pleading, and finally just sobbing.

Francine was not able to hear exactly what was said: she stayed cowering in her bunk, with the pillow pressed over her ears. Sometime around dawn the arguments stopped. (This had later been confirmed by at least three members of the crew. And one of them was to testify that he'd seen

Francine standing at the stern of the boat, staring into the still waters of the Pacific.)

The smoke was noticed a few minutes later. The alarm was raised; but for some reason – either because they were too drunk, or sleeping too heavily – Claude and Mary Lou Faber did not appear. At first the fire was thought to have broken out in the galley, though later the police had been inclined to suspect a lighted cigarette in the Fabers' cabin.

Almost immediately the smoke became so suffocating below deck that the four crew members were forced to retreat. A moment later a Butane cylinder in the galley exploded. One of the crew seized Francine and flung her overboard, throwing a liferaft after her. Then all four abandoned ship.

Later, at the Fatal Accident Inquiry in San Diego, it was hinted that they should have stayed and tried to save their employers. But what happened next seemed to exonerate them from any real blame. Francine had already struck out for the liferaft – she was a strong swimmer – and had just been pulling herself aboard, when the boat blew up.

There had been a quick double thudding noise, echoing across the water, then a deep reverbating *wooomph*, and she had turned to see the whole cabin cruiser burst from bow to stern in a boiling white cauliflower of flame, rising slowly, spreading into that horribly familiar mushroom formation of smoke and flame.

She could not say how long it lasted, or for how long she stayed in the water watching. She remembered the heat and the choking smell of burning fuel. And something else too – something that had caused her to wake screaming every night for months to come. Although the doctors had never been able to establish whether what she said she'd seen had been real, or in her mind, her description of it had never varied. For an instant, at one of the glowing portholes, she had seen a face. She hadn't known whether it had been her mother's or her father's. The face had been screaming and a hand had been beating against the glass: then it had vanished, like a dry leaf in a fire.

By the time the coastguard arrived, what was left of the cabin cruiser had already sunk.

*

Kuzak had heard all this from Francine several years later, after he had been assigned to her case.

The local police and newspaper reports at the time, as well as the San Diego Court records, all confirmed Francine's version of events, which had also been vouched for by the four crew members. The charred wreck of the cabin cruiser had eventually been raised and found to have split open like a sardine can. The exploding fuel tank, together with the effect of the sea water, had destroyed whatever evidence there might have been.

The bodies of Claude and Mary-Lou Faber had been charred beyond recognition. Claude's brother, Amos, had been called to identify the bodies, which he'd done only by recognising an Indian pendant that Francine's father had always worn round his neck. All traces of alcohol had been burned away; and there had been no signs of foul play. For a moment during the Inquiry, a faltering suspicion had been directed at Francine, especially when it became known that she'd been involved in at least one act of arson. If she'd been an adult, this suspicion might have grown firmer.

There had been extraneous evidence too, which the Inquiry judge had reluctantly allowed, that Francine was not a happy child: that her parents had paid little attention to her, and that she'd recently been diagnosed as seriously disturbed. But even the discovery that she was the sole beneficiary of her mother's now much depleted estate, amounting to around eight million dollars, had not been allowed to count against the child.

The judge had concluded, like most other people who'd followed the case, that the whole tragic incident had been the result of a wild night at which far too much had been drunk. A verdict of Accidental Death had been returned, with blame attached to no-one. Public sympathy had been overwhelmingly with Francine – particularly in view of her condition.

For the first six weeks after the death of her parents, Francine had not spoken a word to anyone. She had not even been able to give evidence on video to the Inquiry. To the few people who'd seen her during this period, she'd appeared totally traumatised, moving as though in a trance, eating almost nothing, unable to care for herself, emotionally passive to the point of catatonia.

She was kept in hospital for three months, for observation and treatment, when she was seen by a number of doctors and psychiatrists, all of whom agreed that she was suffering from advanced psychosis, accompanied by clear suicidal tendencies.

One of these was a Dr Georgio Pelaggi, one of the State's leading experts on mental illness – particularly on suicides among children. Kuzak had met with him several times in the months after he'd taken on Francine's case. A grave, elderly man, with the face of a highly intelligent bloodhound, he'd confirmed to Kuzak that the girl's case was serious but that she would probably respond to treatment. What had really worried the doctor was the sudden appearance on the scene of Francine's uncle and aunt, Amos and Marlene Faber.

Until then there had been the problem of what to do with Francine, once she was well enough to be discharged. Whether out of a grudging sense of family duty, or from more sinister motives, Francine's uncle and aunt now volunteered themselves as her guardians. Dr Pelaggi was decidedly dubious. The word of a schizoid child had to be treated with great care; and although he'd listened for hours to Francine's stories about her two relations, and how she hated and dreaded them both, he'd been inclined, professionally, to remain sceptical.

In the event, when he finally met them, the doctor was not favourably impressed by Amos and Marlene Faber. They struck him as small-minded, mean, and almost certainly greedy. He later confided to Kuzak that the uncle reminded him of an albino rat, and his wife exactly as Francine had described her, looking like the wicked witch in the fairytale, an impression which Kuzak had vividly confirmed to him, when he later saw them both in court.

But what had most struck Dr Pelaggi in those early days was that not once, during the two hours they were with him, did either of them show any real concern for their niece's health; nor was there a word of regret at the sad event that had brought them all together. Perhaps even more troubling, however, was the fact that both uncle and aunt had made their appearance just three days after the court in San Bernadino – which administered Desert Hot Springs, the late Claude Faber's official place of residence – had granted full Probate of the Faber Estate to Francine Delacroix Faber, to be held in escrow until she reached her majority. On top of that, the Fabers had arrived well prepared. When Dr Pelaggi met them, they'd already engaged the services of one Ed Milkman, California's most notorious expert on 'family' law – especially custody cases.

Dr Pelaggi had been warned about Milkman, but knew there was little he could do to thwart him. The doctor had no hard evidence of physical, or even mental, cruely on the part of uncle and aunt towards their niece. And they were, after all, her next-of-kin. He could have tried making her a Ward of the District Court; but without more to go on, he only risked sullying his reputation by seeming to obstruct the course of natural justice. He could also have tried for a late adoption, but again faced the problem of having no real evidence.

As soon as Francine was taken in to see her uncle and aunt, she threw a series of violent fits which lasted for two days. At the end of it, she said she would kill herself rather than go back to live on her uncle's farm. Ed Milkman then invited himself in and explained to Pelaggi what the alternative would most probably be: a Court order confining Francine to a State institution for the rest of her childhood, and perhaps much longer.

The doctor felt unable to argue. Soon the papers were drawn up; and Francine was driven off in the back of Amos Faber's car.

Dr Pelaggi actually wept as he watched her go.

Chapter Twenty

Amos and his wife boxed clever. They knew their niece to be in a highly volatile state, and that if they didn't tread very carefully – if they mistreated or provoked her in the least – there might well be dire consequences. Dr Pelaggi at least made sure they understood that much. For what the uncle and aunt feared most was either having the child kill herself, or making such a fuss that the court might rescind the custody order and return her to hospital. Either way they stood to lose all control of the money.

Pelaggi made it an absolute condition that she must be allowed to visit him once every two weeks, and to call him at least once a week at a fixed time – or at any other time, if she felt under stress. The doctor also retained the right to re-admit her to hospital, and to prescribe whatever treatment he thought appropriate. The Fabers had agreed, with ill-grace; but against all expectations, the arrangement had seemed at first to be working well.

Francine's recovery had been slow but consistent. Dr Pelaggi treated her with the minimum of drugs, preferring to spend hours leading her, gradually and with great care, through the memories of her short life, trying to unearth her innermost feelings, particularly towards her dead parents. Soon she came to regard him as a mentor, almost as a guru; until the doctor feared that she might conceive some unbridled passion for him – the older man, the father she'd never really had. Pelaggi had to tread very warily, and altogether found his work cut out for him.

The first trouble arose over his fees. The doctor's time was not cheap, and the accounts he rendered the Fabers were mounting up. At first they disputed the sums, and he reduced his fees, in an attempt to appease them; then they started refusing to pay altogether. Like all good doctors, even in the mighty U.S., Pelaggi worked on the principle of charging his patients only what they could truly afford. His dilemma here was that technically Francine Faber was very rich indeed.

It was after he received a letter from Milkman, virtually accusing him of exploiting his patient's condition by charging exorbitant fees, that Dr Pelaggi began making his own inquiries. He already knew that the $8 million remaining from Mary-Lou Faber's money was held in a Discretionary Trust, to be administered by the court until Francine came of age. He applied to the court, and at least succeeded in getting his fees paid; and he also learnt that, through a legal technicality cleverly exploited by Milkman, Amos Faber was allowed to retain all his brother's personal property. In fact, no sooner had the court so ruled, than the uncle had begun to convert Claude Faber's possessions into ready cash – with Milkman, working on a contingency basis, reaping a fat percentage.

The Fabers decided to sell their fruit farm and move into the ranch-house at Desert Hot Springs. Everything else was put up for auction – apartments, automobiles, antique furniture. Dr Pelaggi could only guess, but by going on current real estate and auction-house prices, he calculated that, within a year, Amos and Marlene Faber must have accumulated well over a million dollars in their personal bank accounts. Yet he remained helpless. Until, and unless, Francine made a direct plea to him for help, the ethics of his profession prevented him from making any move.

And the Fabers had been canny enough to know this. Francine's welfare was their meal-ticket. What would happen when she reached her majority, at eighteen, was something they probably hadn't worked out yet. But for the moment they were determined to keep her sweet, by bestowing material gifts on her – the same impersonal, arm's-length kindness that her dead parents had offered her. Presents, clothes, a car when she'd turned sixteen and an expensive, so-called 'progressive' school in San Francisco, where she'd learnt how to smoke dope and sleep with boys.

Nothing had given Dr Pelaggi – or any other doctor, for that matter – sufficient grounds to complain to the court. No hint of hard drugs, no pleas for help from Francine herself.

And so it went on, for the next six long years, until Pelaggi began to relax, and even think that the girl might after all have been cured. But he continued to keep her case under strict but unobtrusive review.

During this time she continued to visit him at the hospital in San Diego, only at ever longer intervals now – while her uncle and aunt wisely did nothing to dissuade or obstruct these visits. And gradually, as the years passed, the doctor had come to revise his opinion of Amos and Marlene Faber. They were an unattractive pair, stupid and rapacious, but whether they'd been embezzling their niece's inheritance or not, the fact remained, from Pelaggi's point of view, that under their custody, Francine appeared to have made a miraculous recovery.

She had also grown into a beautiful young woman – a pale Renaissance beauty, Pelaggi thought: ascetic rather than sexual. For the good doctor had become very proud of his patient. Her case seemed to represent the triumphant conclusion to a long and successful career.

Yet there were still two things about Francine which continued to trouble the doctor. Francine obstinately refused, over all these years, to talk about that night on the cabin cruiser – particularly the minutes leading up to the death of her parents. Now that she was no longer a child, this refusal had become more marked; and on the few occasions that he tried pressing her on the subject, she flew into sudden, violent rages, even hysterics on the last occasion.

Georgio Pelaggi also noticed that these convulsions were usually followed by a certain remoteness, a detached indifference to all around her, almost a coldness of the heart. She continued to be devoted to the doctor, and to look forward to their now intermittent sessions together – but her affection had become more formal, without the spontaneous warmth and affection of a child.

Pelaggi also observed in her a certain deviousness, even cunning. Sometimes he realised that he was being subtly manipulated by his patient, not an uncommon occurrence for psychiatrists, but in Francine's case he began to feel indefinably uneasy. She'd become aloof, arrogant, but in a controlled, calculating way. He started catching her out lying, but always over trivial, pointless incidents in which there could have been no possible advantage to her in not telling the truth.

Pelaggi wasn't quite able to put his finger on it, but in the few months leading up to her eighteenth birthday he began to suspect her of trying to provoke a crisis. He feared she might be on the brink of a relapse.

The crisis came in later summer, exactly three weeks before her birthday. She'd gone to spend the weekend with her uncle and aunt at her father's old ranch-house at Desert Hot Springs.

*

The storm struck after midnight, on her second night there. The local police were called to the ranch-house by an hysterical Marlene Faber. There'd been a fire in one of the empty guest rooms. Her husband had managed to put it out in time, but it had destroyed the bed and most of the curtains, and the rest of the room had been ruined by the portable fire extinguisher. Then, when he and his wife confronted Francine about it, she suddenly ran amok.

She attacked her uncle with the empty fire extinguisher and knocked him to the floor unconscious. When his wife had tried to protect him from further attack, Francine had threatened her with a steak knife. It was only when the girl could be persuaded that Amos needed a doctor, that her aunt was able to call an ambulance. He was taken to the local hospital and was given sixteen stitches in his head. In the meantime, one of the paramedics had been sufficiently alarmed by Francine's general manner, which he'd later described as fluctuating between hysterical rage and bitter remorse, to call the police.

Versions of what had really happened now varied. It was established that the Fabers and their niece had gone out to dinner that evening in the near-by luxury spa resort of Two Bunch Palms. The waiters were to testify that Amos and his wife had drunk a great deal, and that towards the end of the evening a bitter argument had broken out between them and Francine. She had finally smashed a glass, screamed abuse at them both, and stormed out.

The spa was part of Desert Hot Springs, but the Fabers had both been too drunk to drive, and had taken a taxi the half-mile back to the house. Francine had walked. Her own version of events seemed to confirm the waiters' evidence. Her uncle had been drunk and had started to abuse her: he'd called her 'a dirty little teenage tramp' – that she was a 'taker', a self-seeking little bitch who'd 'been given everything, and gave nothing in return!'

Francine agreed that she'd broken a glass, after she'd loudly accused her guardians of helping themselves lavishly to her poor dead mother's money – that they were both 'blood-sucking leeches who'd only taken her in so they could feed on her inheritance!' She'd screamed that she'd go to the police – get a lawyer – expose them both for what they really were!

Francine's version only varied from Marlene's – and later, when he'd recovered enough to be interviewed, from her husband's – when she came to describe what happened after they'd all got back to the ranch-house. She said that for nearly two hours they'd gone on abusing her, mocking her – calling her a 'psycho', and that as soon as she got a steady boyfriend, *if* she ever go a steady boyfriend, he'd soon find out about her and drop her like a hot potato. *Nobody wanted a girl who was sick*!

Francine told the police that when she could no longer bear it, she'd left her uncle and aunt downstairs drinking – it had been just like that last night with her parents on their cabin cruiser – although she hadn't put it quite like that in her deposition. She said she'd gone upstairs to one of the guest-rooms to smoke some joints and try and calm down. Then, still fully dressed, she'd fallen asleep on the bed. She'd been woken by the smoke.

As far as the assault on her uncle was concerned, she told the police that as soon as the fire was discovered, her uncle had roared drunkenly upstairs and, after putting out the fire, had threatened to strip her naked and whip her. He'd chased her downstairs with the empty extinguisher; and they'd fought, during which he'd tried to tear her dress off her, and Francine had defended herself by wrestling the extinguisher away from him, then knocking him out cold.

The local police had been inclined to believe her. The Fabers had not made themselves popular in the neighbourhood, and although there had not been any evidence of their ill-treating their niece, Amos and Marlene Faber were not, as the local Sheriff put it, with admirable candour, 'The sort of people we like to have in Desert Hot Springs.'

Kuzak was called in a week later – after the dreaded Ed Milkman had made his second appearance, like a dark shadow from the past. The police had decided not to press criminal charges against Francine. Forensic tests had seemed to bear out most of her story. There were marijuana stubs in the guest room; her dress had indeed been torn; and a blood sample taken from Amos Faber several hours after he'd been admitted to hospital showed an alcohol level which the doctors described as 'likely to cause either a blackout or symptoms of violent behaviour'.

But then Milkman showed up again. Retained once more by Amos and his wife, if he hadn't been working all along for them, for a contingency fee. He applied at once to the San Diego Court for a stay of execution in the release of the Faber Discretionary Trust to Francine, as sole beneficiary, on reaching her eighteenth birthday, in less than a month's time. Milkman indicated to the court that he intended to show that Francine Faber was mentally ill and unfit to administer her own affairs; and as evidence he would not only produce the evidence gathered by the Hot Desert Springs police, but also her long medical history.

Dr Georgio Pelaggi was appalled. Not only by her relapse, but by the prospects of a protracted, well-publicised court case, and what effect this might have on his patient – who, he now decided, was far from cured after all. But this diagnosis only made his position vis-a-vis Francine all the more difficult. He knew that by its very nature, his own evidence on her behalf would in effect count against her. What Francine needed was another red-hot lawyer.

*

Pelaggi had always tried to avoid lawyers; but he did have an old friend who was the Senior Partner of a law firm in L.A. His name was Leland McKenzie. And Leland had chosen Michael Kuzak to represent Francine against her uncle and aunt.

The case had gone before the San Diego Civil Court less than four months later – leaving Kuzak barely enough time to complete his inquiries and gather the evidence. But, largely due to Dr Pelaggi, the court officials had been persuaded that the usual delays would risk putting Kuzak's client at grave risk, and destroy all hopes of a further recovery.

Kuzak had thrown himself tooth and nail into the contest, which he'd seen as a duel, a *mano a mano*, between himself and Ed Milkman. Besides, he was bewitched from the start by his new client. He found Francine beautiful, weird and fascinating: totally beguiled by her curious and varied personality – one minute grave and withdrawn, a lover of classical music and the ballet; the next, a hyperactive teenager smoking pot and hanging out with a gang of bikers who operated out of Long Beach. By turns he'd found her an outrageous, clever flirt; a morbid introvert; a well-educated, charming companion; an excitable streetwise kid who could be easily aroused to anger, tantrums, hysterical outbursts which had left her panting for breath and near collapse.

Pook Mike Kuzak! He'd certainly never met anyone like her before, or he would have known that he was dealing with someone with all the classic symptoms of the advanced schizophrenic. Or perhaps he just didn't want to know? After all, she was his client: and this looked like the biggest case he'd ever handled.

*

Milkman did not know it, of course – but on the very first day of the hearing, even before the proceedings had begun, he and his two clients were already dead in the water.

His case before the court was simple. He had already, immediately after the fracas in Desert Hot Springs, gained a temporary injunction preventing Francine from inheriting outright the residue of her parents' money. He now sought not only to have that injunction made permanent, *ceteris paribus*, but went on to tell the court that he intended to show that his clients' niece – for whom they had laboured so long and hard, and against such painful odds! – was suffering from a chronic mental illness that must render her totally incapable of handling her own affairs. He even stated that he would produce evidence indicating that she might be a danger to the public, and for the time being at least ought to be confined to some institution for her own safety.

The only solution – according to the lawyer – was for the court to make a new order, transferring the Faber Discretionary Trust from the control of the court, to be administered instead by his clients, who would continue to care for their niece 'with the same exemplary devotion which they have shown throughout the last turbulent six years – during which they surely cared for Francine as though she were their own daughter.'

Milkman had been suave and persuasive, even calling Pelaggi as one of his chief witnesses. Then Mike Kuzak had gone in for the kill. He had done his homework, no detail ignored, no stone left unturned. It was a text book performance. Guided at every move by Giorgio Pelaggi, and backed up by the evidence of McKenzie Brackman's financial ace, Stuart Markovitz, who, in the judge's own words, 'could sniff out a scam like a pig rooting for truffles', Kuzak had unearthed a Pandora's box of fraud and deception perpetrated over six years by the plaintiffs against a sick and defenceless girl – an orphan, and their *niece* to boot!

He opened that box on the second day. Instead of trying to block Milkman's tactics, and try to refute the charges of madness and irresponsibility against Francine, he'd made a straight appeal to the judge. He intended to prove that over the whole of Francine's adolescence, when she'd been dogged by illness, instead of caring for their niece, the Fabers had been systematically bleeding the Trust dry. A substantial fortune of some $8 million dollars, which should, with interest, have now increased by between thirty and forty percent, now stood at a little over $4 million.

The details of the fraud had been extremely complicated. Kuzak showed that the original order by the San Diego Court, setting up the Discretionary Trust, had been very loosely drafted, and there were at least five clauses which were ambiguous, to say the least. With the help of Milkman, and a murky stockbroker in New York called Jack Melrose, Amos and Marlene Faber had been able, sometimes even legally, to syphon off large sums of the Trust's money for their own personal gain.

At this point Kuzak graciously conceded that while Ed Milkman had been party to this trickery, it was reasonable to assume that he'd not been privy to the full extent of the scam. But the judge took a less generous view. He stopped the proceedings at the end of the third day and ordered a postponement for six days, in which both Kuzak and Milkman would agree to hand over all relevant evidence for the judge to study, before deciding whether to allow the case to continue.

Milkman had not been exactly struck dumb; but he'd looked severely disconcerted. At the end of the six days, the judge duly ordered that the appellants' case had failed, and that, in addition, there was a *prima facie* case of fraud and embezzlement against the Fabers, with Milkman and Melrose as accomplices. He also awarded all costs against the two plaintiffs, and ordered them to repay their niece the total of $4 million.

Next day the D.A.'s office issued a warrant for Amos and Marlene Faber's arrest. They were charged with stealing more than four million dollars from their ward and niece, Francine Faber.

During their subsequent trial six months later, it transpired that they had not only spent freely over the last six years, but had made some bad investments, and could barely raise half-a-million. During the trial a bankruptcy order was made against them; and they were later found guilty and sentenced by the San Diego Criminal Court to between five and ten years' jail. Criminal proceedings were also about to begin in New York against the stockbroker, Jack Melrose.

As for Ed Milkman – the Great Californian Home-Breaker and biggest American agent for the Redistribution of Wealth since Huey Long – he escaped criminal charges, but his file was sent to the A.L.A. in New York and he was in due course barred from practising as an attorney anywhere in the Union for five years.

Meanwhile, Mike Kuzak returned to his office, a star in the L.A. law firmament. His client, however, had not been so fortunate. After the first hearing in the San Diego Civil Court, she cracked up completely. Dr Giorgio Pelaggi told Kuzak afterwards that he could not remember any case involving one of his patients which had so appalled and depressed him. It seemed a wretched consolation that Francine should at last be rich, when she'd also reverted to the state she'd been in during the days just after her parents' death.

In the months that followed the first court hearing, and the indictment of her uncle and aunt, Francine fell into a deep, clinical depression which often degenerated into a coma for several days on end. Kuzak and Dr Pelaggi did what they could for her; but in the end, Pelaggi had consulted his old friend, Leland McKenzie. On Leland's austere bidding, Francine was consigned to 'Our Lady of Mercy' private clinic in Bel Air.

Yet here was this very same girl, just a year later, now sitting next to him in her brand new, Italian sports car – the hood down and her hat off, her burnt sienna hair beginning to lift and billow in the smoggy slipstream.

Kuzak could hardly believe everything had come right.

Chapter Twenty One

Mike Kuzak turned and stretched himself like a cat, his body naked and cool against the pure linen sheet. A spear of brilliant sunlight cut between the drawn curtains. Occasionally a breeze stirred them, and he lay and watched the slow-moving patterns of light and shade on the ceiling. He felt amazingly relaxed. And free. His natural vitality, which was so easily converted into aggression, together with his tendency to become belligerent over moral issues had been dissipated by the events of the night before.

His hangover from yesterday was gone. So was his rage against Douglas Brackman. Instead, he felt a stillness, a sense of almost total serenity. The desert breeze filled the room with the thick scent of the mimosa shrubs out on the terrace. The only sound was the faint splashing of a fountain.

After a time he got up and ran a long cold shower next

door; rubbed himself down with a rough, luxurious towel; then cleaned his teeth with the spare toothbrush he'd salvaged from his desk – perhaps the most useful item he now possessed. Besides, he'd always relished the idea of travelling really light: it belonged to the adventure stories of his childhood.

Then he noticed a man's razor, an expensive one, lying on the glass shelf beside the sunken bath. There was also a wooden tub of shaving cream; it was half empty. Handy though, he thought: shaving tackle was not something he kept at the office.

He shaved; then, with that innate curiosity that most lawyers share with their spiritual kin, journalists, he looked into the medicine cabinet. It was packed with bottles of prescribed pills, most of them from a hospital in San Diego. Kuzak guessed there were at least a dozen separate brand names there. Still, they were all on prescription – and the doctors must know best. There was also a diaphragm in a plastic box, next to a well-squeezed tube of spermicidal jelly.

He shrugged. Nothing wrong with that. A highly attractive, very rich girl living alone in a big luxurious house in California – there'd have to be something pretty wrong if she *didn't* have the odd affair. Yet it still rankled with Kuzak. He knew it shouldn't have done, but it did. Somehow it took the gloss off that wonderful night, waking up in this wonderful house, naked next to this wonderful girl. With a twinge of bitterness, he realised that it had been just another one-night stand – so far . . .

As he finished dressing, as though on cue, Francine came in from the terrace. She was wearing a narrow strip of blue bikini bottom; the rest of her was naked, tall and very slim, her pert breasts remaining firm as she moved. She was carrying a tray with a willow-pattern jug and two matching cups. Above the mimosa Kuzak could smell the roasted coffee, and a discreet whiff of perfume.

Francine was smiling gravely, as she placed the tray on a sidetable. 'You've slept beautifully, Michael.'

'I didn't snore?'

'Of course you didn't. You were perfect. You're the most perfect man I've ever met.' She began to pour the coffee. Her manner was strangely remote and matter-of-fact, almost business-like. If she'd been dressed in a suit, he might have thought she were about to negotiate some deal with him. Perhaps, in a funny way, that was precisely what she was about to do. He was glad he was dressed; he felt it gave him a slight advantage over her.

She gave him his coffee, black, without sugar – just as he liked it. She took hers with a sweetener. She raised her cup to him. '"Black as the raven, strong as life, sweet as love . . ." Do you know who wrote that?'

'A poet, I suppose?'

'Edgar Allan Poe. I *love* his poems. He had such passion, and he was so tragic – so desperately sad.' She sipped her coffee, sitting beside him on the unmade bed, staring across at the half-open curtains leading to a brilliant-white terrace.

'He died when he was only 43. He died lying on a gravestone,' she added wistfully, with the cup poised level with her lips. 'He was a hopeless alcoholic, you know. And he took drugs. That's what killed him. That – and the sadness of losing his young wife. He never recovered from her death. He was *obsessed* by death.'

Kuzak felt vaguely uneasy. This was a rather different Francine Faber from the calm, happy girl he'd encountered yesterday afternoon outside the Moviedome Leisure Room, before being driven off by her to the beach, then a quiet restaurant near San Diego, followed, at her insistence, by the hour's drive inland to the ranch-house at Desert Hot Springs.

Kuzak had been surprised she'd kept the place on, with its memories of her parents, then her uncle and aunt, and finally the awful showdown before the police were called. But Francine seemed not only happy with the house, but positively proud of it. Last night, before they'd gone to bed – an experience that even Kuzak wouldn't easily forget – she'd shown him how she'd entirely stripped and rebuilt the inside of the house. Instead of the rather stuffy, overblown decor chosen by her father, and retained by her uncle and aunt – what Francine called *Empire Décadant* – the place now mostly consisted of a single room the size of an aircraft hangar; granite wall on one side, glass and open brickwork on the other, with a huge log fireplace and jacuzzi, lily pond and a fountain, all sunk into the floor at various levels.

Yet for all its typical Californian 'individuality', it had a curiously impersonal, unlived-in atmosphere, like a luxury penthouse between lets. Perhaps, he thought, with more prescience than he realised at the time, she'd not yet decided on what personality would best fit such a home?

He'd already noticed that the few books she had were on a shelf in the bedroom: a couple of Jackie Collins novels; *Women Who Love too Much* by Robin Norwood; a volume on depression and recovery; Brett Easton Ellis's *American*

Psycho; and the *Collected Works of Ezra Pound* – all in hardcovers. Hardly light bedside reading, he thought: but at least she wasn't lacking in intellect. Kuzak tended to be an intellectual snob where women were concerned.

'So what's the programme for today?' he asked, when she'd finished her coffee.

Without a word Francine put her arms round his neck and kissed him greedily, with her neat cool mouth, then pulled him to her aggressively.

Afterwards, as though the interlude had not taken place, she answered his questions: 'We'll swim. Then have lunch. Then come back here and make love again. Then I'll show you the yacht.'

'*Yacht*?' Kuzak wondered if this were some obscure joke.

'Yes! Didn't I tell you? I bought it after I got well – with all that lovely money you won for me! It's called *Recovery*. Nice, don't you think? It's moored out at Oceanside – just where Daddy's used to be.' *If this is a joke, it is in the worst taste*, Kuzak thought, as she added, 'Just so perfect for watching the sun go down!'

Kuzak tried to smile, but for a moment couldn't. Again he felt a strange uneasiness. 'I've got to get myself some clothes and things first,' he said.

'Of course you have! I've got an account at Pacino's in San Diego. The best that money can buy. We'll dress you like a young prince!'

'I've got some money too, you know,' he protested feebly, remembering that the one time they had come close to quarrelling was last night in the restaurant when Francine had insisted on paying. And her protest had been more than just a formality between old friends – it had been nearer anger, and certainly beyond what the occasion merited.

So again he let it go. If she wanted to spend her money, he wasn't too proud, yet, to stop her. After all, if it hadn't been for him, had she gone to some hamfisted local lawyer, she might now be broke!

'Tell me about your yacht, *Recovery*?' he asked her later, when they were again lying naked on the bed, the sheet stripped off, feeling the warm breeze from the windows flutter against their skin.

'It's beautiful,' she said. 'The most beautiful thing I've ever owned. It's a thirty-foot yawl, smaller than Daddy's, but much nicer. Much more *style!* You couldn't give a party on it – because it's a *real* yacht. Just one small cabin and a galley, and a lovely deck to sunbathe on. I never wanted a big boat, like Daddy had,' she added, with a sort of sleepy ingenuousness. 'I think boats like that are vulgar. Mine's a real sailing boat!'

'Can you sail, Francine?'

'Of course! I've studied navigation and I've got all the charts, right down to the Mexican coast. What about you, Michael?'

'Huh?'

'Can you sail?'

'I don't think I've ever tried,' he said truthfully. 'Except a few times in a motor boat off Malibu . . .'

'Well you must try! I'll teach you. Tonight . . . I'll turn you from a lawyer into a real sailor-boy!' And she kissed him ravenously.

Chapter Twenty Two

The office of McKenzie Brackman and Partners was in chaos. It was the third day since Kuzak had gone A.W.O.L. and James Stewart ('Stoo') Nugent-Ross, a.k.a. the 'Phantom Boot', was here in the office, demanding to know what was happening about his case. The preliminary hearing had been set for a week today and he wanted to make sure he got the full media treatment – nothing but cable and national network coverage would be good enough. He knew that every full-blooded American heart was ready to reach out to him.

Meanwhile, Grace was in her office with her client. The woman was weeping intermittently, her eyes puffed and red from alcohol. Grace said patiently, 'You must understand, Rita – an interim order is merely a formality. In agreeing to it you in no way waive your rights to a full trial and any compensation that the court decides upon.'

'I don't un'stand all this legal stuff!' Rita Turner whimpered. 'I just wan' what's right by my baby!'

'We all do,' Grace said gently. 'I promise you that.'

'How can you promise me anything?' the woman said, squinting with sudden aggression across the desk. 'You got no idea about this! You dunno what it's like, you don't! You got no kids – you're not even married! I want someone older – someone who knows about these things . . .'

Grace gave an internal sigh. She'd been through this half a dozen times, and it was getting her nowhere. No good explaining to the wretched creature that she, Grace Van Owen, had been a judge until recently; and that anyway an older person, a married lawyer wouldn't help. The only person who fitted the bill was Leland, and this certainly wasn't his line of business. Probably Roxanne was the most suitable candidate in the office, but she didn't have the training or the diploma.

Grace felt very tired. She knew that Victor had returned, but he hadn't contacted her. *What was the matter with these men*? Were they scared? Too scared, after a passionate sexual encounter, to tell her they wanted a pause, a bit of space to breathe in? Grace would have understood that. She'd experienced such situations too many times herself. *But surely not Victor*? he was supposed to be different from the rest of the pack: his absurd good looks a shield behind which lay a sensitive and generous spirit. A man easily misunderstood. He'd told her so himself, many times. Yet what was he playing at now? She remembered how she'd said goodbye to him at the airport, on his way to Las Vegas. She had detected in him a certain reserve, a drawing away. Was that really his way of telling her it was the end?

She was aroused from her thoughts by the plangent, slightly slurred voice of Rita Turner, repeating aggressively:

'I don't want any goddam lawyer – I want someone who really *cares* . . .'

'I care,' said Grace softly, aware that while she pitied Rita Turner as a victim, she was also becoming mightily fed up with her as a woman. 'Look, Rita, as your attorney I can only advise you. But believe me – I want the very best for you and your child. To this end, I've already contacted the Triton Corp –'

'The lowdown murderin' *bastards!*' the woman screamed. 'If I ever get my hands on 'em, I'll kill 'em!'

'Now Rita, that sort of talk is not going to do anyone any good. What I propose – *advise* – is that you allow me to negotiate an interim settlement that will in no way prejudice your rights to a full, final agreement as to damages –'

'*Words – words – words!*' Rita Turner yelled. 'Why don't you lawyers ever talk proper English? I don't understand you – all this stuff about interns and prejudicin' my rights . . .! What about my baby lying there in the hospital? What does *she* get out of it, huh? Who pays all the doctors' bills when she gets older? And the special schools she'll have to go to? You tell me that, Miss Lawyer-Lady!'

Grace continued, with dogged patience: 'That's exactly why I'm advising you to accept an interim payment right now, Rita. So you can pay the bills – make plans for yourself and Candy's future. If you hold out for a full court hearing, and Triton decide to appeal, it could take months, even years.'

'How much would this interim payment be?' the woman

asked, suddenly alert.

'I can't tell you right away. It depends on how much I can negotiate. But several thousands of dollars.'

'Several thousand! That's nuttin'! Small potatoes! One of the men from the TV I talked to said I ought to get *millions!*'

'Yes, well maybe you will, Rita. But you need something right away, don't you?'

The woman sighed and her head slumped forward. Grace could not decide how much of the woman's performance was due to delayed shock, and how much to drink. 'Excuse me,' she said. 'I'll be back right away.'

She went out and asked Roxanne to buzz Leland. Roxanne and she exchanged brief eloquent glances. They were two birds of a feather – and sometimes life was just pure hell. Only Roxanne was more cheerful.

Grace found the Senior Partner busy on the telephone. He motioned her to sit down. 'So what can I do for you, Grace?' he said at last.

'I've got that Turner woman in my office, Leland – the mother of the kid – '

'I know, I know!'

'Well, she's driving me crazy. I don't know whether she's drunk, or sedated, or what. But she doesn't seem to understand half of what I say. She also seems to be building up a resentment against me – personally.'

'Any idea why?'

Grace hesitated. 'I think she wants someone older, more mature. Maybe I don't quite fit her idea of what a high-powered L.A. attorney should be like.' She paused. 'I think she resents me, Leland, as a *woman*.'

Leland McKenzie sat watching her shrewdly. 'Anything else?'

Grace swallowed hard. 'She accuses me of not understanding her – because I don't have children myself.'

Leland nodded. 'You've explained about going for an interim payment?'

'About a dozen times. Until I'm hoarse.'

'Well, that's all you can do – for the moment.'

'I have to deal with the woman's moods, her tantrums, her absolute refusal to co-operate. I can't do it, Leland! What that woman needs right now is a psychiatrist, not a lawyer!'

'You can do it, Grace.'

There was pause. 'I'm worried about her, Leland. I'm worried that if she *is* drinking, and probably taking medication too, she's going to foul everything up. If Triton's lawyers get on to it – and they've got a really nice piece of work called Mort Carne who looks as though he'd as easily eat his mother for lunch . . .'

'Partly know the man,' Leland murmured. 'But I say again, you *can* handle all of this, Grace.'

'Not if my client presents herself as a half-crazy lush, I can't! A single parent mother like that, and a blind kid to look after – why, they may try to serve an order under the Child Protection Act and get Candy put away in some institution. They might even be right, for Chrissake!'

Leland studied her some more. He was thinking, *Grace is a great lawyer but she always gets too involved. She is too intense. Everything about her is too intense – including her private life.* In moments like these, Leland McKenzie often found himself thinking of her as a daughter.

'How are you getting on with the Triton end?' he said at last. 'Is this Randolph Miller proving co-operative?'

'So far, yes. That's to say, he doesn't want the case to come to court.'

'I bet he doesn't! But be careful of him, Grace. These big money people can be charming one moment, then, when they think they've softened you up enough, they'll spit in your eye like a rattlesnake.'

'Rattlers don't spit,' Grace said. 'You're thinking of cobras.'

'Cobras, then.' Leland smiled. 'It's all the same. They don't like spending a dime they don't have to – even if it belongs to the stockholders.'

'With Triton it's mostly Miller's own money – on paper, anyway.'

'All the more reason, then –' He broke off, as the sound of shouting came from outside. They heard Roxanne's voice trying to soothe the raucous yelling of Rita Turner. 'Go see what's going on,' Leland said.

But even as Grace started towards the door, it opened and Roxanne came in, her hair disordered, her blouse slightly rumpled. 'She'd going crazy out there, Grace. Your client – !'

'I'll handle it,' Grace said quickly. From outside the hoarse shouting grew closer, louder.

'Oh God!' said Roxanne.

She and Leland heard Grace's voice, quiet and commanding, then Rita Turner screaming, 'You bloody lawyers! All the same! All bloody fancy in your nice clothes, with your big cars . . .!' Then Arnie Becker's voice, followed by a short scream. '*Get away from me, you ape . . .!*' But the yelling now began to subside, the voices to recede. Leland McKenzie looked at Roxanne, who was clearly terrified. 'Not like you to lose your nerve, Rox!'

'I just hate crazy women!' Roxanne said, beginning to shake slightly.

Leland shook his head. 'Better not let Abby Perkins hear you say that.' He looked up as Grace came back in.

'She wants money – right now. Or she says she'll go to the TV people and raise hell.'

Leland nodded and turned to Roxanne. 'Let her have five hundred, Rox. Two-fifty in cash, tens and twenties, and give her a cheque for the rest which she can cash with Welfare.' Roxanne withdrew, still looking worried.

Grace stared grimly at the Senior Partner. 'I think I'm going to lose this case, Leland.'

'You do your best, Grace. And remember,' he added, as she reached the door, 'as Count Tolstoy once said, "everything is experience."'

Easy for you! she thought, as she closed the door behind her.

*

Down the corridor, close to her office, Grace could see a small crowd round Rita Turner. The woman had stopped shouting and was bent forward, weeping hysterically. Arnie Becker had been joined by a second man who'd evidently just arrived in the office. It was Victor Sifuentes. He and Grace saw each other in the same moment. Victor's expression, which until then had been one of tolerant concern for the Turner woman, now clenched into an impenetrable

Aztec mask. He was deeply tanned from the desert sun and the whites of his eyes had a bluish sheen, the pupils black and piercing.

Grace knew she had turned very white. She nodded and said, 'Hello, Victor. Have a good trip?'

Rita Turner lifted her head, saw Grace and muttered furiously, 'Bloody lawyers! Chatting together like it's the bloody country club . . .!' And in that moment Grace was immensely grateful to Rita Turner. At least the woman had provided a vital diversion. Grace took her arm and began to lead her back to her private office, followed by Roxanne.

Victor Sifuentes just stood where he was, saying nothing. Grace didn't look back once. It was over.

Chapter Twenty Three

Grace Van Owen rang the unlisted number and heard the phone answered on the second ring. The man was waiting for her call. He answered in a dry, evasive voice: 'Ye-es?'

'Randy?'

He recognised her voice at once. 'Grace! How very nice . . .!'

'I've got to talk to you, Randy. As soon as possible.'

'Sure. What about *La Poissonerie* down on Sunset?' His voice had changed pitch, and was now altogether too smooth and relaxed for her comfort. Here was a man who controlled a modest industrial empire, which a nine-year-old girl could still bring crashing down, in a duel in which Grace still held all the high cards. Yet he sounded about as tense as if he were taking his latest secretary out for a quick date.

'I feel just like a late lunch of fried oysters and a cold

lobster,' he went on. 'Shall we say 1.45? That gives us an hour to get there . . .'

Grace said, 'Too heavy. *Much too heavy.*'

Randy Miller paused just the right length of time. 'Okay. As you wish. Somewhere a bit quieter. My club? – it's Thursday, which is Ladies' Day. Strictly by invitation, of course.'

Grace gritted her teeth. 'I'd want to gate-crash that club of yours, Randy, like I'd want to try getting into Iraq without a visa!'

She heard a light chuckle the other end. 'I like it, Grace. I really like it! Only I didn't draw up the club's rules, y'know.'

'You didn't have to.'

'So let's say you come to the office and my chauffeur drives us over? 1.45, huh?'

'No. I can make two o'clock, but not at your club, Randy, or anywhere else on the town.'

'Aw hell, Grace! You're not going to try and throw all that stuff at me again about being an officer of the law, and a former judge, and not consorting with the opposition?'

'I mean exactly that. This is official, Randy. And it's important. I'll see you in your private office at two o'clock.' This time there was a longer pause. 'You professional girls are quite something!' he said at last. 'I'll expect you at two o'clock, then.' And he hung up.

*

The receptionist showed Grace through the Mussollini parlour, where Randy Miller met her at the foot of the long stairway. He was dressed in a dark linen double-breasted suit and dark blue polka-dotted tie, which showed up the pallor of his face. In his breast pocket was a white silk handkerchief folded carefully into three identical points. His expression was formal, and slightly remote.

'Grace.' He took her hand in his: it was dry and cold, like a doctor's. Then he led her up the stairway to the platinum-framed glass doors into his office.

'Drink?' He had started towards the bar. 'I've got a *Krug* already on ice.'

She surprised herself by nodding. He poured both glasses, handed her one, then sat down in the high leather chair behind the desk. 'You said it was important? So – shoot!'

'I'm ready to do that deal with you, Randy. An out-and-out payment for the Turner family — fifty percent up front, the rest in six months time. A total of two million dollars. No publicity – case closed.'

He sat looking at her for a long time. His handsome, frigid features were as still as a photograph. He sipped some champagne. 'I'm afraid I've got to tell you, Grace, that the terms have changed.'

She felt herself flush. 'We had an agreement,' she said. 'A gentleman's agreement, I think it's called.'

'We had a discussion over a very nice lunch and decided to avoid the hassle of a court action. Mostly, if I remember rightly, to spare your clients any further time and grief. If that's the agreement, it still stands.'

'So what's changed?'

'The terms have changed. The money.'

There was another silence, icy this time. 'This conversation's being bugged, I take it?' she said at last.

'Would it make any difference if it weren't?'

She didn't answer. She drank half a glass of champagne, then took a long breath. The champagne was dry and not too cold; it was very good. She said, 'What are you offering now?'

'Two hundred thousand dollars. I've already had the cheque made out – to your firm –'

'Two hundred thousand!' she gasped. 'That wouldn't even cover your costs in a court action! You *bastard*, Miller!'

He continued smoothly. 'And another two hundred thousand spread over the next two years. Then as you say – case closed.'

'You bastard,' she said again, under her breath this time.

Randy Miller's face was as impassive, as impenetrable as Victor's had been back at the office. And she felt a great depression descending upon her, like a dark wall. Was she losing her touch? Losing her nerve? L.A. was a hard city to hack it in, and for a competent young woman lawyer it needed the stamina and strength of character of a Marine. She suddenly knew she was no match for Randy Miller. She'd been charmed by him, fooled by him, and had utterly underestimated him. It had been the scarred face that had done it: and that quiet understated charm that she associated more with Europeans than Californians. Again she felt very tired.

Miller was saying, 'Don't let's get sentimental about this, Grace. I like you. I really do. And with people I like I *do* get sentimental. But this is business. Your law firm is business, just like Triton is business. Sentiment just clogs up the machinery. I wipe it away.'

'That's bunkum – pretentious, crackle-barrel bunkum! Save it for one of your after-dinner speeches.'

'Oh I use it all the time!' Miller said, with his wooden smile. 'I'm alternatively a cynic and a romantic. And you know something? – it always works.'

'You think it worked with me the other day at lunch?'

Miller gave a small shrug: more a piece of body language than a movement. 'We all have to play the cards we're dealt, Grace.'

'How good are your cards, Randy?'

'You really expect me to tell you? Oh no! This isn't a friendly game, lady. But that doesn't mean friends can't play poker for high stakes, and still remain friends. Some of my oldest buddies belong to my regular twice-monthly poker school. And the stakes are high there, I promise you! The stakes are high right now, Grace. They're *damned* high!'

'I bet you can drop a couple of hundred grand in a night and not even miss it in the morning. Anyway, with a bit of creative accounting by people like that fat slug Mort Carne on your pay roll, it wouldn't even have to show, would it? As far as paying out damages is concerned, it's still a game. Isn't it, Randy?'

'It's business, Grace.'

'Sure. And the important thing is to win. And nothing else matters – not even a blind kid.'

'I won't argue with that. It's a game. So what?'

'Does winning the game mean trying to crawl out from under a massive law suit, with all the ruinous publicity for your company, and getting away with screwing that little kid and her mother down to a crumby four hundred grand to last the child for the rest of her life? Christ! If she lives another sixty years, that's only $60,000 a year for two people – not taking into account inflation. It's not enough, Mister Randy Miller. *It's goddam well not enough!*'

Miller didn't move; didn't say anything. Grace held up her empty glass. Only then did he rise and move smoothly over to the bar, to come back with two full glasses, his own topped up with Cognac. He gave Grace hers and went back to his chair. 'Business with pleasure,' he said dully, as he sat down again.

'Two million, Randy. Your company can afford it.'

Randy Miller shook his head sadly. He might have been a father having to refuse his grown-up daughter a present she'd particularly hankered after. 'Sorry, Grace. Just can't be done. My directors and stockholders wouldn't agree. They'd want to know why I'm backing down when there's no real case. We've already been through this. There's absolutely no direct evidence to link the kid's injuries to Triton. What there is remains purely circumstantial – and there isn't much of that.

'Besides, as Mort told you last time, those kids were trespassing. They shouldn't have been near that ash-pit in the first place. Any reasonably competent attorney will make a meal out of that, as you well know. Irresponsible single parent, no control over the kid. Lets her run wild in just about the most dangerous area of the most dangerous city in the world – then wants to make out that accidents never happen! And on top of that, this particular client of yours, the mother, is a prize lush. Or perhaps you didn't know that?'

'I know she loves that kid. Candy was all she had going

fo her.'

'Yeah, they all say that – when it's too late.' Miller drank the last of his champagne cocktail, then returned to the bar and came back with his glass, this time full of neat Cognac. He took a long sip. 'Your Mrs Turner's also a drug addict, Grace. She's twice undergone treatment over the past two years, while her kid was farmed off to neighbours. Did you know *that*?'

'Your people have sure been busy,' Grace said, knowing that her tiredness was showing through. Even the excellent champagne was failing to lift her.

Miller said, 'Part of the game, Grace. Man has to cover himself in a situation like this. You should start getting busy yourself.'

'I already have. And I've found out quite a lot. Nothing so routine as booze and neighbourhood drugs. But routine all the same.' She paused. 'You want to hear it?'

'Sure. Why not? That's why you're here, isn't it?'

'You're running a scam, Randy. You and one of your fellow directors. Stealing from your own company. Second-degree felony, with a statutory three-to-five minimum, if they send you down.'

*

Randy Miller reached out, carefully lifted his glass and drained the Cognac in one long swallow. His hand was quite steady; but Grace thought she detected a tiny shadow of anxiety cross his pale expressionless face. He gave a little nod. 'So that's what you were doing all day in the S.E.C. Building? Must have made a lot of work – reading right through my 10-K?'

Grace let out a sudden, grating laugh. 'So that little runt with the moustache *was* working for you? My God! I'd have thought you could have done better than that, Randy! He looked like a bank teller down on his luck – only less inconspicuous. I spotted him the moment I left the building.'

He gave his imperceptible shrug. 'I didn't want to use one of the big P.I. agencies. So I got a small outfit – said it was a divorce job. But what the hell? Who cares? A 10-K is in the public domain – for anyone who can be bothered to look. So what?'

'It's all about a nine-year-old kid, that's what!'

Miller pretended to ignore this. He looked as though he were deciding whether to give himself a refill from the bar; but instead leaned back and gave a deep, exhausted sigh.

'I don't want a case over this, Grace. Perhaps I'm getting old. Perhaps I don't care too much anymore. But the fact is, you're overplaying your hand.'

'Two million dollars? You mean, Triton can't afford that much?' She'd meant to taunt him – to strike at the male executive's most sensitive area, his bank rating. But his reply shook her to the core:

'I mean, *I* can't afford that much. See, it wouldn't be the company that paid. It'd be me.'

'You – *personally*?'

Miller seemed suddenly to reach a decision. He stood up and poured himself that other Cognac from the bar. He didn't offer anything to Grace. Then he sat down, very still and rigid in his high-backed chair. 'Triton's in trouble, Grace. Big trouble. Some of it shows – most it still doesn't.

But a two million *ex gratia* payment would probably break us. That's why if you lean on us too hard, we'll have to fight. And we might even have a good chance of winning.'

'There'd still be the publicity,' said Grace.

'Sure.' Miller drank down his fresh Cognac as though it were beer, but still without any visible effect, except the slight shadow in his eyes had darkened to a frown. 'You're right, of course – we can't afford the publicity. But then nor can you.'

Graced stared at him. 'What does that mean? A law firm's only hurt by publicity when it loses a case – and even then, it depends on the case.'

Randy Miller gave his stiff, frozen smile. 'Unless you found yourself suing someone very close to your own firm.'

Grace felt a hot tingling begin in her scalp and creep down through her neck. Randy Miller had played his best card. *He knew.* For the moment, however, Grace decided to play dumb. There was just the chance that she'd misunderstood him and that Miller was referring to some other obscure connection with McKenzie Brackman and Partners.

She said simply, 'I don't understand.'

'No? Your firm includes a married couple – a Mr and Mrs Markovitz. Right? Stuart Markovitz is one of the best and most respected tax and financial lawyers in California. Squeaky-clean. Not a blemish. Right? And he's married to a woman whose maiden name was Ann Kelsey.' This time he didn't seek confirmation.

'Her old man, Matthew Kelsey, has been a co-director of Triton for the last five years. If I'm guilty of blinding this kid of yours, so's he. That's the shape of it, Grace. I told you, if you force me against the wall, I'll fight. And it won't do your firm one damned bit of good, win or lose – only an awful lot of harm.'

Grace now knew that she'd have to play her own top card. Keeping her voice as controlled as possible, she said, 'I was bluffing, Randy. When I came in here today, I already knew all about you and Mrs Markovitz's father. I've known since yesterday since I got a call from an old friend in the D.A.'s office. He's been digging too – and deeper than just the public files with the S.E.C. Or did your little gofer with the moustache miss that? I'm not the only one, Randy, who's been taking a peek at your 10-K Form and drawing conclusions from it.'

'I see. So you put the D.A.'s Office on to me?' His voice was flat, unemotional; but his eyes had taken on a chilly look and there was now a faint flush on his cheeks. Even from where she sat, Grace could just make out the tiny white scars from the sutures on the side of his face, threading their way along the edge of the damaged tissue like a miniature railroad track on a photographic negative.

She didn't say anything; while Miller sat with his hands spread out on the desktop, his head slightly tilted as though he were listening for something. Grace had a moment of panic. This would be the moment when the heavy mob burst in and took her away.

When Miller finally spoke, his voice was very soft, hardly audible: 'I don't want Matthew Kelsey hurt. I don't give a damn about myself. As I told you, if I could break the habit, maybe I'd get out now. But I won't leave Matt to carry the can. No – *that I will not do*.'

Grace frowned. 'Is he that good a friend?' she asked, genuinely puzzled: for somehow any emotional connection between this man and Ann Kelsey still seemed difficult to grasp.

'He's the greatest guy I ever knew. Everyone else – wives, associates, friends, contacts – they're *nothing*, they count for *zilch!* But Matt Kelsey's in another class. He's what America used to be, what it was always meant to be, before we became a soft, spoilt, neurotic nation of P.R. politicians run by lobbies and single-issue fanatics, gays and drug-addicts and TV chat-show hosts, all with about as much moral fibre as a split fingernail!'

Grace tried to smile at this eloquence. She guessed the Cognacs had at last begun to get through, showing up his scar-tissue now in a livid, blotchy white against his flushed face. 'I told you before, Randy – you should go into politics! If you can't beat 'em . . .' She paused. 'But tell me – what did Ann Kelsey's old man do to deserve this special honour among your affections?'

'He saved my life. Pulled me out of a burning plane in Korea. He didn't have to – most of the crew, except the pilot, had already bailed out. The pilot was Matt Kelsey and he managed to land the plane before the tanks blew. By rights he should have jumped with the others. I was trapped in my seat, about to roast. Matt thought I was dead. He started to climb out – at the same time as I started to scream. So he came back and lifted the whole seat and half the fuselage off me – he's a strong man – and carried me bodily out of the flaming wreckage. It was like a goddam movie! It was only afterwards that I found out his legs were full of shrapnel.'

He paused, staring at his empty glass. 'We were both in hospital for months. And they gave us the usual medals – Matt even got a Silver Star. But a medal counts for nothing in a war like that. Everything afterwards – success, fame, money – they get to seem kind of hollow, pointless.' He relapsed into silence.

Grace said at last, 'When did you decide to hook Matt Kelsey into this scheme of yours?'

He looked up at her, as though roused from a deep sleep. When he answered, it was as though he were talking to himself. If the conversation was being taped, he didn't seem to mind. Mort Carne had looked the type who'd blackmail his own child in order to extort chocolates. But Randy Miller was past caring now.

'We kept in touch after the war,' he went on, his voice flat and weary, but still sober. 'You know how it is when you're trying to get established in the rat race? Matt started his own crop-spraying company, doing most of the flying himself, and I put a lot of business his way. Selling him pesticides and so on, at a discount. Maybe that's where I got so good at cooking the books!' He gave a little dry chuckle.

'We used to meet once, twice a year. I got to know the family a bit, but not well. I met his daughter, Ann, a few times – in the school vacations when they went skiing or up to a lake in the Rockies. She used to call me "Uncle Randy-Pandy" when she was small.

'Then, after I took over Triton, we kind of drifted apart. But we still kept in touch. Matt was a lucky bastard. His was the original marriage made in heaven! And I heard his daughter was doing well here in L.A.?' He glanced quickly at Grace. 'Crazy world, huh?'

'When did the racket start?' she asked.

'It wasn't so much a racket – more like paying off a very old debt. And screw the stockholders! When the Chinks had twenty U.S. Divisions bottled up in the Pusan Peninsula, most of those rich cats were probably back Stateside claiming to be "students", so they didn't have to get dirty sleeping in six feet of freezing mud every night. Aw, to hell with the stockholders!

'Anyway, about five years ago, during the slump in the Mid West, Matt Kelsey's crop-spraying outfit started running into trouble. He was a darned fine pilot, but I guess he was maybe a lousy businessman. Anyway, I fixed it so we both got a series of loans from the Corporation so as to buy real estate abroad. Instead, we stashed the stuff away in a couple of banks in the Caribbean. But I reckon you know all that?'

'More or less.'

He nodded. 'I cut myself in out of greed, I guess – though it may have been partly because it seemed safer because Matt didn't know the ropes. Anyway, as I said, I did it to pay off an old debt – and more recently, to save Matt and his marriage from bankruptcy. His wife would never have survived the shame of that.'

'You know the marriage has been on the rocks?' asked Grace.

'Yeah, I did hear something. Matt called me about a month ago, said he'd got hitched up with some grasping little bimbo who'd taken him to the cleaners. I had to okay the cheques, as co-signatory. And you know how much he spent on the bitch? Nearly a quarter of a million bucks in just a couple of weeks! The crazy dope! But who am I to grudge an old man his last cup of poison?'

'He and wife are back again now,' said Grace.

'I know. He called me again a couple of nights ago to tell me. Said he was taking her round the world.' He glanced again at Grace, his face pale again, and solemn. 'You don't want him to get back and find the Sheriff's men waiting on the dockside, do you?'

'I've still got a job to do, Randy. And I've still got those same two clients. The kid's blind and the mother may be a crazy old soak, but all they've got is each other. They need a break too – like Matt.'

'Sure. Sure.' Randy Miller suddenly stood up. 'You'll hear something from me in about two days.' He paused, fingering the three sharp points of the handkerchief in his breast pocket. 'Two million, huh?' He sighed. 'Still, it's only money. No use to a guy if he's turned into a lump of charred meat in a burnt-out aircraft.'

He looked at Grace and came forward with both hands held out. 'You know, if I was twenty years younger, or I'd maybe met you ten years ago, I'd have thrown my hat in the ring for you. My God I would! And I wouldn't have looked at another woman in the whole damned world!' He sounded almost as though he really meant it.

He looked at the copper-faced clock on the wall. 'It's getting late. Are you sure you don't want that lunch?'

'I'm sure, Randy. I've got to get back to the office.'

He gave his stiff, wounded smile as he watched her walk to the door.

Chapter Twenty Four

As soon as Grace was done, Miller returned to the desk and punched a button on the intercom. 'Mort?'

'Mr Miller, Sir!'

'Mort, I've got to leave town. Personal business. I want the Caddy out front in thirty minutes, fully fuelled. I'll be gone a few days, so cancel all appointments. If anyone wants to know where I am, play dumb. I'll need an overnight bag with a change of clothes. Summer things. Okay?'

'Okay, Mr Miller!'

'And call my wife. Tell her I've been called away on urgent business and won't be back for a couple of days at least. Only you know nothing. Don't worry! Use that famous charm of yours – she can't bite your throat down the phone. But don't call her till I've gone.'

'It'll be done, Mr Miller.'

He pressed a second button, to his private secretary in some inner office. 'Joan, I want a pot of black coffee, no sugar, and one of my "keep-awake" pills. And I don't want to take any calls.'

'Right away, Mr Miller.'

While he waited he drank a pint of iced water from the bar, then sat down at the desk, took a copper pen out of the copper pen set and wrote a short note on the company's writing paper. He folded it into an envelope, addressed it in his own hand and gave it to his secretary when she came in.

He drank a cup of fresh steaming coffee, then lifted the phone and dialled a number on Grand Cayman. The conversation lasted ten minutes. He hung up, swallowed the little blue pill his secretary had left in an enamelled box; then took his keyring out and unlocked a drawer in the desk down by his right knee.

He took the folded silk handkerchief out of his pocket and lifted out a heavy object from the drawer. It was a well-oiled Colt .45, U.S. Army issue, 1951, with the serial number still stamped on the side of the breach. Nothing fancy – no special gadgets, like a silencer or custom-made hand-grip. Just a routine, well-tooled killing machine – the same as was carried by a million men in that war.

He tested the firing pin, then held the gun at arm's length, getting the feel again of the hard matt-black handle, the firm, steady weight of the gun, which can blow a man's head off at thirty feet. He laid the weapon down on the handkerchief spread out on the desk; then reached again into the drawer and brought out a small sealed box of standard .45 blunt-nosed ammunition, "for target shooting only". It had been bought two weeks ago, using his Gun

Certificate, at a local sporting shop on the Wilshire Boulevard.

He broke open the sealed box and selected three of the slightly greasy rounds, snapped out the magazine from the handle and pressed the three cartridges under the spring-slot, rammed it back in, feeling the first round slot into the breach; then, almost by instinct, checked the safety catch was on, wrapped the gun in the handkerchief, and slipped it and the ammunition box into his briefcase, which he locked.

Already he could taste the dry, enervating effect of the pill beginning to work on his brain. He felt tense, yet also relaxed. He was ready.

The intercom buzzed. It was Mort Carne's oily voice again: 'Car's ready, Mr Miller, Sir. Everything you want is packed in the trunk.'

'Thanks. I'll be right down.' Randy Miller drank what was left in his cup, picked up the heavy briefcase, and strode out of the room.

Yes, he was ready!

Chapter Twenty Five

The court had opened ten minutes late, on account of the packed Press benches and clusters of TV crews with their tackle of lights, cameras and sound equipment. There was also a strong contingent of local supporters, who'd come to cheer on the plaintiff in this great battle between the citizen motorist and the indiscriminate power of City Hall.

It was now 10.25 and Judge Barry Savory was looking angry. He was a big, well-muscled man, famous for his bad temper and for not suffering fools gladly. Leaning forward in his black robe, his jowly face glowering down at this chaotic audience below him, he looked like a buzzard about to go in for the kill. He was angry not only because the case was running late, but on account of half the court officials' car lot outside being closed off for some building work. The remaining places had all been taken when he'd arrived, and the judge had to leave his official car in a side street at the back of the courthouse.

'Miss Lamb!' Savory shouted above the din. 'If your client is not here in the next five minutes, I propose to postpone your case, and also warn you that your client stands to forfeit a substantial part of his bail money.'

C.J. Lamb was on her feet, careful to make sure her profile was half turned to the TV cameras. 'Your Honour, I can only apologise once again for my client's absence. Last night he gave me no reason to suppose that he would not be attending court today.' She did not add that her client had made a vigorous and not very subtle pass at her last night – which was why she hadn't done him the courtesy of driving him to court this morning.

'Well he'd just better be here!' Judge Savory growled, just as an excited movement began at the back of the court. There was a loud murmur of voices, then a burst of clapping and cheering. Girls' necks craned; cameras clicked like castanets; flashes went off; the TV cameras started to roll; and the reporters began shouting their staccato questions, as the gorgeous blond hunk of James Stuart ('Stoo') Nugent-Ross – a.k.a. the 'Phantom Boot' – made his lordly entrance.

When he was halfway down the aisle he gave Savory a friendly wave. 'Sorry, Judge! I had a little problem with the cops. Just had my car immobilised by the Boot!'

A roar of laughter went up from reporters and spectators alike, interrupted by the furious hammering of Judge Savory's gavel. The man was beside himself with rage.

'If this behaviour does not cease *at once*, I shall clear the court! As for you, Mr Nugent-Ross, it may be you find this whole thing just a mighty big laugh, but this court is not a theatre and we are not here to provide you with any grandstand on which to indulge your ego! Nor do I intend to act as your Press agent!' There was a titter of laughter across the court and a girl's voice called from the back, 'We're with you, Phantom – all the way!'

'Can that noise *right now!*' Judge Savory snarled; while Nugent-Ross, still smiling, made his way up to the front of the court and sat down next to C.J. Lamb. She whispered something quickly to him and he shrugged, but stopped smiling. A court official then read out the charges:

'James Stewart Nugent-Ross, you are charged that in the city of Los Angeles, between June nine and August ten this year, you did deliberately inflict malicious damage on nineteen vehicles belonging to the Los Angeles Police Department . . .'

Nugent-Ross had risen languidly to his feet, before the official had time to finish, and said, 'Your Honour, I wish to address the court . . .'

'*Siddown!*'

'But your Honour, this is pertinent to my case . . .'

'*Siddown and shuddup!* If I have to reprimand you once more, young man, I will cite you for contempt.' Savory turned to the court official. 'Proceed.'

'The defendant is also charged with wasting police time, obstructing the police, and with assault on a police officer. How does the defendant plead?'

'*Not guilty!*' Nugent-Ross cried, starting to get up, when C.J. yanked him down into his seat by the back of his sports jacket. Her client continued, undismayed, 'It was the police officer who assaulted *me*! He's the only one who should be here to answer charges!'

'That's *enough!*' Judge Savory glanced down, first at C.J., then at the Prosecuting Counsel – a rising young star in the D.A.'s Office, called Lavery, who was wearing, under a striped blazer, a pink shirt with matching striped braces.

'Do either of you know anything about this?'

Lavery stood up, tossing his bouffed hair. 'Your Honour, a complaint has been received by the Beverly Hills police, but has been most emphatically denied. It appears the defendant, on being first apprehended, tried to taunt the officers. Then, at the Precinct House, on being arrested and charged, he became abusive and threatening, and struck a senior officer.

While Lavery was speaking, C.J. laid a hand on Nugent-Ross's arm. The young man frowned but said nothing. Judge Savory now turned to C.J. 'What have *you to* say about this, Counsel?'

C.J. stood up gracefully and paused, for dramatic effect. She was no longer worried about her client, but was thinking hard how she could get through this without embarrassing McKenzie Brackman and Partners. For it was tricky territory – since Douglas Brackman, without consulting anybody, had effectively kicked any assault charges into "touch". Besides, the only traces of the assault on Stoo Nugent-Ross was a swollen lip, which gave his otherwise sullen, babyish good looks a touch of Jean-Paul Belmondo – for those in court who still remembered.

'My client maintains,' C.J. began, 'that when he was caught – right outside the Beverly Hills Precinct House – he had every intention of being charged with this misdemeanour. He was making a point, your Honour.'

Judge Savory shook his head; but when he spoke, it was in a gentler tone – he was well-known to mellow at the sight of a pretty face. 'I'm afraid, Counsel, that matters of personal principle, if that's what this is, do in no way alter the facts in a case. What I am interested in now is whether your client intends bringing a civil action against this senior police officer?'

From behind her Stoo Nugent-Ross bawled out from his seat. 'Damn right I do!'

'*Shuddup!*' yelled Savory.

This time the blond hulk, with C.J. frowning pointedly beside him, maintained a smug, exaggeratedly solemn expression, while Prosecuting Counsel Lavery broke in:

'Here I think it relevant to state that the defendant's original attorney, a certain Mike Kuzak, apparently resigned from the case –'

C.J. sprang to her feet. 'Objection! Totally irrelevant! My colleague's absence from this court today has absolutely *nothing* to do with these proceedings. He is away for strictly personal reasons,' she went on, as though enjoying this huge fib.

'Objection sustained.'

C.J. sat down again, feeling slightly flushed. *Thank you, Douglas Brackman! Thanks for nothing!* she said to herself, almost aloud.

Judge Savory turned again to Prosecuting Counsel: 'May I take it, Mr Lavery, that the defendant will be instituting private proceedings against the police in this matter?'

'I have no knowledge of that, your Honour' – Lavery began; but was cut short by the deafening voice of Stoo:

'Damn right I am! I'm gonna sue the bastard – !'

‘*Fined five hundred dollars!*’ roared the judge; and there were some faint boos and hisses from the back of the court.

C.J.’s proud, erect body sagged in its seat; she almost put her head in her hands, as Judge Savory now turned to the court official:

‘I propose the assault charge be put aside, pending further investigations, and that we proceed with the initial charge, involving malicious damage to the nineteen squad cars.’ He had turned to Lavery, when Stoo climbed to his feet yet again. C.J. only noticed when it was too late. Her client was already booming:

‘Judge, I protest!’

‘You *protest*, do you, Mr Nugent-Ross?’ Savory looked like a big snake about to swallow a handsome bird. ‘Well, listen here, young man. I’m fining you a further one thousand dollars. Furthermore, I order the court officers to stand by you, and to remove you physically from this room the very next time you open your big mouth!’

Two tough uniformed men in shirtsleeves, hands on their holsters, moved purposefully forward, taking up their stand behind Stoo’s chair. C.J. felt furious and humiliated; and only with great restraint did she remain seated while her client began whispering urgently in her ear. Finally she stood up.

Judge Savory gave her an indulgent nod, evidently feeling for her.

‘Your Honour, I submit, firstly, that this second fine is excessive . . .’

‘Overruled . . .’

C.J. nodded, giving herself time to choose her next words carefully. ‘I further submit that my client has raised a point with me that may materially affect the nature of the misdemeanour. I shall ask, therefore, that he be heard.'

Judge Savory considered her for a long moment. Not only was he pleasantly struck by her looks, but he found her English accent entirely beguiling.

'I must remind you, Counsel,' he said at last, 'that your client supplied the police with a full, signed confession when he was arrested. And you yourself, just now, suggested – if only by implication – that he is guilty. So may I ask, therefore, whether you now agree to your client's plea of Not Guilty?'

C.J. went back and conferred for a few moments with Stoo. When they'd finished, Stoo was smiling broadly. But C.J. looked a lot less happy, as she stood again in front of Judge Savory and said, 'Your Honour, my client does not deny that he immobilised nineteen squad cars. But he objects to the wording of the charge.'

Savory looked irritated: in spite of her charms, this English girl was beginning to get on his nerves – almost as much as her client. 'Counsel, the wording of the charge is quite simple. Would you like it read out again?'

'No, your Honour. But may it please the court' – and a titter went up from the crowded floor, while Judge Savory scowled – 'if I submit that it would be sufficient that my client is permitted to make a short statement –'

Judge Savory gave a loud sigh of impatience. He'd also sensed that the audience was growing restive too. 'Counsel, I've heard quite enough of your client's voice for one day. And if he wishes to comment on the charge, *providing* it's relevant, then he must do so through you. As his attorney, you should know that.'

'Your Honour, I do know that. But as for my client's behaviour, I submit that not everyone in this city is a lawyer. Not everyone here has been in court before. Furthermore, my client has a blameless character –'

The judge gave an audible snort. 'Blameless in the law, maybe. But my opinion is, he's come here with the deliberate intention of enjoying himself and making a monkey of us all. However, it seems he is not only to be indulged, but positively *suffered* by this court, like a boil on the ass!' This time he made no effort to suppress the laughter all round.

C.J. squared her padded shoulders. 'Your Honour, I most strongly object!' *My God! She could just imagine an English judge making such a comment at the Old Bailey! He'd be up before the Lord Chancellor before he had time to wipe his nose.* 'I do not accept,' she went on, 'that my client should be subjected to personal remarks, amounting to verbal abuse against him as an individual, when these remarks have absolutely nothing to do with this case.'

Judge Savory gave her a thin smile. 'Objection sustained. But I still don't want to hear another word from your client – except in answer to questions.'

'I thank your Honour.'

'So if you have something to say on behalf of your client,' the judge continued generously, 'then you may do so now.'

She turned and walked slowly forward to face the court, like a model on a catwalk, with Stoo Nugent-Ross eyeing her swaying buttocks with approval. C.J. addressed the court, oblivious of the ogling face behind her:

'May it please your Honour' – more tittering – 'But my

client points out that he is accused of causing deliberate, malicious damage to a number of squad-cars. He denies this most vehemently. That is to say, he challenges the word *damage*. He challenges it for the simple reason that all he did to those cars was put the boot on them.' There was a cheer from the back of the court, C.J. pressed quickly on, before Savory had time to quell the noise, which this time was obviously in sympathy with Stoo.

'My client further wishes me to point out, with what I consider commendable logic, that if, by immobilising these vehicles with a boot, he is subsequently convicted of causing malicious *damage*, then, I submit, half the population of Los Angeles will be free to sue the city authorities for millions of dollars!'

This time the applause exploded as though at the final curtain of a triumphant show – though whether in response to C.J. herself, or for her client, was not immediately clear. At first Judge Savory looked as though he'd been hit on the head with a heavy sack falling from a great height. Then he leaned forward and banged his gavel. The noise subsided at once. Nobody wanted to spoil the fun and get the court cleared at this critical point.

Judge Savory recovered at last; but he was obviously in a quandary. C.J. resumed her seat, again without once looking at Stoo. The Judge watched them both from under his thick-lidded eyes, deciding, with satisfaction, that there seemed little love lost between attorney and her insufferable client.

'I grant you may have a point in logic there, Counsel – if not in law,' he said at last, as though to add: *Let no-one say that Judge Savory isn't a fair judge*. He turned now to the court official. 'I order the first charge be dropped, and we shall proceed with only the second – obstruction and wasting police time.' He looked again at C.J. 'Does your client plead guilty to this charge – in its present wording, Counsel?'

'Guilty by law – innocent by common justice!' Stoo boomed again, this time turning to the audience with a huge grin of triumph.

Cries of '*Two– four – six – eight! Who do we appreciate? The Phantom!*' began to reverbate from all sides, with a growing number of '*Viva la Fantoma! Olé! Olé!*'

Surprisingly, Judge Savory endured this uproar for several seconds. He seemed to be in a benign trance. Now it was his turn not to want to spoil things by clearing the court. He waited until the crowd had had their fun, then reached wearily for the gavel. 'Will the defendant stand!'

Stoo stepped forward, turning to the crowd and smiling at the cameras like an actor who's just won an Oscar.

'James Stewart Nugent-Ross,' Judge Savory intoned solemnly: 'You agree to be sentenced by this court? Or do you wish to exercise your rights and go before a grand jury?'

Perhaps for a fraction of a second The Phantom hesitated. Then he smiled broadly at Judge Savory and said, 'I'll take my chance with you, Judge!'

Savory nodded. 'You will pay a fine of two thousand dollars which makes three thousand, five hundred, with the two previous fines during this hearing. And I order you to pay the Los Angeles Police Department two thousand dollars, plus all costs.' He paused:

'I also sentence you to ninety days in the County Jail.'

There was a stunned silence. Nugent Ross's jaw dropped open and he stood gaping around him. He didn't seem quite able to take in what Judge Savory had just said. C.J., who had been about to go and talk to him – if not to congratulate him, at least to say she'd done her best, and *my God, she had!*, now stopped in her tracks. *Ninety days!* But suspended, surely? Had Savory said, 'Suspended?'.

Just then pandemonium broke loose. A small phalanx of shirt-sleeved guards moved forward, arms akimbo, to hold back the furious crowd of spectators and the eager, determined Pressmen scrambling for instant sound-bytes. Judge Savory had already slipped quietly through a small door behind him.

C.J. was particularly shocked, because only yesterday she'd been advised by Douglas Brackman himself that her client might expect a heavy fine, but that for a man with Nugent-Ross's background – and considering the publicity his case had excited – a custodial sentence was highly unlikely: Californian jails not being nice places for good-looking beach boys.

She started through the crowd towards where her client was still standing, and bumped into the pink shirt of Lavery, the Prosecuting Counsel. Her hand touched one of his pink braces. 'Did I hear right, Mr Lavery? *Ninety days*? Not suspended?'

'Not suspended,' Lavery said smugly. 'But if he's a good boy, he could be out in less than two months. Unless you delay it by going to appeal.'

'We're going to appeal, don't worry!'

'I won't. But he sure didn't do you both any favours in here just now. *Wow!* what a bad-mannered young client you picked! And Savory's old man used to work on the railroad. This is one judge who doesn't like playboys. Pity nobody told you. But of course, you're new here . . .'

She looked round and saw a couple of sheriff's deputies walking towards her client, break through the crowd round him and put a hand on each arm. Nugent-Ross had recovered sufficiently to have shut his mouth, and he was now glaring stoically at his enraged admirers; while a pack of reporters also closed round him: '. . . *How does it feel, Phantom . . .? Are you still glad you did it . . .? Were you expecting a jail sentence, Mr Ross . . .? You'll be taking it to appeal, of course . . .?*'

Another, smaller crowd was trying to swarm round C.J.: '*You feel the Judge was prejudiced against you being a woman, Miss Lamb . . .? What's the C.J. stand for, Miss Lamb . . .? What's your real opinion of your client . . . speaking as a woman . . .? D'you think he'd have done better being defended by a man . . .?*'

She tried to answer as politely and obliquely as she could, as she forced her way through the milling crowd to reach her client. One of the deputies turned and stared at her. They hadn't quite put the cuffs on yet.

'I thought you'd left with the sinking ship?' Nugent-Ross said, half resigned, half truculent.

She took his arm, saying to the two deputies, 'You can leave him now. I'm Mr Ross's attorney – C.J. Lamb.' She showed them her card, and they went on staring at her. One of them touched his cap, as C.J. began to hurry her client away.

'Where are we going?' Stoo said, sounding slightly dazed.

'To post bail and file the appeal papers. They won't make any trouble – not with all the media people here. But if they do, I'm going to blow them out of the water.'

Stoo Nugent-Ross followed submissively, while the Press closed in again – the TV crews lugging their cameras and sound-booms, and trying to keep up; and the newspaperman scampering along beside them, still firing off their salvos of futile questions: '*How d'you think you'll make out in jail, Mr Ross . . .? So how d'ya find our American justice now, Miss Lamb . . .?* They squeezed through the courtroom doors and emerged, in a breathless, struggling scrum, into the main hallway of the courthouse.

The only one who remained cool and unruffled was C.J. She led the way to a dark mahogany door with gilt lettering carved into the wood: COURT ADMINISTRATOR *Bail Applications*.

At once they cry went up.`'*So you're gonna appeal . . .?'*

'You're damn right, I'm gonna appeal!' Stoo bawled at them. 'I'll take it right up to the Supreme Court, if necessary!'

C.J. had opened the door a foot or so, and now pushed her client bodily through the narrow gap, followed herself, then slammed the door in the reporters' faces. Some of them tried to follow, but a patrolman intervened.

The bulk of the reporters now began to disperse – some hurrying off to the phones to file their copy; others to make their way back to their various offices. The fun was over. Any details about the bail proceedings would be picked up by the wire-agencies.

*

But they were wrong. The fun was not over. The best part of the story was still to come – just round the back of the courthouse. From here there now came the sound of raised voices, swearing and shouting. A moment later the figure of Judge Savory appeared, waving his arms and walking very quickly, as though he were about to break into a run – only restrained by the knowledge that a judge *never* runs.

The man was apoplectic with rage. Devoid of his gown, and the grim solemnity of the courtroom, he now looked like a furious little storekeeper who's just discovered that his stock's been stolen. 'My God! Somebody's head's going to roll for this!' he huffed, as they reached the corner of the courthouse. 'I want someone to call the Traffic Department *and* the Commissioner's office . . .!'

It was here that the judge's party collided with a lone journalist – the chief crime reporter on the L.A. *Sentinel*, called Sangster. He at once moved in and tried to interview Savory. But the judge wasn't having any of it. He was still bawling out instructions, fuming against those '*goddam cretins in the Traffic Department!*' 'On second thoughts,' he went on. 'I'll speak to the Commissioner himself!'

Sangster asked what was wrong. 'What's wrong!' roared Judge Savory; and some of the officials around him started smirking behind each other's shoulders. One of them whispered to Sangster, 'The judge is real mad! He's just had his car booted.'

James Stewart Nugent-Ross and his beautiful English attorney were at once forgotten. Sangster had the story of the day. He could already see tomorrow's banner headlines: 'PHANTOM BOOT' JAILED. 'PHANTOM' JUDGE BOOTED.

Chapter Twenty Six

It was Mike Kuzak's fourth day at Francine Faber's ranch-house at Desert Hot Springs; and he'd almost lost track of time. Like a prisoner in a golden cage, he felt he should mark the passing of each day – perhaps in Francine's Esteé Lauder lipstick on the bathroom mirror?

For each day was the same. Waking next to the same cool slim body, with the same steel-blue sky outside; the same splashing fountain; the same pot of black coffee, which Francine always prepared. There were servants in the house, but one of the strange things about these days was that Kuzak never seemed to see any of them. He began to have a vivid idea of what it must be like for a Latin American general living under luxurious house arrest, or a 'material witness' being guarded from the Mafia.

Yet another strange thing about these days was that Kuzak was not bored. Idle, yes, but even in California, this

W.A.S.P.'s Babylon, many people rated idleness as a great virtue, if only because it signalled huge reserves of wealth and leisure. A couple of times he wondered if he were suffering from some mild form of breakdown. Such a thing was not uncommon in these parts, after all. Driven by the frenzy of city life; pressured inexorably by at least one woman in his own office, and tempted by several more outside; then the stresses of the office itself – neurotic clients, desperate clients, arrogant clients who were never satisfied, rich clients who refused to pay. Not to mention that bastard, Lieutenant Slazenger, and that bang on the head he'd given Kuzak, in the privacy of a police cell. Was there any wonder if he really *had* suddenly cracked?

Perhaps it had been Slazenger who had triggered it all off? A slight concussion, no obvious complications, then next day the man has a fight with his Senior Partner, storms out of the office, and within *minutes* allows himself to be picked up by an ex-client and driven off by her into the desert. Just leaves, without going home; without collecting his car from the lot; without even making a single phone call. Just vanishes . . .

He wondered how long it would take for people to start worrying? Grace? – Roxanne? Even Douglas Brackman himself? Then there was James Stewart Nugent-Ross and the case of 'The L.A.P.D. vs. the Phantom Boot'. When he thought about it, which wasn't often, surprisingly, he felt guilty: but not on account of his former client, who was a foolish young man with too much money.

No, Kuzak felt guilty because he'd skived off from a case, and the fact that the case was trivial, the client worthless, did not eliminate the fact that his behaviour had been thoroughly unprofessional. For whatever else he might be – reckless, wild, impetuous, – at heart Michael Kuzak was a puritan, sometimes even a prude. But now all that was mysteriously gone – washed away in the dazzling sunlight, the desert air, the dry salty smell of Francine's body, and all the other worldly delights that went with this strange, beautiful house.

Francine had described his situation the other day by the pool, reciting from a poem which she'd then forced him to learn by heart:

Here with a Loaf of Bread beneath the Bough,
A Flask of Wine, a Book of Verse – and thou
Beside me singing in the Wilderness –
And Wilderness is Paradise enow.

In the hard-boiled luxury of California, Kuzak decided, beautiful girls who were rich and unattached, *and* given to quoting ancient Persian poetry, were at something of a premium. You might still find one among high-class call girls, or on New York's Lower East Side, where the 'art-set' still dress like tramps and go to their psychiatrists five days a week. But these were mostly fakes. Kuzak thought he very much preferred the Desert Hot Springs version.

Kuzak was attracted and fascinated by Francine, and believed, naively perhaps, that all her virtues, and her oddness, her eccentricities, were at least genuine. She hadn't put on this show of reading poetry just to impress him. *Or had she?*

Perhaps it was that bang on the head again – but Kuzak didn't really care.

*

The routine of these first few days hardly varied. They

woke with the sun and made love again; then Francine went to fetch breakfast, while he showered and shaved – with the man's razor, which was never mentioned. Mornings they whiled away by the pool, sunbathing, swimming, kissing, then drove out in her slinky, high-powered convertible for lunch in some restaurant – always exclusive, expensive, and always paid for by her. In the afternoon they either made love again, or drove down to the beach near San Diego where *Recovery* was moored.

The boat was just as she'd described it: a graceful forty foot yawl with a lot of warm varnished woodwork and polished brass, and a tiny cabin with a bunk so narrow they had to cling to each other, feeling the gentle heaving of the ocean beneath their bodies. It was comfortable and very tidy. Kuzak saw no evidence of a crew, a servant – anybody who might help her keep the boat in its pristine condition.

There was only one jarring note. At the back of the cabin was a tiny shower and toilet, what she insisted on calling 'the Heads', that was again so small that only one person fitted in at a time. Here, on the shelf above the lavatory bowl, Kuzak found a second diaphragm, with its tube of spermicide – almost but not quite untouched this time. But at least there was no man's razor.

The lovers' daily routine was suddenly interrupted, when Francine ordained they go into town to do some shopping. Here, in less than three hours, Kuzak was left gratified and slightly aghast at having accumulated more expensive clothes, with accessories, than he'd ever owned, or even thought of owning, in his entire life.

Then, on the fifth day, after breakfast on the terrace,

Francine calmly advised Kuzak to hire a car. She didn't, surprisingly perhaps, offer to buy him one: just said he must have his own car so he could be independent. Then, without further discussion, she appeared in a smart tailored suit, kissed him and told him she was going to San Diego to attend to some private business.

For a brief moment Kuzak felt a twinge of uneasiness, even jealousy, perhaps, like a shadow left when a cloud passes in front of the sun. He heard Francine's car roar off towards the town; then went indoors and looked up the number of a local hire car company.

He could, of course, always go back to L.A. and collect his own car, a Porsche, from where he'd left it in the parking lot under the building in which Mckenzie Brackman had their offices. Later he could never decide for sure why he *hadn't* gone back. Maybe it was the fear of running into someone from the firm – Rox or Douglas or Leland, to all of whom he owed elaborate, exhausting explanations, which they might not believe anyway.

Or he could have called up Grace and tried once again to re-ignite their old passion. But instantly he thought of Francine, and somehow his mind's image of her wiped out everything else. He booked a two door hatchback with sunroof and overdrive, and waited for them to deliver it. Then he watched an old French film on cable TV.

He only began to worry slightly when it began to get dark, and Francine had not even phoned. In his male arrogance, he assumed that his own passion for her was reciprocated in every detail. The idea that she might operate on a different wavelength from him – that she might even have an entirely different set of values, even morals – had not yet properly occurred to him. He fixed himself something to eat, then watched more TV. He couldn't read – even if there had been anything in the house that he wanted to read.

At eleven o'clock he began to get slightly angry. But still only a small cloud across the sun. At two in the morning the cloud had got bigger: Kusak was becoming seriously worried.

He couldn't sleep. He went out for a swim, with the underwater lights in the pool dancing wildly under him till they made him feel giddy. He had a headache when he got out, and found a bottle among Francine's medicines in the bathroom which he took to be a form of aspirin. Then he listened to some tapes from Francine's collection by the empty log fire. She had a curious selection, consisting entirely of the heavier German classics and the latest cheap pop. It was not very restful.

At three o'clock, exhausted now by his old, revived anxieties, Kuzak called the local police precinct and asked if there had been any accidents reported in the San Diego area. He gave Francine's name and the registration number of her car. The police said they'd check with Highway Patrol and call right back. A couple of minutes later the phone rang. He grabbed it.

'Michael, darling? Oh Michael! My darling Michael!'

'*Francine!* – where the hell are you?'

'I'm very happy, Michael – but I miss you so!' Her voice had a sleepy, far-off tone, and for a moment he thought she was drunk.

'Francine! Where are you?'

'I'm very happy, darling . . . So relaxed –'

'For Christ's sake, Francine! *Where are you?* Are you

safe, darling?' He paused. The awful thought of those pills in the medicine cabinet hit him in the chest like a body blow.

'I miss you, Michael. You're the most wonderful man I've ever met.'

He gripped the handset, trying to keep his breathing slow and steady. 'Now listen, darling. *Don't scare me.* Just tell me where you're speaking from?' No answer.

'Francine, there isn't a phone on the boat – *is there?* There's only the Ship-to-Shore. So where are you calling from? *Please*!'

'Oh, I'm sorry, Michael. I must have frightened you. I've been on the boat all evening,' – she sounded suddenly quite normal –' most of the afternoon too, actually, and I've been so lonesome, so I decided to come ashore and call you. I'm in that café-brasserie place on the plaza opposite – the one that's open all night. I've just stopped in for a milkshake.'

'I'll come right out and get you. I hired that car this afternoon, like you told me to.' He paused. 'You do want me to come, don't you, Francine?'

'Oh Michael, *yes!* I miss you so much.'

'I'll be with you in less than an hour!' He'd hardly put the phone down, when it rang again.

A man's voice said lazily: 'Koo-sack?'

'Speaking.'

'Hot Springs Police – we checked on Miss Francine Faber. Highway Patrol reports no accident in the Southern Californian area involving anyone with that name or automobile registration . . .'

'Thanks!' Kuzak slammed down the handset, then grabbed his jacket and a loose sweater. These desert nights could be very cold.

Chapter Twenty Seven

Kuzak took the Expressway out of Desert Hot Springs and set the cruise control at just under sixty – slightly above the speed limit, but too low to be tracked accurately on radar. He drove carefully, checking every few seconds in both mirrors for a patrol car coming up behind. But it was that dead hour before dawn, and there was almost no other traffic.

The outskirts of San Diego were like a ghost town. As he approached Oceanside, and came closer to the *Recovery* and Francine, he began playing over again in his mind their phone conversation, trying to fathom her motives: but now that he was so close, his previous anxiety began to be replaced by a puzzled anger. *What the hell was she playing at?* Had she always intended staying out the night? Hadn't she realised that he'd be worried? Was she totally irresponsible? Or had she just not cared enough to stop and think what he'd be feeling?

He didn't stop until he reached Oceanside and the little waterfront plaza where *Recovery* was moored. But to his alarm she wasn't tied up on the jetty. He parked and got out in a panic. The Pacific was still shrouded in that pitch-darkness that seems to fall just before sunrise. There were no lights out to sea.

He was sweating as he ran over to the café-brasserie opposite. He hadn't expected her to be there, but to be waiting back on board. He crashed in through the door and found the place empty except for a Mexican waiter who was reading a Spanish paper behind the counter. He hardly looked up, as Kuzak burst in.

The Mexican was his only hope, he decided. He approached the counter. 'Have you observed a young lady? Very pretty, well-dressed – she got off a boat out there – ' He waved rather desperately at the dark windows.

The Mexican looked sleepily back at him. '*Quiere café, Senor*?' He was already reaching for a cup and saucer from under the counter.

Struggling to hold himself under control, Kuzak began again: 'A young lady – a *Senorita* – she came in here about an hour ago to use the telephone. Did you see where she went? Did you see where the boat went? A nice sailing boat . . .?' And he started trying to describe *Recovery* in mime, using the same gestures he would for tracing the hips of a sensuous woman.

A kind of comprehension seemed to cross the man's flat, expressionless features. *Four in the morning – a telephone – a beautiful woman.* He shrugged and gave Kuzak a sad-eyed smile. He regretted – he regretted very much – but it was not possible. It was too late. Tomorrow perhaps? '*Mañana tal vez!*'

Kuzak walked out, half-crazy with worry and frustration, and began heading for the deserted jetty. Ahead, a very thin, pale margin of light was beginning to show along the rim of the ocean. Kuzak strained his eyes for a glimpse of the slender two-masted yawl. There were no ship lights to be seen anywhere – which in itself was ominous.

It was just over an hour since Francine had made that call from the brasserie. She'd said she'd be waiting for him and now she was gone. Was that just another impulse? Or had she planned her departure – getting *Recovery* all shipshape and ready to sail *before* she made that call? He didn't know how fast the yawl could go: but on a still night like this, she'd have to use the outboard motor. And how fast and far could that take her? Would she already be out of sight? And if she weren't, why was she showing no lights?

For already another dreadful scenario was forming in his mind. She was a rich girl living alone, in a fairly lawless corner of the U.S.A. Her lifestyle was eccentric, her habits unpredictable. Was there an altogether more sinister explanation for her behaviour? Had Kuzak been lured out here and left stranded on the empty waterfront, an hour's drive from her house, so that some horrendous crime could be committed against Francine?

As an experienced L.A. lawyer, Kuzak not only knew that such things happened – they were even commonplace. And her voice had certainly not sounded normal over the phone. Was she being held somewhere? Forced to make that call? Did that po-faced Mexican pimp back there have something to do with it? He'd fit the part.

It was cold out here by the ocean, and Kuzak shivered in his sweater. He had reached the start of the jetty. The band of light along the horizon was broadening, seeming to grow brighter even as he watched. He strained his eyes through the half-darkness and for a moment thought he saw something: an irregular smudge against the smooth dark waters. Perhaps half a mile off, perhaps a mile – distances were hard to judge in this light. If indeed there was anything there at all. He felt the hairs beginning to prickle on the back of his neck.

Suddenly he swung round. A car swished across the plaza and pulled up outside the brasserie. It was a long, dark Lincoln Continental. The door of the driver's side opened and a man got out. He was shortish, slightly stooped, wearing a dark suit and tie. He seemed to be alone. Kuzak watched him walk into the brasserie. Something about that walk, and the slight stoop, struck him as dimly familiar. The man certainly didn't *look* like a gangland hood. He might have been a salesman grabbing himself some coffee before his last leg up the coast to L.A. – except that salesmen don't drive around in the small hours in Lincoln Continentals. If they're that rich, they get someone else to do it for them.

Kuzak had turned again towards the huge empty ocean, wondering if he should ring the cops again at Desert Hot Springs and get them to check Francine's house? And then the San Diego Coastguard – after all, the girl's boat was missing, and so was she.

Kuzak was about to turn back towards the brasserie, when he saw something flicker far out to sea, just below the horizon. It was at about the same spot where he thought he'd seen something flicker a few moments ago. A boat, perhaps? Then he saw it again, suddenly quite clearly. No doubt this time. The slim profile of the *Recovery* was lying low in the water. Then again he saw that flicker of light – larger this time, dancing like quick silver. Only it was not an ordinary light, certainly not a standard ship's light.

The thought crossed his mind that it might be someone trying to signal – but again, there was something wrong. The light was wrong – a livid yellowish glow, beginning to leap now along the edge of the yacht. This time he stared in horror, feeling his whole body turn cold. He was looking at flames.

From behind him the brasserie door opened and the man from the Lincoln Continental came out. But instead of getting into the car, be began walking across the plaza towards Kuzak. At first Kuzak didn't hear him, could hear nothing except a furious roaring in his head.

He saw now that the yawl was not as far out as he'd first thought. Perhaps three hundred yards, no more. The flames were catching quickly now, not only licking along the beautifully polished mahogany deck, but also beginning to catch below. And he saw the single porthole beginning to glow a deadly orange.

The next moment he'd torn off his sweater, kicked off his shoes, and begun to race down the jetty. He heard a man's voice shout behind him: '*Michael!*' But he seemed not to hear it. He reached the end of the jetty and dived smoothly in. As he came up, he felt a loud thud against his eardrums. But he could only concentrate on Francine – alone out there, about to be roasted alive. *Could she swim*? he wondered. *She must be able to swim?*

The whole yacht was burning now from bowsprit to stern, and flames were beginning to lick up the masts which were denuded of their sails; but there was no sign of anyone on board, or trying to get clear. Kuzak struck out in a powerful, frenzied crawl. He didn't hear the explosion at first – just a strong thump of air against his face – then a great booming noise reached him even through the roaring in his ears. He slackened his pace until he was almost treading water. He felt a heavy agonising weight pressing against his chest; and at some stage he was aware that he was screaming and crying – yelling Francine's name over and over again.

Recovery was burning like a paper boat now, the lines of her deck and stern curling up at the edges and flaking off into showers of bright sparks and embers, some of them drifting upwards like giant fireflies, others spattering down into the water which was now full of floating pieces of wreckage. Everywhere was the stench of fuel, hot metal and burnt wood. Kuzak was sick twice, the vomit washed away with the salt water.

What was left of the *Recovery* was already settling in the water and beginning to go down at the stern, with a horrible hissing of steam, like hundreds of snakes. Kuzak remembered thinking afterwards that the yacht must have been carrying a huge amount of fuel to have provided such an explosion. But Francine would have known all about that.

Kuzak swam round, his body as heavy as stone, limbs already numb. On the jetty ahead a crowd had collected. Out in front, he could see the stocky shape of the man with the Lincoln Continental.

Chapter Twenty Eight

The first person Kuzak recognised was the stocky man from the big car. 'Michael,' the man said: 'There was nothing you could do – believe me.'

'Yes, Giorgio. I believe you.' Kuzak sat on the paving at Dr Pelaggi's feet, feeling the water trickling out of his trousers and running away in rivulets down the gaps between the concrete paving. In the early light the water looked black, like blood. Behind him, all that was left of the *Recovery* was a scattering of smoking wreckage.

'There was nothing I could do,' he echoed Pelaggi.

From a distance, Kuzak could hear the wail of a siren. He had not bothered to look for his shoes and sweater, and now felt so heavy with exhaustion that he didn't think he'd be able to stand up. The crowd stared balefully down at him. Several of them were wearing coats over their pyjamas. They had that sterile expression – half puzzlement, half fascination – that you see in crowds around a car accident.

Vaguely, Kuzak was aware of a woman arriving at the back of the crowd, her body wrapped in an Indian shawl. Her hair was straggly and wet, as though she'd just got out of the shower. *What people would do to join in the aftermath of tragedy*! he thought, without malevolence. Dr Pelaggi leant down and took him under the arm. Kuzak struggled, panic-stricken, as though in a nightmare where you try to move, to stand up, and your muscles are like jelly. A couple of men came forward to help. 'You okay, Mister?'

'Fine.' The siren was getting closer. Kuzak straightened up and tried to focus. Just behind Pelaggi was the girl in the Indian shawl. She was smiling. Kuzak stared at her, than at Dr Pelaggi. The squad-car had turned on to the plaza, its siren dying. The girl in the shawl suddenly laughed. It was a beautiful melodious laugh and the crowd all turned to look at her. Two patrolmen were hurrying towards them. The girl let go of the shawl and it opened. Underneath she was stark naked.

Kuzak and Pelaggi were looking at Francine Faber.

*

'To attempt to explain everything,' Pelaggi said later, in the hospital, 'would require a whole book. I made a mistake about Francine. We both did, I guess. Only you're not an expert. I am – or am supposed to be'

'She set the whole thing up.' Kuzak said, resting on the upright pillow, feeling pleasantly light-headed from sedation. 'She rang me an hour before and told me to meet her on the boat. But you didn't have so far to come?'

Pelaggi nodded his solemn bloodhound head. 'She rang me ten minutes before the flames caught. She must have timed it to the second.'

'But that call to you? She couldn't have made that from the café, or I'd have seen her?'

'No. She made it from her carphone. She was parked at the far end of the waterfront.'

'Ah.' A nurse came in and gave Kuzak two small pills and a glass of water.

'Don't worry,' Pelaggi said. 'It's just something mild to help you sleep.'

'And Francine?'

'She'll have to stay in hospital for a long time, I'm afraid.'

'Will she be in trouble – with the law?'

'I don't think so. There may be some minor charges – but as a lawyer you know more about that than I. The insurance people may kick up a fuss, of course.'

She must have set the charges about the time she rang me.' Kuzak said. 'Tied to go off in one hour. Then she loosed off and swam back to shore, where she holed up in her car and waited?'

'It seems so,' said Dr Pelaggi.

'But she didn't hurt anybody?'

'I don't think so. They're sending divers down to make sure. But I don't think Francine wanted to kill anybody – except her own alter-ego. Poor girl!' Pelaggi himself looked close to tears.

'Did she kill her parents?'

The doctor considered the question for a long time; then took a drink of Kuzak's water. 'I don't know. I'm not a policeman. My job's to help people. In this case I seem to have failed – rather lamentably.'

'But what's wrong with her?'

'From a simple medical point of view' – the doctor spoke lugubriously, without looking Kuzak in the eye – 'she suffers from advanced paranoid schizophrenia, with distinct suicidal tendencies. That's what happened back there. She killed the other, younger Francine.'

'Can she be cured?'

'I don't think so. At least, not completely. But there are always new drugs coming on the market . . . So maybe there's hope.'

There was a long silence. 'Will I be allowed to see her?' Kuzak asked finally.

'It would be very unwise – at least, for several months.'

'But she'd recognise me, wouldn't she?'

'Maybe. But probably not from tonight – or even the last few days. She'd remember you as the handsome young attorney who won her case for her. That's all.'

There was another silence between them. Then Kuzak said, trying hard to sound casual, 'What about me? Will I be alright?'

'Nothing that can't be fixed with a few days in bed. Just delayed concussion and shock. We'll be running a brain-scan on you tomorrow, just to make sure there's no permanent damage. But it'll only be routine. If the results tally with those at the L.A. hospital, you should be out of here and back in your office within a week.' He gave his wise, hangdog smile. 'That's right – I took the liberty to call

Leland McKenzie and explain what's happened, but without going into too much detail.

'Leland was very understanding, as I expected him to be. He wants you back – and not just because you've got a firm contract. He wants you back, Michael, because you're a damned fine lawyer! And he'll be very hurt and insulted if you don't go.'

Kuzak was feeling too weak and tired to argue. 'And he wants you to know,' Pelaggi went on, 'that he's furious with Douglas Brackman. He thinks that police lieutenant from Beverly Hills should be tossed out on his ass!'

'Yeah, well –'

Pelaggi patted his arm and stood up. 'Now you get some sleep.'

Just as he was dropping off, Kuzak remembered something else. 'I wonder if running into the girl again like that was just chance? Or was that also a set-up?'

'Oh, my guess is she'd been planning to pick you up for days! Once the idea got into her head, she'd probably decided to track your movements in and out of the office, waiting for her best chance. But when the meeting did happen it probably *was* accidental – in that she'd slipped out for coffee, before continuing her vigil outside.'

'But *why*?'

'Who knows? I'm only a psychiatrist, Michael. The human brain is a very extraordinary machine. It's like the computer that's so vast it's never been built. Only unlike an ordinary computer, it programs itself. And when that programming starts going wrong, nobody really knows what happens.'

But Kuzak was already asleep.

Chapter Twenty Nine

Morning Conference began with Leland McKenzie holding up a thin piece of paper that might have been a receipt for some restaurant bill. 'We have to thank Grace for this! It's a rather unusual gift that came with this morning's post.' He paused dramatically.

'It is a banker's draft,' he continued. 'Drawn on the French *Banque Creole et Occidentale*, Grand Cayman, and made out to this Partnership for the sum of no less than *two million and twenty thousand dollars*. This is by way of full and unconditional settlement of our case against the Triton Corporation, brought by Mrs Rita Turner . . .'

The whole Partnership, less Kuzak and Ann Kelsey, rose excitedly to congratulate Grace, who acknowledged their applause and admiration with some embarrassment. It wouldn't do, after all, to probe too deeply into how she'd managed this legal feat in less than two weeks. She caught

Stuart Markovitz's eye and said, 'Thank you! But I should make it clear that Stuart here played a vital role – and as a personal favour, too!'

They all watched Stuart cringe with modest satisfaction.

'I should add,' said Grace, 'that the deal is subject to a complete news blackout. We announce only that "substantial damages" have been agreed between our clients and Triton. Any more and the deal is nul and void.'

'Till we cash the draft!' Becker said slyly.

'The man must be a goddam nut-case!' Stuart was shaking his head in disbelief. 'Crazy! Absolutely crazy! For a man in his position . . .'

'Oh – and I should add,' said Grace, 'that the twenty thousand is to cover all outstanding expenses.'

'My only other comment,' Leland went on, 'is to observe that the otherwise odious Triton Corporation appears to contain at least one true gentleman, after all. As for the details, let's just say that we go by results on this one. The means are something else – I'll leave that to Grace, in the certain knowledge that she's acted throughout not only with extraordinary speed, but that her methods have been entirely ethical.'

She nodded blankly. 'Thank you, Leland.' From further down the table, she and Victor were avoiding each other's eyes with a studiousness that was visibly painful.

Opposite her, Stuart was beginning to calm down again. For Stuart Markowitz liked crooks to behave like crooks, and felt almost personally offended when they didn't. But he was expecting Ann back from Colorado later in the day, so he could afford to look cheerful from now on.

Leland continued, 'I'm also glad to announce that

Michael Kuzak comes out of hospital tomorrow and will be rejoining the Partnership next week.' Only Brackman betrayed no enthusiasm at this news.

C.J. Lamb then gave them the bad news. Stoo Nugent-Ross had been released again on bail, pending his appeal against the jail sentence. Now he'd gone on an indefinite trip to Indonesia and Thailand. It wasn't only worry about the threat of the sentence being sustained that prompted him to "up sticks and scarper". He'd been mightily galled by the Press reports following his trial, in which the unfortunate Judge Savory had hogged most of the billing: while Stoo and his cause were largely ignored, even ridiculed. The *Los Angeles Times*, for instance, had written a short, humorous leader on the case, concluding brutally: '. . . *Meanwhile, Mr Nugent-Ross remains a wealthy young playboy of whom it may safely be said that such men are not destined to change the American Constitution . . . After his ordeal, he would do well to take a long trip abroad – preferably on a bicycle.*'

A warrant for Nugent-Ross's arrest had now been issued and his new bail, set at $5,000, was forfeited. Since half the original bail money, set eventually at $3,500, had been posted by Brackman when he'd sprung Kuzak from the Beverly Hills lock-up, Douglas was not cheered by this second piece of news either. A sum of $1,750 was petty cash to a firm like McKenzie Brackman, but it was the principle that mattered. No lawyer likes to lose a case: much less, have his client skip bail while awaiting appeal.

Arnie Becker was not making much progress either – though he was having rather more fun – representing a 'married' gay who'd broken up with his lover and was trying to gain custody of two lion cubs.

'My preferred solution is to send the cubs to a zoo and give the quarrelling couple a japanese *tozo* each,' he told them all with a grin.

Ten minutes later Conference was over. Stuart Markowitz immediately rushed up to Grace, saying in a conspiratorial whisper, 'But how did you do it, honey? I mean, you *got* to tell me – I was in on the case right from the beginning, remember?'

'How could I forget, Stuart?' Liqueurs and soft music, it had been, as the Iron Duke said, 'a damned close-run thing'. 'Just let's say it was mostly down to you, Stuart, for pointing me in the right direction. As well as a lot of luck – and a little bit of feminine intuition.'

Stuart looked disappointed. 'There must have been something else? Some hold you have over him?'

'Yes, Stuart.' She smiled brightly. 'I made Randy Miller fall in love with me. But don't worry – we never got further than first base.'

'By the way,' she added, 'I'm so glad about Ann and her father. Wonderful news!'

'Yes, isn't it!'

*

It was after 11 am. Roxanne opened Grace's door and said breathlessly. 'Grace, it's been on the Morning News! Quick – they're doing an update now . . .'

'What – ?'

'It's your Randy Miller . . .!'

Grace ran after Roxanne to the TV room, where Stuart Markowitz was already watching. As Grace arrived, the screen was showing a long closing shot of a Cadillac in the middle of what looked like empty desert. There was no sign of damage to the car. It was like the final shot of an art-movie.

The reporter's voice-over was saying: '. . .*when his body was found shortly after eight this morning by a passing farmer. There were three rounds in the gun, but only one had been fired . . .*'

Grace stood staring in horror at the screen, which now showed a patrolman holding the .45 in a plastic bag, then panned in on the interior of the car:

'. . . *Police found a half-empty bottle of Bourbon on Miller's lap, and believe death occurred between eight and ten yesterday evening . . .*'

Roxanne had gone to fetch Victor, who now slipped quietly into the little room, but Grace did not seem to notice him. She had sunk down on a chair and was watching the TV screen with the knuckles of one hand thrust into her mouth.

From the screen the hard, glacial face of the late Randolph D. Miller now stared impassively down at her. '. . . *Police are treating Mr Miller's death as suicide . . .*' Grace took her hand from her mouth and began to sob. '*Oh my God!* The poor, poor bastard . . .!' And she thought, *If I'd accepted that lunch date yesterday, he might still be alive.*

Victor moved forward and lifted her firmly by the arm. 'Come on, honey. There's nothing you can do here.'

As they left, they were pursued remorselessly by the voice-over: '. . . *to counter recent rumours that the Triton Corporation is facing serious financial problems. And only two weeks ago nine-year-old Candy Turner was blinded on one of Triton's . . .'*

The door closed behind them. Victor put his arm around her shoulder. He said gently, 'C'mon, I'll drive you home.'

*

'But you didn't even call me. Not once in five days! What happened, Victor?'

They'd hardly spoken in his car, on the way back to her apartment. But now she'd recovered enough to confront Victor on her own territory. The news of Randy Miller's death had made her suddenly bold and aggressive. 'And I want the truth! I'll know if you're lying.'

Victor stood glumly on the defensive; he looked tired and sallow after his trip to Las Vegas. 'I got obsessed, Grace. I hardly ate or slept properly in the last three days. I was half out of my mind!'

'Who was she?' Grace said. 'A tramp? A hooker? Can I expect to get AIDS?'

Victor flashed her his pirate's smile. 'Not from this lady, you won't!'

'Then who is she, for Chrissake! One of the Vestal Virgins?'

'Lady Luck – the Goddess of Fortune. And Patron Saint of Las Vegas.' Without being invited he poured two stiff drinks. 'Here's to happiness, Grace!' – and he raised his glass to her.

She stood frowning, waiting for him to go on.

'It was like this, honey. I had dinner with my client on the first evening, and I guessed at once that he was guilty as hell, and that the casino had only erred in taking so long to rumble him.

'My client, Xavier Istaquez, is an old-fashioned card sharp. Only he's also a blackjack dealer, so he can work both sides of the table. He got slightly drunk during our dinner and explained how it's done. He has a memory like a computer, so he can memorise every card that's dealt, and can calculate the odds until all eight packs have gone from the shoe.

'Having the eight packs, instead of one, cuts the odds right down. But the court cards, counting as ten, are the important ones – followed by the low cards, the aces and twos. After he or the dealer have got through six of the eight packs, and if most of the court cards are out, or still to come, the odds can shorten up to sixty per cent against the house.'

'But don't the casinos know about that sort of thing?'

'Sure they do! But the only really effective action they can take is to bar anybody who starts winning too much, and too consistently. Every table is monitored on closed-circuit TV video, which is fed into a computer and studied almost simultaneously. If one table starts showing consistently high winnings by one, or a group, of customers, the house will move in, pay them off, and ban them.'

Victor was speaking with a quiet, single-minded intensity, like a professor lecturing an impersonal audience of students. Grace felt he hardly noticed her.

'So no-one can get away with it for long?' she said, feeling more interest than she showed.

'Sure. But it takes a few days. And the money has to be serious – or the casino would get the reputation of not paying the winners, which is instant death in a gambling city like Vegas. So the trick is to play for low stakes, varying your play and changing tables – but not too often – and quitting when you're not too far ahead. You work, say, a dozen places, but only about two or three on any one night. That way, with luck, the computers don't pick up a pattern – until it's too late.'

Victor took a deep drink, to whet his dry mouth. 'Well, I'd heard about this sort of thing, but I'd never seen it done. I've got a pretty good memory for figures, as you know, so after that first dinner my client took me along to one of the big places where he reckoned he wasn't known as a dealer – Vegas is full of Istaquez lookalikes, all with shades and gaucho moustaches. For an hour or so we worked a couple of tables – just for fun.'

'Sure – just for fun.'

Victor ignored her. 'I played, and Istaquez stood a little aside and signalled me when to draw or fold. By the time I'd started getting the knack of it, I was seven hundred bucks up. I was also hooked. We went to another place next morning and played till well after lunch. I was getting so good, Istaquez left me to play alone for a bit, and so vary the pattern. By the end of that afternoon, we'd cleared nine thousand dollars. Split both ways, of course.'

'Of course.' Grace had poured herself another drink. 'So did you go on winning – or were you thrown out?'

Victor lifted his jacket off the back of the chair, took out a fat crocodile skin wallet and counted out a stack of hundred dollar bills. 'Forty-two thousand, eight hundred and sixty dollars,' he said. 'All winnings. I paid my expenses by credit card.'

Grace sipped her drink and gave him a long, cool stare. 'So that's why you didn't call me?' she said at last. 'For a goddam pack of cards!'

'Honey, for most of the time I didn't even know if it was day or night. One morning we came out of a casino when people were already driving to work and I thought it was just after midnight! I'd wanted to get at least one decent night's sleep.'

'And Douglas Brackman thought you were working all this time?'

'Douglas is a fool. But I don't want any of this to get out, Grace. I'm a Partner, like you. Leland and Douglas would have me out on my ass if they found out.'

'Oh I don't know. They might take a lenient view – providing you agreed to join Gamblers' Anonymous.'

He put down his empty glass and advanced towards her. 'C'mon, let's go to bed.' He started to put his arms round her and kiss her on the mouth; but she broke gently away.

'First there's something I have to do, Victor.' She went to the phone and dialled the D.A.'s office, asking for Sam Ohls. 'Sam . . .? Yes, Sam, I heard . . .'

'You notice there was nothing about a suicide note?' the D.A.'s man said excitedly. 'Suicides *always* leave a note. Miller didn't.'

'Oh yes he did, Sam. He wrote one to me.' It was a barefaced lie, but it was all she could think of. 'I want you and your boys to drop it now, Sam. The other angle, I mean – the second half of the scam . . .' She kept her voice down so that Victor, who was already in the bedroom, couldn't overhear them. Grace was wary, anyway, of saying too much on an open line.

Sam didn't answer for a time. 'Are any investigations into Miller's affairs already underway?' Grace went on.

'I dunno. Sorry.'

'Ah come on, Sam! No-one even picks his nose in your office, without you being in charge cf the production! So let's have it?'

'If anything here goes any further, Grace, it won't be down to me.'

'Of course it won't, Sam!' she said, with raw sarcasm. 'Like it wasn't down to Goebbels or Himmler . . . But you're not like that, are you?'

There was a long pause. Then Ohls sighed loudly down the line and said, 'All right, sister. Miller's dead. Case closed. So we won't be turning up any other skeletons – providing the party in question promises to keep his head way down deep in the ground . . .'

'Thanks, Sam.'

'Buy me a strawberry vanilla cheesecake when you see me next, huh?'

'Grace!' It was Victor's voice from the bedroom. She thanked Ohls again and hung up.

'Come here, honey.' Victor's dark naked arms reached out to her from the bed. He smiled. 'Lucky in cards and lucky in love.'

'There's something wrong there, Victor.'

'There's always an exception to the rule. I'm the exception.'

Grace got into bed beside him.

'And you're going to spend all that casino money on taking us round the world.' she said later.

He chuckled. 'Like Ann Kelsey's parents?'

'Like Ann Kelsey's parents,' she said.